Meet Pat Silversol, a science fiction writer who discovers a gateway to another dimension where he gains certain powers that can help him save lives as well as become rich.

When Pat and his friend Eric travel to a world in this other dimension called Owega, they accidentally stop a thief who is wanted by the city of Clarissa, and prevent him from getting away on his latest robbery. Pat and Eric end up receiving a cash reward and a free seven-day vacation package to a famous sporting event in Wiktona. They find out that the robber was no ordinary thief, but happened to belong to a gang of terrorists.

After learning of a tragic event that took place back in Clarissa, they're advised to leave Wiktona and travel to a country that's several thousand miles away. Pat soon discovers that the terrorists have developed a weapon that could wipe out humanity on Owega. He realizes that the sweet scent that helped him to discover the gateway wasn't put there by accident but was there to lure him over and so he could find a way to stop them before it's too late.

When a bombing incident occurs in Lavinia, Pat's hometown on Earth, he soon wonders if his new Owegan girlfriend is someone who was hired by the gangsters to help turn Pat over to them.

 Will Pat be able to save Owega and become a famous hero, knowing that a billion lives will be sacrificed if he should fail? Or will life on Owega seize to exist if the gangsters mission becomes a

Gateway to Owega World

To Cheyrl

Prologue

The sweltering sun shone down on the world-famous beach resort. The tropical heat caused purple-black thunderclouds to build up on the horizon. The northeast trade winds would soon bring them towards Solinga Bay.

The kids were still on their New Year's break and most of them were hanging out at the beachside with their families.

Among them was an eight-year-old boy swimming alone in the one-metre-deep area. He had difficulty executing basic swimming movements. His father had gone to a nearby bar for a few drinks. This was his hundredth-or-so time to the beach — the last couple of times, with only his dad.

Bobby, known as the local bully, noticed him standing around in the chest high water. He decided to tease the young boy by offering him swimming lessons in the deeper section just beyond the rope the lifeguards put out each day.

"Here, put your hands on my shoulders and float along with me, into the deep end," said Bobby, when he reached the boy. He did as Bobby suggested, and they went out into the three-metre-deep area.

The boy was a little nervous of Bobby — because he was bigger than him, and a bully. It was only two weeks ago that Bobby had gotten him into trouble by putting a piece of paper, that read 'Do not Pee on Mr. Greenlee', into the school bathroom trough. Mr. Greenlee, who happened to be on duty that day, saw it and accused him of doing it, for Bobby had run off on him. He ended up getting the wooden paddle on his rear.

For a few minutes they floated along nicely. Suddenly Bobby pushed the boy just hard enough to submerge him. Out of shear panic, to get his head above water, the boy started pushing on Bobby. His fear of drowning was so great, he didn't realize that Bobby was now submerged.

Since they were floating near the lifeguard lookout stationed in the three-metre deep area, the on-duty lifeguard dived in and grabbed the boy, "Hey, stop pushing him under, else you'll have to get out." The words 'get out' were music to his ears at this point, as it would mean less chance of drowning, but the thought was short-lived as Bobby led him away from the lifeguard. They were only approximately ten metres from the lookout.

The boy found himself once again being forced just below the surface. In a state of panic he pushed on Bobby's head to raise his own above the surface, while at the same time, trying as much as possible to drift towards the lifeguard, so he could yell for help. However, Bobby pushed him downward with strength superior to that of his own.

His heart was palpitating, like a thousand horses galloping at full speed, in his chest. He fervently wished he had the power to push Bobby away and out-swim him to the shore. Operating on pure, undiluted adrenalin he won the struggle, bringing his head above water, while subconsciously still holding Bobby's head under. In this state, he lost track of how long Bobby had been submerged.

The lifeguard once again grabbed the boy, pulling him away from the now dead Bobby. The lifeguard rolled Bobby over onto his back. Feeling for a pulse and finding none, he yelled: "You're in deep trouble now, son! I'm taking you to the authorities. That was my younger brother you just murdered!"

As they approached the beachfront bar, the boy's father stepped in, yelling: "Hey! Let go of my son, you moron."

"Sir, he just drowned my kid brother out there," pointing as the other lifeguards carried the dead body to shore.

"He was only defending himself from your bully brother. Now let go of him before I lose my cool."

The boy was scared witless at the idea of going to jail or reform school. Without thinking, he bit the lifeguard's wrist that had been holding him in a vice-like grip.

The lifeguard, crying out in pain, let go of the boy and tried to grab him by the neck, but failed. The boy's father, seeing him prepare to make his move, drove a solid, teeth-shattering blow into his left cheek.

The lifeguard started to bleed from both his mouth and wrist. He struck out at the boy's father, landing a blow just beneath his eye. They started exchanging blows. The crowd panicked at the sight of the scuffle and the amount of blood the lifeguard was losing, particularly from his wrist. Somebody called the emergency line, 5-1-1.

The boy started to run, now terrified by the entire scene. Blinded by panic, he tripped over a picnic basket and banged his head, passing out from the impact.

When he would come to later, he would have forgotten everything that had happened to him and would find himself living in a world that was totally unfamiliar to him.

Month 14, day 03, year 13-006

For the third consecutive night, Carrie Orangesand had the same dream. In her dream she was at the Westside Gardens and it was well into the night. Most of the evening visitors were home.

As she sat relaxing on a bench, a woman with flawless beauty and a congenial personality approached her. "Carrie Orangesand, I'm Solinga, and I have chosen you to help my lost son find his way to the portal, so that he can come home to the world in which he belongs."

Carrie was rather flattered and a little nervous. She had read many books about ancestors, from a dozen-or-so millennia ago, who had lived in a different dimension on a planet teeming with an abundance of life in all shapes and forms, very much like her own planet, Owega. She learned that legend had it; a supreme race had led them from the other dimension to their present one, by going through a portal built into the cave in West Side Gardens. She was having mixed emotions about letting a stranger in from the other world. She had heard numerous rumours that many of the people on the other side were as hostile as Soapy and his men.

As though reading Carrie's mind, Solinga said: "Do not fear, my son is one of the good ones. He is just lost over there. He needs to be encouraged to walk through the portal. He must save our world from a terrible fate that awaits, in the sky."

Carrie speculated it had something to do with the comet scheduled to pass in the next couple of weeks. She had learned in her history class that a comet had once hit Owega, only a couple of hundred leagues north of the city, on the east side of Orthnus Lake, around five millennia ago.

"You must take this bottle of perfume and spray it so that it penetrates the other world," said Solinga as she brought forth a small bottle filled with an amber coloured liquid.

She led Carrie into the cave and towards the other end. As they approached the end, Solinga waved her hand and a rectangular, rainbow-coloured frame, surrounded the exit of the cave. The outside of the rectangle emitted blue sparks that arced towards the cave walls. When Carrie looked at the framed exit, she saw a dark area with trees barely beginning to bud, instead of West Gardens.

"Just spray some of the perfume to the other side," encouraged Solinga, standing behind her.

Carrie complied with her request. The image began to ripple when the fragrance penetrated the thin layer separating the two worlds.

When Carrie had emptied the bottle, Solinga whispered: "You did well. Maybe he'll come through tomorrow."

Carrie turned to answer but was amazed to find herself alone. It was as though Solinga had vanished into thin air. She began to walk out of the cave, as she had the other two nights. On her way out, she tripped and fell to the muddy floor. She awoke, to find herself in bed with her husband, John. She got out of bed and turned on the bathroom light. A shiver rippled down her spine. Her nightgown was muddy. She put it down to having sleepwalked to the garden, until she discovered the empty perfume bottle in her dressing gown pocket. She put the bottle to her nose and went cold when she recognized the fragrance from her dream. She was left pondering the question: "Was it really a dream?"

Chapter 1

The Gateway

It was April 13, 2002, when thirty-eight-year-old writer, Pat Silversol, took his daily walk through the woods. He lived in a small town, Lavinia, just five kilometres east of Beamsville, Ontario. He had blue eyes and dark brown, fairly short hair, parted to the left of his double crown. His weight was average for a man of his age. He had a tendency to smile frequently. In high school, his friends and teachers had called him 'Smiley'. He was a full-time writer of science fiction and fantasy books and usually made the walk part of his daily routine to relax his mind, before going in to write and fix dinner.

The snow, from a surprising late season cold spell, had finally melted away in the shady areas and some of the trees had started to bud. The bright, clear air filled with the buzzing of bees, other insects and the calls of numerous birds were the perfect setting for Pat to let his mind wander and review his life.

He used to work in a travel bureau where he would spend most of his time booking vacations for other people. At first he found the job quite intriguing. He enjoyed looking at the brochures of different vacation resorts and asking people, upon their return, how they had enjoyed their trip.

After a while, Pat grew envious of the clients who went to resorts where snow and ice were only found in a snow cone and drinks. The fact that he wasn't making enough money to go to the resorts or take ocean cruises, depressed him. He made so many mistakes his manager advised him to seek professional help to snap out of his depression. He was running the risk of losing his job with Blue Planet Travel.

At first, he thought the group-therapy sessions, and his meetings with Dr Graham were a waste of time, until he befriended some of the people there. One of them was a guy named Bill, a couple of years younger and in a deeper state of depression than Pat. They couldn't do things like go to a nightclub, where they may have been able to meet women, because Bill had recently become a married man.

About the fifth week of their friendship, Bill suggested they both put their imaginations to work and co-write a book, under a single pen name. Pat jumped at the idea because he felt that with Bill's experience as a former room steward on Royal Cruise Lines and his own at a travel agency, they could spin out a novel set on an ocean liner. The theme would be about a former employee of a cruise-ship company who decides to take a cruise, throw the captain overboard, and eventually cause the ship to sink. Bill kept telling Pat: "If you're going to dream, dream big!"

Alas, the book never got published. A movie with a similar plot, '*Speed 2: Cruise Control*', was released. Bill became more depressed as the days went by and was put on medication which resulted in him sleeping for over fourteen hours a day. Pat also became more depressed, but for a different reason. On a Monday in early November '97, the president of Blue Planet Travel went to Pat's place of employment. He announced they were closing the Beamsville office and laid Pat and the other five employees off. Instead of taking medication, Pat found that writing a new book helped him feel better. This time he opted for a science fiction/fantasy genre instead of an action-thriller. He tried to persuade Bill to be his writing partner again, but Bill wanted nothing to do with writing another book.

Four days before Christmas that same year, Pat came home after watching a Buffalo Bills game at a local sports bar. The little red light on his answering machine was ominously blinking. He listened to his messages. Bill's wife had left a distressed message: "*Pat, please call me as soon as you get home.*" He immediately called. She told him Bill had jumped from the bridge that crossed over the Queen Elizabeth Way highway. His mother and younger brother had rushed him to St. Catharine's emergency, but the medics could do nothing to save him.

Pat befriended Bill's widow, Terri, helping her deal with the loss of her husband. She inspired him to continue writing his book by saying that one day a publisher would buy it from him. They went out as friends, on and off, for about six months, after which she moved to Vancouver to work as a registered nurse. A shortage of nurses in British Columbia ensued better pay and benefit offers.

In the spring of 2000, Pat picked up a book he thought was rather poorly plotted. He figured the publishing company would publish any manuscript that crossed their desk. He sent his manuscript to them and six months later received the first fifty dollars of a five hundred dollar advance, in addition to an offer of twenty percent for each copy sold.

Unfortunately, the one-woman publisher went bankrupt and couldn't pay Pat the balance of his advance. Feeling bad about it, she met Pat for drinks in Oregano's Bar at the St. Catharine's Holiday Inn, which was close to where her publishing company had been. Later Pat walked her to her apartment and ended up spending the night.

Pat never found another publisher, but was able to make a few bucks by selling his book as a downloadable e-book on the Internet as well as through a print on demand publisher. He wasn't too concerned about finances. He was collecting welfare and had inherited a little two-bedroom house from his grandparents.

It was around this time that he was hired at a new travel agency, which had opened in downtown St. Catharine's. It was called Fantasy Travel, and dealt mostly with Canada 3000 airline tours of the same name. In the wake of the September 11 terrorist attacks on the World Trade Centre and the Pentagon, the job came to an abrupt end in November. The demand for travel had sharp declined and caused the company to close its doors.

His thoughts turned to his grandmother, whom he had admitted to a nursing home due to Alzheimer's. She had passed away at the age of ninety-three, a few days after Valentine's Day. Her death left him feeling he had lost both a mother and a grandmother, as she had raised him after his mother's death from a mysterious illness, when he was six. His father had never recovered from her death. He became an alcoholic, went insane, and disappeared shortly after the last holiday to the beach, when Pat was eight. His grandmother had told him all he knew, as he had no recollection of his younger years.

He was no further than two hundred metres down the path when the smell of a sweet perfume brought him out of his reverie. He couldn't associate the fragrance with any of the several hundred different smells his nose encountered, on any given day. He had noticed the perfume the last few times he reached this particular part of the trail. He had spent the last two weeks trying to determine the source of the smell. He felt a brief flickering glimmer, a mere whisper of memory, that it was something he had smelled a long time ago, before his head injury. Perhaps, somehow one of his memory cells had survived.

He cut away from the path and went over towards the escarpment, following the trail of the perfume, which appeared to be stronger today than it had been on any of the other days. The escarpment, which ran along the southern shore of Lake Ontario, was known as the Niagara Escarpment.

When he got to the hill, he noticed a cave opening in the side. The opening was high enough, prompting him to walk in and explore. Finding it dark, Pat wished he had a flashlight with him. As he walked further, it curved to the left and appeared to be a backward-'c'-shaped tunnel. Ahead he could see light coming from the other end. The scent grew stronger, the deeper he went. "Aha!" Pat said aloud, without realizing it. It was so intoxicating he was reminded of the time he had once tried smoking a joint in high school, to see what all the hype was about. His grandmother had somehow found out about it that same day, and gave him a long lecture about what could become of him if he developed a habit of smoking it. She told him he would be thrown out of her house if she ever caught him smoking it again.

Suddenly, so surprised at the vision that met his eyes, he stopped short of the tunnel exit. He closed his eyes for a second — then re-opened them. The sight remained. Instead of seeing the woods with budding trees on an overcast day, Pat was seeing trees with autumn foliage on a sunny day. There was a concrete path instead of the dirt path, and a fair number of people were either walking, jogging or riding tricycle-like bikes with large front wheels, similar to the ones dating back a hundred years. The scene itself was a little distorted. It was as if he was looking through a frosted glass windowpane. He couldn't hear any sound coming from the scene. The strangest thing was a vertical, rectangular, glowing, rainbow-coloured frame, large enough for a tall person to walk through, surrounding the entire scene. In the frame, several blue electrical sparks arced outward. They emitted no sound, which confused Pat even more, as electrical sparks should give off 'snap', 'crackle' and 'pop' sounds.

Pat turned around and went back the way he had come. He decided to go home and investigate, on the Internet, what he had just seen. He didn't want to try walking through it; he was afraid it might electrocute him or something equally unpleasant.

* * *

Fifteen minutes later, Pat arrived at his small bungalow. As usual, his cat, Pedals, was curled up on his sofa. Pat gave her a quick pet and she answered with a short meow. Pedals has been his faithful feline companion for the last five years. His neighbour's friend had found her as a stray lurking around the

16

video store he worked at. Concerned she wouldn't survive on her own, he had brought her home, and Pat had agreed to adopt her.

After taking his coat off, Pat went into his spare bedroom, which served as a writing room. The room actually looked more like an office, with a desk on which rested a PC, printer, scanner, and high-speed cable modem that allowed him access to the Internet.

Pat turned his computer on, went on-line and searched for sites on alternate or parallel universes. His aim was to establish whether the portal he had seen in the cave was a one-of-a-kind or if there were others.

The search revealed only a handful of sites that mentioned alternate or parallel universes. One referred to them as a world with the same places and people, only sometimes zagged rather than zigged. One example they gave, was a world where the *Titanic* veered around the iceberg in the nick of time, and sailed safely to New York harbour. The other type was where someone goes back in time and does something that has an effect on today's world. It stated how the *Back to The Future* movie was a prime example because the son went back thirty years and taught his wimpy dad to be more assertive and self-confident. When he returned to his own time, his parents' place had fancier furniture and his father had published his first book.

Pat couldn't find much else on the Internet, so he shut down his computer and checked the time: it was only four in the afternoon; an hour had passed since he had been in the cave. Since his friends wouldn't be over for another three hours, he decided to go back to the cave and have a closer look at the scene with his binoculars.

Like someone at a ballpark watching the game from the nosebleed seats, he once again saw the same scene. There seemed to be more people this time. The area looked like an urban park. The trees appeared to be similar to the ones Pat saw everyday. There were maples, oaks, and others that grow in the woods. Most of them were in bright orange, yellow, and red autumn foliage. It was as if this place was either behind or ahead by six months.

In the distance, Pat spotted a white train with tinted windows travelling on an elevated track, much like the shuttle trains that run behind the hotels in Las Vegas.

Pat took a closer look at the people on the path, and noticed the men and boys wore light-coloured puffed shirts and dark pants. It reminded him of a *Seinfeld* episode, where Jerry had unwillingly worn a puffed shirt on a morning TV show. The girls and women wore dresses of all shades and colours. Apparently, these people dressed more formally than North Americans. The scene brought to mind how, in the early 1900s, his grandparents had dressed up to go out, even if it was to an amusement park on a hot, humid day in July.

Pat decided he had had a long enough look for now and his grumbling tummy reminded him he had not yet eaten. After putting the binoculars back in their case, he returned to his house.

* * *

Later that evening, Pat's two friends came over and watched the Toronto Maple Leafs take on the Buffalo Sabres. His friends lived only a few blocks away.

Eric Aberdeen, currently unemployed, kept himself busy doing odd jobs for people such as shovelling snow and mowing their lawns. Though, looking at him, one wouldn't think he did all that. He was, like Pat, five foot eight, but lanky and the only one who smoked.

Tony Wilburt, with dark hair and hazel eyes the same shade as Eric's, was a computer technician. He was the shortest of the three and the only one to wear glasses. They had brass coloured frames. He was a big sports buff. About fifteen years ago, Tony and Pat were at a house party watching the *Peewee's Big Adventure* video, when Tony got up and went to the upstairs living room, to check the score of a hockey playoff game in progress.

Toronto ended up beating Buffalo four to three, after Sundin scored the fourth goal, with only seconds left in regulation. They discussed the game, having a couple of beers apiece. Pat summoned up the nerve to tell them about his discovery in the cave. They stared at him in disbelief.

Eric, making a grab for Pat's beer, "That's it, you've had enough. No more for you."

Tony laughed aloud. "You're putting us on," he said, adding "Yeah, right. Tell me another."

"I'm telling you the truth," Pat declared emphatically.

"Seeing is believing," Eric called Pat's bluff.

Pat, getting tired of being mocked and becoming frustrated, "I can take you there."

This seemed to have the desired effect and they were silent for a few moments. Each busy with their own thoughts.

"Did you try going through the frame?" asked Eric, breaking the silence.

"No, not yet. I was worried I wouldn't make it back."

"I would be afraid to go over myself. Anything could happen. You could catch a virus from them and die," Eric retorted with a hint of sarcasm. He was amazed Pat would pass up, what he considered could be, the opportunity of a lifetime.

Tony, in his bland, bored voice, added his two cents worth. "Yeah, like when Europeans brought disease to Hawaii. They caused the deaths of many natives by introducing whooping cough, measles and small pox."

19

Pat took two potato chips, almost identical in size, from the bowl he had put out during the game. Holding one up he said, "Here's my theory about this parallel world. Picture these chips as universes," taking the other chip and placing them side by side so they touch, he continued, "These two universes are so close to each other they touch at some spots, creating a portal between them. The only thing separating them is, perhaps, time."

"If your theory is correct, it could explain why it appears to be autumn there," suggested Eric.

Pat offered another alternative, "Or, maybe they're in the same time frame, but their axis is tilted the opposite way, thus giving them opposite seasons."

"Maybe we should go have a look tomorrow," Eric suggested with reserved excitement.

Tony, unable to muster courage, piped up; "I can't make it tomorrow. I'll be working all day doing some networking in Toronto."

"You and I can go, Pat. Maybe we can cross over for a few hours and Tony can make it some other time," said Eric enthusiastically.

" Sounds good. Tony will have to look after my mouser if a few hours turns into a few days," Pat nonchalantly said.

"We shouldn't be that long," said Eric hopefully.

"I'm just saying that in case there's some kind of time warp, when coming back," Pat stated to calm him. "Also, anything we've discussed tonight is confidential. The last thing we need is all kinds of people checking this thing out, causing a big commotion. Do I have your word on this?" Pat asked with a hint of threat. They agreed not to say anything about it.

"Why don't we go and check it out now? I'm dying to see this thing, man," Eric prompted.

"I've got to go home soon. 6:00 A.M. comes quickly," said Tony peevishly.

"Well then (making a raspberry sound) to you," Pat said and they giggled as the beers began taking effect.

"Let's just have a quick look, Pat," said Eric eagerly.

"I'll have to find my flashlight. It will be very dark out there."

After getting the flashlight, and giving Pedals a few pets, Eric and Pat went to the cave. Tony went home, taking one of Pat's spare keys, so he could feed the cat, in case Eric and Pat decided to go over and weren't back in time.

They carefully worked their way to the other end of the cave. It was dark on the other side too, and few people were out and about. There were nice bright yellow and pink lights strung on some of the trees, creating the atmosphere of an amusement park.

"Pretty cool, I wonder if they can see us?" whispered Eric, awestruck.

"I don't think anyone has noticed me yet," Pat replied, hoping he was right.

Cautiously Eric put his hand through the rectangle, causing a ripple effect. He pulled it back and motioned Pat to do the same.

Pat stepped forward. He felt a vibration as though he had touched an electronic massager.

"Cool! I guess we should go over tomorrow morning so we could have the whole day to explore. Gee, I'm starting to feel like Columbus or Cartier," Pat said, barely able to contain his excitement.

They began heading back the way they had come. Suddenly they stopped dead in their tracks. In front of them were two pairs of glowing amber eyes with oval-shaped pupils, much like a panther's.

With fear constricting his throat, Eric hoarsely whispered, "This leaves us only one option. You lead the way."

At breakneck speed they ran towards the gateway to the other world.

Chapter 2

To Catch a Thief

They leaped into the portal and encountered a slight resistance as they crossed over. It wasn't enough to slow them down however, instead, it appeared to speed them up as though it was eager to expel them.

They hit the ground running, and found themselves in a cave; similar to the one they had just left. They were fast approaching the exit and would have to slow down before they reached the path and knocked someone over. At the same instant Pat emerged from the cave, a man, who looked to be in his forties and carrying a small sack, ran across Pat's path, left to right. Pat, still trying to slow down, collided with him in much the same way a defensive lineman would tackle a running back.

Pat wasn't hurt but the impact fractured the other man's right leg. The man was left immobile from the shock and pain of injury. Pat got up. A man about Pat's age, wearing a dark uniform with a badge pinned to it, put handcuffs on the fallen man. Pat concluded he had to be a policeman.

"Pat, are you okay?" asked Eric, who had come over to where Pat was standing.

"Yes, just a little shaken."

"Sir, you just stopped a man wanted for several counts; including grand theft, murder, and rape," the cop said in normal, slightly accented English. "I'm Officer Blackberry. What is your name?"

Pat, a little surprised to find he could understand the officer, hesitated slightly before answering, "I'm Pat Silversol, and this is my friend, Eric."

"Pleased to meet you cats." Another officer came along and escorted the thief away.

"Are you taking me to the friggin' hospital?" they heard the thief yelling at the officer. They couldn't hear the reply, as the pair had moved out of earshot.

"Did you two come through the portal?" Blackberry asked.

Pat briefly explained about finding the cave and their remarkable 'forced' entrance.

"It has been many years since someone has come through the portal. We thought they had lost their power."

"Where are we now?" asked Eric.

"You have entered the world of Owega (pronounced Oh-way-gah) and are now in the outskirts of the city of Clarissa. I'll take you to an inn, and in the morning, at eleven, I'll take you to our mayor to collect your substantial reward."

"Cool, he must have been seriously wanted to have a big price on his head," said Pat.

"He stole over five million krayohs in jewellery and rare coins." They whistled at the amount, but had no idea how this related to their own monetary system. Their questions would have to wait.

After a few minutes of walking along the path, they came to the parking lot. The front half of the cars were triangular-shaped. The backs were square and they had no wheels. The cruiser was bright yellow with 'Clarissa Police Dept.' written on it in black letters. Pat figured the cars hovered above the road, just like the vehicles in the *Phantom Menace* movie the kids had raced around on that sandy planet.

Pat was relieved to find that not only did they speak comprehensible English, but their written language was readable too. Pat and Eric were forced to sit in the back as the front seat was narrow and had only enough room for the driver. When Blackberry started the car, it emitted a nice smooth hum, similar to the sound of a computer fan.

"Is this an electric car?" Eric inquired.

"No, it actually runs on air. The motor converts oxygen atoms into energy and after the energy is spent, it is converted back to clean oxygen," Blackberry explained.

"In other words, it causes no pollution." Pat declared.

"None at all," Blackberry confirmed. "We used to have petrol-driven cars, but they always broke down, whereas these cars hardly do."

Pat realized this created little need for a repair garage, and at the same time, no headaches like the ones in his world.

Blackberry slowly entered the main road from the parking lot. On the road were a few stores and restaurants with strange names. One was called Weans and Beans and looked a lot like a fast food joint. After passing the restaurant, they entered what appeared to be a major highway. The sign declared it to be the King Timothy Motorway, and it was very similar to the Queen Elizabeth Way highway linking Toronto with Fort Erie, and bordering Buffalo, New York.

Looking ahead, they could see several skyscrapers. The buildings were all lit in different shades of green and yellow. This scenario reminds me of Toronto, Pat mused.

"Wow! Looks like a big city ahead," Eric exclaimed.

"That is Clarissa, the capital of Venus, which is a province of Corvus," Blackberry pointed out.

"In our world, Venus is a planet second from the star known as the sun, in our solar system," Pat remarked.

"When you get to the inn, you'll be able to learn more about our world and country on the Info-Screen," Blackberry informed them.

Pat imagined the Info-Screen to be their version of the Internet.

"Here's the inn, boys," Blackberry announced, as they came to a stop. The Oaks Inn was a one-story building with the check-in lobby at one end, and a small diner at the other. Behind the lobby was a larger two-story building which contained the rooms.

"I'll check you in," said Blackberry as they approached the check-in desk. "The police department will pay since you really took a large load off our hands back there."

Blackberry went to the desk, checked them in, and came back with a key that looked like an old-fashioned nineteenth-century key. The key was stamped with the number 227. At least the numerals are no different to ours either, Pat thought to himself.

Blackberry took them as far as the building their room was in, and told them he would call them in the morning to arrange their trip to Clarissa and the meeting with the mayor.

After he left, they went upstairs to their room. The room had two double beds, and a couple of chairs. The only difference to a typical inn room, was the absence of a TV. In its place, was a two-metre-wide screen built into the wall, opposite the beds. Just below the screen was a bench table and a keyboard, with keys in a different sequence to those they were familiar with.

Pat tentatively pressed a white button below the screen, turning the computer on. In seconds, the screen displayed the inn logo with a red graphic instruction button. Pat touched the screen with his fingertip and a choice menu appeared: The Corvus almanac, the network directory, and the room-service menu.

Pat decided to look at the almanac. The first thing to catch his attention was a map of Corvus; a landmass unlike any on Earth. A large country, which appeared to be two continents, shaped like two slices of steak, side by side. Also part of Corvus was an island further west.

Pat's journey of knowledge was interrupted when Eric called him into the bathroom. "Where's the toilet?" asked Eric. There was a long trough with water flowing down it like a miniature river.

"I guess we just use that," said Pat, pointing to the trough.

Disconcerted, Eric asked: "What if we have to do more than pee? Do we use the sink or the floor?"

Pat laughed at Eric's outrageous suggestion, then indicating a toilet seat next to the sink he had discovered, pointedly said, "Or maybe we use this."

"Oh, they must do things this way for hygienic reasons," Eric lamely commented.

Pat returned to the Info-Screen and resumed his research on Corvus. The country's population was about three hundred million. The government consisted of a king and queen at the throne, below them governors from each of the twenty provinces. It sounded similar to England's monarchy, except the king and queen shared sovereignty. If one were to pass away, the other would remain on the throne.

Eric came into the room and Pat filled him in on what he had learned. "So the biggest difference thus far is that they have different land masses," Eric summarized, lighting a cigarette.

"Yep. Their ancestors appear to have come from our dimension, and that could be the reason they speak English."

"Anyway, that's enough for me to digest tonight," Pat said, looking at his watch and yawning. "I'm going to hit the sack. It's past midnight and those beers we had earlier are making me sleepy." He returned to the main menu and turned the screen off.

Five minutes later, they were in bed and Pat was thinking about what would be in store for them tomorrow when they went to meet the mayor. He imagined the mayor to look like either Prime Minister Jean Chrétien or President George W. Bush.

Pat felt greatly excited at the thought of having discovered a whole new parallel dimension. He considered himself to be on a priceless vacation and toyed with the idea that not everyone could transport themselves into a whole new dimension. From Blackberry's comments, it would appear that nobody else had found the portal, or if they had, they hadn't been courageous enough to step through. These thoughts left him feeling superior to historical explorers such as Columbus, because he had discovered a whole new planet that supported life, as advanced as Earth's.

Memories of Bella crept into his mind. She would have been in seventh heaven if she were here; in this place they called Owega with scenes that made it a modern version of the Garden of Eden. Bella was a woman from Youngstown, New York, he had dated on a regular basis, ten years ago. He had met her at Niagara-on-the-Lake, where she was painting a picture of the clock tower erected in the middle of downtown Queen Street. After dating for a year, she accepted a job in San Francisco, working for an art firm that specialized in scenes for fantasy books. She was thrilled about the job, as fantasy and gothic were her favourite subjects. They lost contact shortly after the move.

Eric had a few things going through his mind too. One concern he had was what he was going to do when he ran out of smokes. He hoped that if they didn't have cigarettes, they would have either pipes or cigars. The worst-case scenario, which he didn't feel quite ready to face at this point, was the possibility they didn't have smokes because of the health hazards they posed. The other concern was what they would do, if for some reason, they could never go back to their own dimension, or they were thrown into another dimension or even several dimensions. He was thinking about the TV series *Sliders*, where they slid from one dimension to another, without making it back to their own. His concerns quickly faded as the day's excitement took its toll on him and before he knew it, he was sound asleep.

* * *

Pat dreamt he was a kid again, at the beach with his dad. A bully named Bobby, was pushing him below the surface. At this point he awoke, breathing heavily and sweating profusely, feeling as if he had just run a marathon. Pat couldn't remember this event happening. He had always thought most dreams of childhood were of events that had actually happened. He wondered if somehow, crossing over into Owega had awakened forgotten memories.   A few minutes later, he drifted into a dreamless sleep.

Chapter 3

Carrie

Carrie awoke and prepared breakfast for herself. She pondered the empty rooms in their bed-and-breakfast and hoped she would soon have new guests, as she disliked eating alone. John generally left for work long before she was up. She had the Info-Screen set to the news channel, as she would on any given morning. She had put it on out of habit. It was something she did so her guests could catch up on the latest news while enjoying their breakfast. Normally she didn't pay much attention to it.

A newswoman was talking about a man who had made a citizen's arrest on a member of Soapy's gang. Carrie became attentive at the mention of the man's name: Patrick Silversol.

"My gosh, she was right about her son," Carrie said aloud, before she could stop herself. She called the police station to find out where Pat was staying. She felt she had to invite him to stay at her place, partly because he was in danger of being attacked by Soapy's men, and partly because the lady in her dream had insisted that it was a matter of life and death that Pat remained unharmed.

* * *

The ringing phone on the night table woke them. From the image displayed on a little screen next to the number keypad, Pat could see the caller was Blackberry. He briefly informed them he would meet them in the diner.

Five minutes later, Eric was showering. Pat decided to listen to the news on the Info-Screen. The newswoman was reporting the arrest of a thief who had been tackled by two men, at Westside Park. She confirmed the perpetrator was part of a band of criminals wanted on several counts of murder, rape, and grand theft. She declared the kingpin was known as Soapy and that

31

anyone who brought him in, dead or alive, would receive a 20,000-krayoh award. She moved on to other news. Pat was reminded of a nineteenth century gangster who had terrorized Alaska - only a US territory at the time and ungoverned. His name had also been Soapy.

Pat changed to the weather screen. The prediction was the day would again be unseasonably warm, with temperatures approaching 250 degrees. Pat was clueless what this meant because he wasn't sure what the equivalent was in either Celsius or Fahrenheit. The weatherman predicted tomorrow would have showers and thunderstorms with temperatures dropping late in the day.

It was Pat's turn to shower. The shower was very much like the ones he was familiar with, except the soap was already mixed in with the water. Pat thought this sucked, as they wouldn't have a bar of soap to take with them when they checked out.

While Pat was in the shower, Eric stepped out to look around. Two hours had passed since sunrise. Beyond the parking lot, he could see houses much like the ones in his own neighbourhood. Each of them had what looked like a TV aerial with a small round dish on their roofs. Eric inferred they were for the Info-Screen system, and assumed the signal was broadcast through line-of-sight. Some broadband Internet companies at home used this method, instead of using cables or phone lines.

He walked around to the side facing east, where the morning sun was shining in the northeast. This didn't make sense; the sun should have been in the southeast, since the trees were in their autumn foliage. This indicated they were in the Southern Hemisphere. He looked ahead and could see the highway and the train track that ran parallel to the highway. For the last twenty minutes, a powder-blue car had been parked outside the inn. There were two occupants watching their room like hawks. Eric returned to their room without noticing the car.

* * *

The diner was busy with the morning crowd. They mostly seemed to be tourists who were most likely on their way to see the city. They were all dressed as the people in the park had been yesterday.

"There he is," said Pat, spotting Blackberry seated at the third booth from where they were standing. Blackberry waved them over. Sitting with him was a woman in her twenties.

Blackberry introduced the woman when they arrived at the table. "Guys, this is Carrie Orangesand." They shook hands with her and sat down. "She's going to be your tour guide or chaperone for the remainder of your stay. She'll be able to answer the ton of questions you probably have."

Pat noticed he pronounced her name as *Car-ee*. He referred to this as the Ottawa Valley accent because it reminded him of a time he had visited friends near Perth, Ontario, and an hour's drive from Ottawa. At dinner, one of them had pronounced the name 'Carrie' the same way.

Carrie was tall with golden brown, shoulder length hair, and hazel eyes. She was well tanned, suggesting she frequently spent time in the sun.

"I have to be going," Blackberry said. "I have other assignments to look after. It was nice meeting you. Maybe some day our paths will cross again. This is on me." He left a silver coin on the table, and quickly left.

"There's a few things we'll need to do first," Carrie said. "We'll have to go shopping and get you clothes that won't be so conspicuous."

"You mean we'll have to get some puffy shirts and dress pants?" Pat asked incredulously.

"Oh yes, definitely!" Carrie responded. "However, we'll eat first."

A tall, dark-haired waitress stopped at their table to take their order. They both deferred to Carrie who ordered the daily special, something similar to an omelette, with ham and green peppers in it. Carrie called it an egg sandwich, pronouncing it as *sing-widge*.

"What if the food makes us sick?" Pat asked after the waitress had gone to place their order. "After all, if I were to go to a country, on Earth, such as Mexico and drink the water, I could become very sick. Whereas the same water is harmless to the Mexicans because they're immune to it."

"I don't recall any other people, who had crossed over before you, getting ill. Besides you don't need to worry, all the food here is freshly prepared and free of all harmful bacteria and germs," Carrie allayed their concern.

Their food arrived and they found it delicious. They didn't talk much because Carrie didn't want to run the risk of having their conversation overheard or exposing that Pat and Eric were from another dimension. In addition, they didn't want to spend the entire morning in the diner.

After their meal, they returned to their room so Carrie could brief them on the basics of Corvus. As they started up the stairs, Pat glanced out the door and saw a powder-blue car with a man in it. He was certain the car had been there earlier, when they were heading in to the diner. Only then, there had been two people in the car.

As Pat opened the door, a man with a black mask, standing near the Info-Screen, suddenly lunged at him with a switchblade, aimed at his chest. Pat quickly jumped aside, but was not fast enough, and the knife grazed his right upper arm, giving him a shallow cut.

"Freeze!" Carrie yelled at the thug. She held a pistol in one hand and a small remote device in the other. The thug stopped in surprise and she pressed a button on the device. The thug went stiff, as if he had just stepped on a live wire, and fell unconscious to the floor.

Pat checked his upper arm and saw a 2 cm cut on the front of it. It started to bleed a little.

Carrie took the device, put it to her mouth, and said, "I have a 320 here. Please come right away." She handcuffed the thug and walked over to the window, careful to stay out of sight. Knowing Soapy's thugs never worked alone, she looked for an accomplice. She scanned the street, spotting the blue car and recognizing the man behind the wheel. She stepped outside, pointing the device towards the car.

"That'll hold him until the police get here," Carrie said, coming back into the room.

"Are you a cop too?" Eric asked.

"Not exactly, but it's part of my duty to make citizen's arrests when necessary. I also carry the zapper for protection. Most women in this area need one. Some of the guys working for an organized-crime club, known as the Dandoyhee, come down from Squid Bladder Island and have been known to rape women walking alone in isolated areas. They also raid shops in nearby villages. Anyway, I must get you out of here. It's not safe. Those two were part of Soapy's gang, which is a violent breakaway group of the Dandoyhee. They're the troublemakers. The others are quite safe, providing you don't cheat in their casinos found in several Corvus cities."

"What happens if they catch you cheating?" Eric asked.

Carrie drew her finger across her throat. Pat and Eric looked at each other; both licked their lips and swallowed. They had received the message loud and clear.

"Where are we going?" Pat asked.

"I'm going to take you back to my place, but we can't talk in the car, it might be bugged. Those cats are very clever."

"How far do you live from here?"

35

"Just three leagues to the west or about a ten-minute drive from here. It's a nice neighbourhood, not too far from the lake. You'll like my neighbourhood — it's nice and safe with a security gate we have to pass through."

Carrie drove west on the King Timothy Motorway. Pat and Eric could see the exit for the park they were in last night. All around the trees were in full autumn foliage and the sky was a nice, clear, azure.

About five minutes later, Pat noticed a lake to his right that was so huge he couldn't see the furthest shore. It looks like an ocean, he thought. At Lakes Erie and Ontario, you can see the opposite shore. He also thought about the many times he had been in Port Dalhousie's Lake Side Park. He would look straight across Lake Ontario and see the Toronto skyline.

"That's Orthnus Lake," Carrie said when she noticed Pat eyeing the view. "Ten leagues to our left is Outhsus Lake. They're called the twin lakes because they are almost equal in size and oval shaped. The Orthnus is about only fifty square leagues bigger."

"I imagine you get a lot of snow here," said Eric.

"In this area we get about a hundred cubits on average. One winter it was pretty mild and only fifteen cubits fell. The rest of our precipitation comes in the form of rain."

Pat took note the people of Corvus used cubits and leagues for measurement, just as people on Earth did, two thousand years ago. He concluded some of their ancestors had crossed over in the days of the ancient Romans and Greeks.

Carrie exited the highway, headed north towards the lake and made a quick turn, coming to a security gate. After being cleared for entrance, she drove down to the end of the street, where the road widened into a circular court, and pulled into a driveway.

The house was a white semi-detached - similar to the rest of the street, although the others were painted various pastel colours. Her house appeared to have two stories and a basement. Pat discovered that besides working as a tour chaperone, Carrie had two bedrooms with a queen-size bed in each, which she ran as a small bed-and-breakfast. Pat and Eric would each take a room, as they felt uncomfortable sharing the same bed.

"I'm going to get you something for your arm, Pat," Carrie said, after they got out of the car.

Pat checked his arm and saw the cut had almost vanished. There were only a few spots of dry blood remaining. That's weird, he thought, it's like there was never a cut in the first place. "Actually, I don't think that'll be necessary."

"What do you mean?" Carrie asked, a little confused. "Even if it's not a large or deep wound, it still needs to be disinfected." She came over, looked at Pat's arm, and raised her eyebrows. "It has been known that people who cross into our world sometimes receive powers." She was now certain Pat was the man Solinga had referred to in her dream. She remembered her saying he would possess certain powers. "I guess you were one of the chosen." She made light of it, not wanting to overwhelm Pat with his importance to Owega.

"You mean like healing powers?" Pat asked, astonished.

"Yes, and others, such as strength and the ability to move small objects."

"Cool! If I returned to my world, would I still have them?"

"I'll explain in a few minutes when I show you the beach, where I like to hang out. First, let's see if I can dig up more appropriate clothes for you."

They entered the living room. It was bright green with a dark plaid sofa and chair set. A lot like the '70s style, Eric thought. On the wall was an Info-Screen exactly like the one at the inn; only this one had several different coloured buttons and a computer mouse.

Carrie brought out a box containing an assortment of men's clothing. "These are some of my husband's old clothes he had planned to donate to charity. Try them on and see if you find anything to your liking."

After picking out the clothes they liked, they found they fitted perfectly. Carrie was glad because this eliminated the hassle of taking them to the shops, in their strange attire which would have made them stick out like sore thumbs, and would surely have attracted the attention of Soapy's gang.

Carrie led them to a beach through her back yard. She took a grassy path that led through the bed-and-breakfast section. They crossed a road running along the beach. The beach had clean white sand, which reminded Pat of the shores of Cancun, Mexico. They sat down on beach mats Carrie had brought with her.

"First, if you stay in our country for more than thirty days, you must apply for a passport card allowing you to live on our planet, otherwise you'll be deported to your own dimension or to one of the islands where things aren't as good."

"Could we go back to Earth and return for an additional thirty days?" Pat asked.

"Most people don't go back to Earth once they are fully settled. Once they live here, they are delighted by our clean and spacious world. They also prefer our government system because we don't pay any income- or sales tax, as you do on Earth."

"Hmm, how can your government afford to run the country?" Eric asked.

"Well, when our government mints the money, they make enough so that twenty or thirty percent of the coins and bills go directly to them."

"So, for example, if the king and queen wanted to build a bigger castle, they would use the funds from their twenty or thirty percent, rather than taxing the people?" Eric queried.

"Exactly. The other thing your people like about our world is the fact that they feel healthier and more energetic due to the clean air."

"What's the population of Owega, Carrie?" Eric enquired.

"There are about one billion."

"That's it?" Eric was very surprised. "On Earth there are over six billion and the population is growing each day, so in a few years, our planet will surpass the seven-billion mark."

"Man has only existed for thirteen thousand years on Owega. According to historical records, much higher intelligent beings discovered our world and acclimatized it, based on your atmospheric conditions. They then led our ancestors here through the portals, from your world. I have an old high school history project which you can read."

"Sure, anytime it's convenient for you," Eric said. "Would I be able to go back to Earth for a few hours to get some cigarettes? I'm down to my last one," pointing to his pack.

"We can stop there on the way to the shops," Carrie replied.

"Oh yeah, how do you measure time here?" Pat asked.

"We have the same length of days as you do, except our days are divided into ten equal cycles. Each cycle has one thousand milo-cycles. At this precise moment the time is 4.896."

"I have 11:45 on mine," Pat said, chuckling.

Carrie continued, "As for the calendar, we have eighteen months. Each has only twenty days. At the end of each year, we have 'extra days.' There are about five every year, with a sixth every fourth year. These fall during the shortest days surrounding the winter solstice day. On these days, most people are off and all shops are closed. On the first day of the New Year, we have a big holiday. People exchange gifts and attend the annual carnival festival."

"So the calendar is based on the Southern Hemisphere seasons, instead of the north like we are used to?" Eric asked to confirm his earlier deduction, while lighting his last cigarette.

"Yes, most of our people and landmasses are south of the equator. In fact, our latitude coordinate is 46.788°S, with zero representing the equator and one hundred representing the South Pole. Our longitude coordinate is 24.225°W, with zero representing the capital of Corvus and two hundred representing the other side of the globe."

"You mentioned cubits and leagues earlier when measuring distance. Could you please explain them?" Eric requested.

"A cubit is about the length from a person's elbow to the tip of their middle finger or about 22 inches, and a league is about 8,640 cubits."

Eric calculated a league to equal about 5 kilometres and a cubit about 2 feet or roughly 56 centimetres.

They lay down on the beach mats and absorbed the warm noon sun. There were no clouds in the sky, which was a blue Pat liked very much. Back home, the sky was always a lighter blue because of the pollution haze.

"Holy Toledo! What in the Sam Hill is that up there?" exclaimed Eric, startling the others.

In the sky, towards the east, was what looked like a bright blue cruise ship with a large rectangular metal board above it. On each end of the ship shaped structure was a propeller rotating at about the same speed as that of a helicopter rotor.

Carrie laughed. "That's an airship. It flies from Clarissa to Rainbow Falls, which is about six hundred leagues north northeast."

"Don't they have jet planes here?" Pat asked.

"They do, but they're not much fun to fly in. People prefer the airships, which offer more seating space, casinos, and entertainment."

Pat thought they should have something like that on Earth. He used to enjoy flying very much but had lost interest because of the narrow seating space. It was always a nuisance getting up. It meant asking people next to him to get up so he could get past them. It was tougher when the people next to him were sleeping or eating. The solution was taking an aisle seat in favour of a window seat. This had its own set of problems; being bumped by the flight attendants when they rolled the food and beverage carts by. Therefore, it was a catch-22. It didn't matter where you were seated; you were bound to encounter a problem of one kind or another.

"Do they fly above the clouds?" Eric asked.

"The pressurized ones do, but not the ones that have the flat top on them, like the one you see now. They only fly about two to four hundred cubits above the ground. They have to land when a severe storm front passes through, else the wind sheer could slam the ship to the ground and smash it to pieces."

"That could be very unhealthy," Eric dryly observed. "Wouldn't it be hard to land on the water or does it float like a boat?"

"They are built to sail when there's rough weather, especially in the winter when we get gale-force winds over the ocean and twin lakes."

After watching the airship until it was a mere speck in the sky, they returned to Carrie's place for lunch, which consisted of ham sandwiches and fizzy drinks, similar to Coke or Pepsi.

"Sweetie, I'm home," a male voice announced from the direction of the living room. A few seconds later, a tall guy with reddish hair came in and sat down. Carrie introduced him to Pat and Eric as her husband, John, and briefly explained their situation to him.

"I heard about you on the news this morning," John said, taking a bite of his sandwich.

"Yeah, I saw the report this morning," Pat said. Carrie recounted to John, the run-in they had had after breakfast, at the inn.

Pat and Eric learned John was an accountant for many bed-

and-breakfast places in the immediate vicinity, the town of Serie Beach, a popular vacation spot for the Clarissa area.

After lunch, John went back to work, and Carrie took them to the portal so Eric could return for cigarettes.

* * *

The portal they were going to use to return to Earth was the only two-way portal in Clarissa, and the same one they had arrived through. Carrie told them all the other portals only went one way. As they approached the cave exit, they looked into the window, expecting to see the woods with budding trees. Instead, a tropical forest with vegetation so thick they couldn't see much of the sky, greeted them.

"This isn't right," said Pat alarmed. "That's not our home area."

"It looks like Soapy's men have been tampering with the coordinates. There's another set of portals to and from your world, but it's halfway around the globe, on Emerald Island."

Chapter 4

Tony's Wild Entrance

"How much would it cost to fly there?" asked Eric.

"On a jet plane about fifty krayohs, the equivalent of an average person's earnings for five days."

Eric made a snorting sound. "Wow! That's pretty reasonable," he exclaimed.

"The airship from Rainbow Falls to Emerald Island is one hundred krayohs, which includes meals. On the other hand, there's the all-inclusive rate of one-fifty, which includes food, drink, and gratuities, but it'll take a week or five days to get there. By the way, I forgot to tell you we have five-day weeks."

"Are there any places that sell smokes here? I couldn't go five hours, let alone five days without one," Eric chuckled.

Carrie laughing, replied, "We have cherry-flavoured cigars that are popular. They are healthier as very few people who smoke them suffer from lung disease or other ailments."

"Yeah, I'll try one of them," Eric said, chuckling again.

"Now we'll go shopping for clothes and then we have an appointment with the mayor at seven cycles. It is now just after six," Carrie declared.

The shops were in a typical mall. Large stores such as Zellers or The Bay were absent. This reminded Pat of a mall in Cancun with only specialty gift and souvenir shops.

The first shop they stopped at was a man's clothing store called Clothes That Make the Man. When they entered, a young blonde sales woman attended them. They purchased a few puffy shirts and some pants each.

They quickly stopped at a bookstore called Book Worm Books and picked up a small travel book on Corvus. The book was electronic; it was illegal to print paper books on Owega.

* * *

Tony was having a rather bad day. He found a parking ticket on his windshield because he had parked on the side of the street in front of his apartment, disobeying the winter by-laws which were still in effect. He was livid. He didn't think he would be ticketed, as the snow on the street was all gone, except for a few inches left along the embankments.

The next stroke of bad luck hit him when he got to work. He was called in to see his manager and informed he was one of five people to be laid off indefinitely because of the declining networking industry.

When he arrived home that afternoon, he decided to give Pat a call to grumble and inform him that he, too, had now joined the ranks of the unemployed. All he got was the answering machine. He tried Eric's number and got his machine too. He then remembered Eric and Pat talking about going through the portal last night, and that they had planned it for today.

Tony contemplated crossing over to join the others, now he no longer had the responsibility of a job. He found Lavinia depressing at this time of year and hoped it would be more exciting over there.

He didn't know exactly where to find the portal. He went to Pat's place, intending to find it by following Pat's directions. Tony headed east on the path for a few minutes and cut off, heading towards the hill Pat had described.

Aha! He thought to himself, as he saw the cave entrance 10 metres ahead. He walked in and found it curved, just as Pat had said it would. As he approached the other end, he saw the scene Pat had described. He was relieved and astonished to find Pat had been telling the truth. He watched the sunny autumn scene with people walking and riding tricycles.

He took a deep breath. It's now or never, he thought to himself as he stepped through. He encountered a glass wall, so clear and clean, it was almost invisible. He tried a second and third time without success. He was confused because the others must have been able to go through, or he would have heard from them by now. He reasoned then they too, may have been unsuccessful and were out doing errands somewhere, which explained why he hadn't been able to get hold of them. He decided to try again just before dark, if he hadn't heard from them by that evening.

* * *

The city hall was a large, white, rectangular, fifty-story building. On either side of the building was a large red triangle of transparent glass, fifty-five stories tall and two or three feet thick. Glancing at it from the side, the triangle made the building appear red.

The elevator was a lot different than any on Earth. It was the width of the entire building instead of a small cubicle. This made it practical for someone entering at one end and having to go to an office at the other end on a higher floor: they could walk, in the elevator, while it was ascending, and be on the desired end when the designated floor was reached.

The mayor's office was on the 49th floor, one floor below the observation deck, where the tourists usually went to view the city and the southern shores of Lake Orthnus. His desk was crescent-shaped with a large 21-inch flat monitor, hooked up to the Info-Screen system, on it.

The secretary led them into the office and introduced them to the mayor, Jack Bluewood. A man of average build with a short brush cut and black square-framed glasses making him look like an army general.

"So where are you from?" Bluewood asked after they had all shaken hands.

Eric answered. "We're from a different dimension, a planet called Earth."

"It's not often we see people from your dimension in Clarissa. Not everyone from Earth is capable of coming to our dimension. They usually end up in Dimension Three, which has a planet similar to Earth and ours. However, it is a very hostile world consisting of mostly plains and mountains with very little water. That is of course if they can cross over at all, because most of the portals won't activate, if the person lacks the power."

"How many people live in Dimension Three?" Pat asked.

"There's no official census, but the estimated population is about twenty billion, give or take twenty-five percent."

"Holy Toledo!" Eric whistled, surprised at the figure. "How do they survive with very little water?"

"The natives have evolved in such a way that they don't need much water. They know where to find as much water as they need, but because of the scarcity, they guard the locations very closely. Therefore, the people from Earth or dimension one, that end up there, tend to return to Earth out of fear they would die of thirst before gaining the trust of the natives and the knowledge of the locations for the water supplies."

Pat decided it was time to change the subject. "I couldn't help noticing how 'cool' the red triangles on either side of this building look," pointing with his thumb.

"The triangles are filled with a gas that colours when charged with an electrical current. As the current's intensity is changed, the colour changes. In this way it can be set to different colours on different nights."

"That's pretty cool," said Eric. "Are there miniatures available as souvenirs?"

"Oh, definitely, they can be purchased in the ground-floor gift shop as well as many of the city's shops," he replied while pulling out what appeared to be money. He presented them with 720 krayohs each. He explained the average worker in Corvus would have to work six out of the eighteen-month year to make the same amount.

That would be more than enough to buy a ticket on the airship from Clarissa to Emerald Island and leave some for spending, Pat thought.

* * *

Tony returned to the cave. He stepped into the portal, but still couldn't get through. He considered it might be controlled by the cycle of the moon or something similar. He decided to return home and try again the next day.

As he was about to head back out of the cave, a deep, soft voice startled him. "I see you are having trouble getting through."

He spun around. The light emanating from the portal was not enough to completely illuminate the cave. He could barely make out the person behind the voice. He could see a man in his fifties with reddish hair showing signs of greying. He wore a puffy shirt and dressy pants. He introduced himself as Steve Bloomstein and led Tony out of the cave.

"Are you from the other dimension?" Tony asked.

"You're exactly right. I'm from dimension two, as we call it, and our world is called Owega. The city and country I'm from is Clarissa, Corvus."

Tony recalled an evening he had been chatting with a girl, in a chat-room, who had used 'Corvus' as her handle. He had found out her real name was Darcy and she was originally from somewhere in the U.K., but living in Corfu, the small Greek island to the west of the mainland. The other thing he remembered was Darcy telling him the chat-room was named after a small amusement park, known as Lunar Bay Park, which had once existed near Southampton, England. Her parents had taken her there fifteen years ago and she had gone on most of the rides.

"As you may have guessed, your two friends are already in our dimension," Steve continued, bringing Tony out of his reverie. "They came through last night and were lucky not have injured themselves because they didn't use the portal tube." He briefly explained the portal tube as a train-like device that goes through the portal and safely stops when it is in the designated dimension.

"Do they like it over there so far?" Tony asked.

"Yes, they do." Steve described the citizen's arrest they had made by accident and the reward they were going to receive. He also mentioned the run-in with two other gangsters at their inn, and how they were most likely in danger.

"If you're ready to cross over we can go in a couple of hours. We'll have to use the portal in the States, just outside Buffalo."

"How did the others get through if I couldn't?" Tony asked, perplexed.

"Only people that have the power to activate the portal can cross here. These are usually people born on my planet. There are some on Earth that have the talent or power in their genes, just as some people inherit the talent to sing or write and others don't."

"My friends were born here on Earth as far as I know," Tony said, giving a little laugh, hoping he was right.

"Maybe one of them inherited the power to cross. Anyway, we should go. Those gangsters may have someone here on Earth working for them, and there's no telling what they may do to you."

"Can we stop at my place to get some things to take with me?" Tony asked.

"That would be rather risky. For all we know, they may have planted a bomb or bug in your apartment. These gangsters like to create small incidents, so as not to draw the attention of the police and risk imprisonment. I was sent to ensure your safety."

They got into Steve's rental car, a dark blue Grand Am. Tony assumed they must have cars in Steve's dimension since he seemed to have no problem driving this one.

During the one-hour trip, Steve, making conversation, told Tony his grandfather had been a scientist. One day a stranger from Corvus had crossed over and offered him a job designing and improving electronic items such as cars, trains, and even the existing computer network. He had accepted and crossed over with his wife to have a much better life, because at the time, it was 1938 and Germany was on the verge of war.

Tony's mind wandered as he studied the passing Buffalo cityscape. Something caught his eye and he looked back for a better view. Steve was busy telling him that he and his wife, Carol, had lived on Earth for a year, to see what it was like, and had visited Germany for a month. The other eleven months they had lived in Lavinia. Tony hadn't heard the last part of the conversation as he had been studying the blue car which had caught his attention.

They were on the I-190 expressway going south when Tony, a little worried, remarked, "That blue car has been following us since we cleared customs."

"Yeah, I think we have company," Steve said while getting a zapper device out of his pocket.

Suddenly a bullet shattered the back window, hitting the back of Steve's headrest. The car swerved a little but Steve quickly regained control, sped up, gave the zapper to Tony, and told him to quickly aim it towards the driver of the blue car and press the red button.

After Tony pressed the button, the blue car behind them suddenly veered out of control and hit the barrier wall a few times before finally coming to a stop on its side. A few other cars, unable to avoid it, crashed into the blue car.

50

"What did I just do?" asked Tony concerned, yet at the same time excited.

"You just rendered the driver unconscious and caused a rather ugly accident. Don't worry. No one will have a clue what we just did. The police will probably conclude the driver lost control of the car. There aren't any bullet holes in the car to make them think otherwise."

To prevent encounters with any more hit men, Steve took a roundabout route by going south over a skyway bridge, then going east on another road, until they were in the country. They headed north into a small town, which had a pleasant looking downtown with nineteenth century buildings.

"The portal is on this road," Steve said, turning right and heading east again down a residential street. Most of the houses had two stories. A few were old and partially hidden behind overgrown pine trees; others were fairly new with well-kept yards.

Beyond the residential area, Steve turned into the parking lot of an old abandoned factory. There was no name on the building but a sign with a picture of an apple, suggested that 'apple', may have been part of the name.

They entered the building and Steve led the way around the machinery that had been left behind. There was still a sign on the wall stating the place had been accident-free for three hundred days. At the other end of the large room, they came to a flight of stairs and descended three sets.

They walked into another large room. About twenty feet in front of them was a white cylinder-shaped train car on a monorail track. Steve pulled a set of keys from his pocket and pressed a button, opening a set of doors. They stepped in, Tony took the front right seat, and Steve took the engineer's seat. Steve pushed some buttons on the panel in front of him and the engine started up.

"Have you been on any roller coaster rides?" Steve asked with a twinkle in his eye.

"Oh yes! Quite a few, such as the ones at Cedar Point, when I was there eight years ago," Tony enthusiastically replied.

"This portal train will feel like a fast roller coaster when we switch dimensions."

"Sounds good to me."

"Hang on now," Steve said as the train started to move.

The train backed up for, what Tony guessed to be, about half a kilometre, stopped, and started forward at an accelerated speed that reminded Tony of a jet plane becoming airborne. In about twenty seconds, they zipped past the area where they had boarded the train. At this point, Tony guessed they had to be going around 120 km/h.

As they went into a dark area, ahead of them they could see a spinning green vortex. The train shot into the vortex and they suddenly started dropping at a sharp 80° angle. This made Tony think of a roller coaster going down its first hill with no bottom to it. They finally reached the bottom, levelled out and came out of the vortex into total darkness, which made it feel like they weren't moving. After a few seconds, the train started spinning sideways and flipping end over end at the same time.

"This tops any of your theme-park rides," Steve yelled above the whining noise.

"You can say that again," Tony answered and hoped it would calm down soon.

The train stopped spinning and flipping, and entered a pink vortex, started dropping and going around sharp turns. Tony was reminded of the water-slide, at Canada's Wonderland, in an enclosed tunnel that had many turns and small drops until it reached the pool at the bottom,.

The train came out of the vortex and gave a small bump as it connected to another set of tracks. The train came to a quick stop and the doors opened. They were in another station similar to the one they had left.

"We're now in Owega," Steve announced. "I see you survived the ride."

"That was awesome," said Tony, a little shaken.

They rode an elevator, exited, walked down a long hallway into what appeared to be a bookstore, and continued into a mall. Tony looked behind him and noticed the bookstore was called Book Worm Books.

"I'm going to take you to my place where my wife Carol, and I run a bed-and-breakfast," said Steve. "It is also within walking distance of my friend John, and his wife Carrie, which is where your friends are staying."

They exited the mall and got into Steve's own car, a bright red and white '50s car with fins on the back. Tony marvelled at the shape of the car and wondered how it ran without wheels. Steve started up the electric motor and Steve's unasked question was soon answered when he saw the car gently rise off the ground. They drove to Steve's place while Tony drank in the view of the city of Clarissa.

Chapter 5

Steve and Carol

After seeing the mayor and stopping at a store so Eric could buy cigars, Carrie took them back to her place. They went to the beach while Carrie did some housework and prepared dinner.

Pat noticed a tree close to them he had never seen before. It was an average-sized tree with banana-shaped leaves; pinkish in colour with black veins. He wasn't sure whether it was in its autumn or regular foliage.

With the sun low in the western sky, they headed back. Carrie would soon be serving dinner and neither one felt overly comfortable about being in the dark without a guide.

Along the way, Pat saw a girl who was perhaps in her twenties. She had straight dark hair tied in a ponytail at the base of her neck. Her skin was dark, giving the impression she was from the tropics. She was dressed in a bright blue outfit and accompanied by a large white dog that looked a bit like a wolf. For a split second, she reminded Pat of Bella. His question about dogs and cats on Owega was half answered.

Back at the house, they had a good dinner, consisting of roast beef, squash, and potatoes. They noticed Carrie and John pronounced squash as *squarsh*. This reminded Pat of his uncle who pronounced it the same way.

The doorbell rang just as they were finishing their vanilla pudding. John went to answer it and announced, "It's Steve and Carol."

Carrie introduced the couple as good friends. Carrie told them Steve and Carol also ran a bed-and-breakfast called The Beachside Manor, which was situated behind their place on the grounds they cut through when going to the beach. To Pat they looked like a couple he had met somewhere before.

"Pat, do you remember us?" Steve asked. "We used to live next door to you when you were a kid."

This remark jogged Pat's memory. He remembered when he was about ten, his next-door neighbours had gone overseas for eleven months, renting their place out to a young couple with a cat and dog. There was another young couple, Dave and Barb, who had visited them frequently, accompanied by a dog and cat. Pat couldn't place the names of the pets other than a white cat named Chien, which he had found strange as it was French for 'dog'. He remembered them living a hippie lifestyle because they had many candles in their place and had dressed in shirts with bright painted patterns. They had also worn beads around their necks. He remembered Carol had then looked a lot like the actress/singer Cher. Now her hair was short and showing grey streaks, like Steve's. He asked how long they had been living on Owega.

Steve laughed. "We have always been from Owega. I work for the government. We crossed over to your dimension to study the people and environment. To fit in we dressed like hippies. Anyway, why don't you guys come with us? We have a little surprise for you."

They went with them while Carrie and John stayed behind to watch a movie on the Info-Screen. Steve led them to the guest living room.

"Surprise!" yelled Tony, who was sitting in front of the Info-Screen.

"How did you get here!" asked Eric.

Tony explained everything: from first seeing Steve at the portal to their arrival at The Beachside Manor.

"So, do you like it here?" asked Pat.

"Yeah, it's pretty cool. My first impression is that the air is much cleaner here and everything is different."

While they talked, a big white dog came down the stairs and into the room. Pat realized he had seen the dog earlier, with the dark-haired girl.

"That dog belongs to one of our guests," Steve said. "She won't hurt you." It went to Pat first and he petted its head.

Pat mentioned he had seen a young lady walking the dog earlier. Carol told him she was staying with them to familiarize

56

herself with the Clarissa area. She wanted to write a book with the area as its setting"I write books too," Pat exclaimed.

"Maybe we'll introduce you to her tomorrow. She's out this evening with a personal tour guide, who also happens to be our daughter."

"We should be heading back to John and Carrie's," said Eric. "Are you staying here tonight, Tony?" he asked.

"Uh, yeah. I'm in a single room upstairs. There are about five rooms here all together."

Pat asked Tony if he had met the girl yet. He replied he hadn't, but probably would during breakfast.

"Gee, Pat, you have girls on the brain again," teased Eric.

When they got back to Carrie and John's, Pat borrowed her project about the first people to arrive in Owega. It was an essay a little over four hundred words in length. She had written it for a history assignment when she was about nine years old. He quickly read it.

The First People of Corvus
By Carrie Orangesand

About 13,000 years ago, in Dimension One, on planet Earth, there existed a race of people known as the Atlantians. They lived on an island called Atlantis. They lived in peace and harmony with nature and their surroundings.

As the years went by, they became bored with their lifestyles and felt their lives needed excitement. Some of the men formed an army, fought battles with other nations, and won. The others started abusing their natural surroundings; causing pollution and having many parties where they got drunk and became violent.

A small part of the group wanted to preserve their custom of living in peace. They moved to the other side of the island and built their own village.

One day a foreigner, wearing strange clothing, told the people he was from a far away place where they had advance knowledge. He explained how his people had found a way to travel to this other dimension where there was a planet similar to Earth, but with different landmasses and bodies of water. He urged them to come with him, saying the gods planned to destroy Atlantis because the people on the other side of the island were living in sin.

They agreed to go with him. He took them in a round ship, and flew them far north to an area where there was snow on the ground.

The stranger led them through a cave towards a portal to the new world. Before crossing over, they were all given injections so they wouldn't be in any danger of not surviving the crossing.

When they arrived in the new world, they were flown in another airship to an island, which became Emerald Island. On this island, they built a city. It was an exact replica of their beloved Atlantis.

They explored their new world and discovered a landmass, far bigger than their island. They claimed it as their country and named it Corvus, which meant 'the land of the free'.

A few generations later, most of the people were killed from a plague-type virus. The ones who survived had discovered a way to move through the portals to another alternate dimension, later named Dimension 3, they made their homes on this third planet, similar to Owega, but with less water and more land. Others stayed on Owega and hid in caves until the plague had run its course.

After they had both read the essay, they watched a sitcom on the Info-Screen called *Funny House* and drank a brand of beer called Eyrus, which meant 'king' in one of Owega's languages.

Eric asked Carrie if it was possible for them to use the portal Tony had come through earlier, instead of having to go halfway around Owega.

"I actually forgot all about that portal. I'll talk to Steve in the morning and see what can be done."

Just before midnight or zero cycles, they had all turned in for the night. Pat and Eric each had their own rooms.

Pat was very curious about the girl he had seen earlier on the beach, because she reminded him of Bella. He wasn't looking for a substitute for Bella, but would like to have a relationship. Her hair reminded him of Bella. Meeting someone in a different dimension, intrigued him. On the same token, he was concerned that, if he decided to return to Earth after the thirty days, he would never see her again unless he came back. He would have to use the other portal in the States because Soapy's gang had tampered with the one behind his house in Lavinia.

* * *

Later that night, Pat again dreamt he was eight years old and walking along the path behind his grandparents' place. A storm was moving in. He wasn't concerned because his grandmother had said the odds of being hit by lightening were rather slim. She had stated that being in the path of a struck tree was more dangerous. The storm came closer and it started hailing with high winds. Dangerous lightning struck closer each time. He discovered a cave and walked in.

The cave had another exit at the other end. He could see the hail coming down heavier, turning the ground white. The scene seemed a little rippled, as if he was looking through a thick glass window.

Someone pulled at his left arm, he turned around and saw his grandmother with a rather angry look on her face, which meant he would be spanked when they got home. He woke from his dream, taking quick short breaths.

He now realized that in the dream he had been looking through the portal. It seemed strange because he hadn't discovered the portal until yesterday and felt he would have remembered it, if he had seen it back then.

Pat glanced at the window. Through the blinds, he could see the sky glowing a reddish colour. He checked the digital clock: 1.20 cycles, which meant it was just before 3:00 A.M., and yet the white blinds glowed with a reddish hue, suggesting it was just before sunrise.

He quietly got up to check his watch; it read 2:54 A.M. This confirmed the clock was set to the right time. Looking through the windows, he could see the northern sky was dark, but the lake, trees, and other houses glowed red.

He quietly went downstairs and looked out the south facing living room window. He saw orange and red lights that looked like a huge set of billowing curtains, in the sky. It has to be the 'southern lights,' he thought. Maybe they cover more sky in this world, because on Earth he would have to be closer to the one of the Poles to see them this bright. He had never once seen them on Earth, because whenever they were visible in southern Ontario, the sky always seemed to be overcast.

He went back to bed while wondering if he, by any chance, had gone near or through the portal when he was a kid. He couldn't remember events that had happened before he was eight because, one day at the beach, he had tripped and hit his head on a rock. He lost all memory of anything that had happened in his life, before that incident.

Pat fell asleep. This time he dreamt he went back home to check his e-mail. There was a message advising him to leave food and other supplies hidden in the cave where the portal was, just in case he couldn't make it home when he returned to Earth. This didn't make any sense because the portal was within walking distance of his house. He wondered if the dream was a message telling him to take precautions.

Chapter 6

Lightning Bolt.

The next morning at breakfast, Pat told everyone about the lights he had seen during the night and mentioned he had never seen them on Earth, because most of the time they're only visible in or near the Arctic and Antarctic circles.

"Yeah, I saw them too, but they were in different shades of green and blue," said Eric.

Carrie explained they have much larger magnetic fields at their poles, so when there's a solar flare, the lights can be seen at the equator.

"Steve will be coming by shortly to take you back to Earth. If you want to come back, which I'm sure you will, you can make arrangements with him."

The phone rang. Pat and Eric speculated it had to be good news. Carrie was saying things like: "Oh my goodness," "What time would they leave?" and "I'm sure they'll be looking forward to it."

About five minutes later, she hung up. "There's some good news: the mayor has enough tickets for up to eight people to attend the annual Bluewood Cup game taking place in the city of Wiktona, tomorrow evening. However, John and I can't go, as we need to look after our bed-and-breakfast, but feel free to contact us if you have any problems."

"Wow! How are we going to get there?" asked Pat, excited.

"It's a package deal consisting of a ride on the high-speed rail and a week's stay at the Panther Resort outside the city, at the famous Wiktona Beach. I'm just waiting for the mayor's office to call back with the rail times."

"Also, if anyone asks where you're from, say you are from the Clarissa area and you both have your own town house, next door to each other. This is because, though some Owegans are aware of the other dimensions, they are suspicious and fearful of people from Earth. They have been told people from Earth are mostly like Soapy and his gang."

"If they know about the other dimensions, why don't they cross over and find out the truth for themselves?" asked Pat.

"They have no desire to cross over. They are taught Earth has certain countries where they could be sent to prison for not having a valid passport. Also they are afraid of being bounced to Dimension Three, where they could die of thirst."

About ten minutes later, the mayor's secretary called back. Carrie wrote the rail times down.

"Okay, here are the times. You leave tomorrow morning at 2.5 cycles and arrive in Wiktona Beach at 5.2 cycles. Check into the resort, then ride a shuttle to the stadium at 7 cycles and the game starts at 8 cycles," Carrie announced.

"What type of sport is it?" Eric asked.

"It's a game where the players kick a ball to each other and try to score on their opponents by picking the ball up and throwing it into a net. A defender tries to prevent it from going in."

Eric told her it sounded a lot like soccer except for one major difference. In soccer the players aren't allowed to touch the ball with their hands, only the goalkeeper or defender.

Steve came over with Tony. Pat and Eric joined them and were driven, in Steve's car, to the portal Pat and Eric had come through. It had been fixed and was now safe to use.

Steve informed them he had received permission for them to pass back and forth between dimensions. He quickly explained the two dimensions line up perfectly every forty days and when they do, crossing is as smooth as walking through a normal tunnel. On the other days, it's risky because the high-speed vortex that carries them through creates the danger of crashing into a tree or person, when they land at the other end. On these days it would be advisable to use the portal tube.

The weather was fairly warm with a hint of rain in the air. The weather station was predicting a sharp cold front would come through later in the afternoon with a good chance of severe thunderstorms.

They went in and quickly crossed over to Earth. The only effect they encountered was a brief flash, like that of a camera flash. On Earth, it was unseasonably chilly and there were wet snowflakes in the air.

"Holy Toledo, it's freezing here! Let's do what we have to and get back to Owega," said Eric, shivering.

While Tony and Eric stopped at their respective homes, Pat and Steve quickly went to his place, checking for new voice- and e-mails. His cat, Pedals, meowed to be fed. He gave her some fresh food and water and she started purring while eating.

There was still close to an hour left before they were to meet the others at the portal. This gave Pat enough time to arrange with his next-door neighbour to feed Pedals once a day. He briefly told his neighbour, a widow in her sixties, that he planned to be overseas for a month. He told her he was working on his current book and needed to see the area he planned to use as its setting. He didn't want to tell her the truth, as they had all promised Steve not to say anything about the other dimension. Besides, he thought, she would think he had lost his marbles and would probably blame it on his sci-fi writing.

Thirty minutes later, they were all back at the portal. Each of them had suitcases with toiletries and extra clothes that wouldn't be conspicuous in Owega.

"Looks like you have enough smokes to last you a year," Pat said to Eric, who was holding a bag with three cartons. The three of them giggled at Pat's remark.

"Okay, you cats, let's get going," urged Steve, anxious to get back to Owega.

* * *

Twenty minutes later, they were back at John and Carrie's place. The passage back to Owega had been nice and smooth, just as their earlier crossing had been.

The weather at noon was sunny and warm. Clouds were building up due to the approaching cold front. Pat guessed the temperature had to be around 25°C or 77°F.

The three friends went for a walk along the beach. They didn't feel like sunbathing, partly because the clouds were blocking out the sun, and because they wanted to explore the area as much as possible.

"Here's this neat tree," said Pat to the others as they approached the tree with pink banana-shaped leaves. "I imagine we'll see some other strange flora and fauna in this world."

"You mean like pigs that fly or pink elephants?" asked Eric, laughing uproariously.

"Anything's possible," answered Pat.

"I wonder if they have the same religions here?" asked Tony.

"I don't see why not," said Pat. "Perhaps after God had created our universe, He decided to create a few more and put them in different dimensions. It's kind of like an author writing more books if his first is a roaring success, or because he likes creating new stories. The other possibility is that there's only one universe spread over many dimensions."

"What if this dimension was created by some other supreme beings or race?" asked Tony.

"You mean somebody such as the 'Lords' in Philip J. Farmer's *Tier Worlds*? That's also possible, because on this planet, the land features are different than Earth's. It doesn't seem to be anything like that *Sliders* TV series, which featured people sliding to different 'Earths' with the same countries, date, and time, but different political parties or situations."

"I remember that show," said Eric. "They had this device that looked like a TV remote with two things on the front end shaped like batteries. The device was called a 'timer', because it counted down the days, hours, minutes, and seconds to the next slide window. If they missed that window, they would have to wait twenty-nine years before the next slide window came up. Once the slide window opened, they would press a button, a vortex appeared, and each of them had to jump into it."

"I saw one episode where they went through the vortex and landed in a cleaning closet. And another where the place they were on had a king of the U.S.A. instead of a president," said Pat.

"Guys, we should turn around. I just felt a couple of drops," Tony informed them.

"I hope they weren't acid rain drops like the one *Sliders* show where the rain had enough acid to burn exposed skin," said Pat, half teasingly.

"I don't think so. The air here is cleaner and my skin is fine. They don't appear to be any different to the drops on Earth, but there's no use us getting soaked if it should decide to come down in buckets."

They turned around. Two minutes later, there was a flash of lightning, followed by a crash of thunder that sounded like it came out of the lake, about a kilometre away.

"That was a little close," said Pat, a little nervous. He subconsciously looked at the pink-leafed tree, which was only a hundred feet from them. He had spoken too soon, a second later he saw a huge lightning bolt hit the tree. The bolt was so bright and orange in colour he had to squint. The thunder came a fraction of a second later, and sounded like a group of big cherry bombs going off. There was the smell of sulphur, which he associated with the static electricity he got when pulling off a wool sweater.

"Man, if that was any closer we would have been fried like bacon," said Eric, shaken.

"I think I see a dog behaving strangely at that tree," Tony pointed out.

67

As they got closer to the struck tree, Pat saw the now familiar white dog and a shiver went down his spine. On the ground next to a big severed, smouldering branch, lay the girl he had seen the day before. Pat guessed she had been walking her dog when the lightning had struck both her and the tree.

Eric and Tony took the dog that was shaking like a leaf with them when they ran to Steve and Carol, to have them call for an ambulance. It started raining hard while the lightning and thunder drifted eastward.

Pat went up to the girl and checked for a pulse, but found none. He attempted to do CPR, even though twenty-or-so years had passed since he had learned the techniques in high school. He couldn't resuscitate her.

He remembered his cut healing. He put his hands on either side of her head and felt a vibration pass through his hands, like that of a power massager. A few seconds later he checked for a pulse — she was still unconscious, but a weak pulse fluttered.

Eric and Tony came back with Steve and they asked if she was alive. Pat briefed them on the situation. Steve put a blanket over her so she wouldn't catch cold from the heavy rain.

The ambulance arrived and two attendants, a man and woman, came over quickly with a stretcher and put her on it. Pat and Steve followed the attendants to the red and white ambulance, which looked a lot like a late '50s station wagon, but without wheels.

"Are you the host of her residence?" the female attendant enquired.

Steve gave her an affirmative answer. The attendant told them they were taking her to the Serie General Hospital and requested Steve come along to sign her into a room where they would keep her for observation.

The rain let up as the ambulance rushed off to the hospital and the sky started to brighten a little. They went over to Steve and

Carol's to have some hot tea and cookies. They needed to dry off since they were all soaked to the skin.

"Is she okay?" Carol asked, a worried frown creasing her brow.

Pat quickly explained the girl had had no pulse and after putting his hands on either side of her head, her pulse had somehow been restored, but she remained unconscious. He asked the girl's name.

"Her name is Maili (pronounced my-lee). She's from up north in the tropics, a country called Ixlezem (pronounced ee-lay-zaym)."

"Sounds a lot like a Hawaiian-type nation," said Pat. He once remembered corresponding with a pen pal from northern Pennsylvania who had the same name and had been born in Hawaii. They wrote letters once a month. After a year of correspondence, he didn't hear from her again. He remembered her last letter had mentioned she had gone to Greece as a nurse, met someone there, and become engaged. He surmised that was probably the reason their correspondence stopped.

Pat was brought back to the present when Carol spoke again. "Actually, they are descendants of the true native people of our planet, known as the Zemians. About 50,000 years ago, the planet suffered a large meteor hit and a lot of them died from starvation. The survivors went over to your world to live on Bornea Island, near Kuching, Malaysia. They later became the ancestors of the Orient races. In Ixlezem they speak our worldwide language called Pihanos, (pronounced pee-hah-noss), which is a combination of several native languages, and is just as common as the Corvic language, or as you call it, English. They also speak their own native tongue, which is Zemish."

"Were they transported to Earth in the same way the Atlantians were brought to Owega?" asked Eric.

"Their legend has it that they were taken to Earth by a superior race of aliens they thought to be gods. They were led to a place somewhere in South East Asia. They eventually returned to Owega thousands of years later because they were being attacked by Mongolian races."

"Is the portal still there?" asked Pat.

"When we were on Earth we went to Kuala Lumpur, the capital of Malaysia, and did some research in the libraries there."

"Oh yeah, I remember when I was a kid, you and Steve went there in the winter of '73 and brought back a map of Malaysia," said Pat, who had been fascinated by maps when he was a kid.

"We determined the portal was possibly located somewhere on Borneo Island in the rain forest area, about 20 kilometres from a resort called the Damai Lagoon, which is close to the city of Kuching. However, there were no records of a race of people from a different planet living there. We tried looking for the portal but couldn't find it."

"Isn't there one here that goes there?" asked Eric.

"If there is it would probably be somewhere in Ixlezem."

"Look how dark it's getting out there," said Tony. The others looked out the kitchen window and the sky was blackening quickly, making the inside of the kitchen dark in a matter of minutes.

Pat got up, looked out the south facing window, and saw dark, quick-moving grey clouds, which indicated a wind shear. He saw a flash of lightning, followed by thunder that sounded like a roaring lion. Just after the thunderclap, the classical radio station declared a twister watch for the entire Clarissa area, and a severe thunderstorm warning for the Serie Beach area. A louder roar of thunder followed another flash of lightening. Eric got up and took a look too.

" I think we'd better get away from the windows," said Carol, pronouncing it as *win-ders*. They stepped away and went to sit in the living room. As they did, the wind picked up to gale force and they could hear what sounded like stones being thrown at the side of the house. From where they sat, they could see what looked like a blizzard outside, but were actually hailstones blowing in the wind, at what Pat figured had to be well over 100 km/h, maybe even 120 km/h. Besides hail, there were leaves and small branches flying around as well.

Pat was so busy watching the storm that when he felt something brushed his left leg he assumed that it was his cat back on Earth. However, the rubbing had also felt a bit like an electric massager. He looked down and saw the white dog that was still shaking as bad as it was out in the earlier storm. He started petting it on hopes that it would settle down.

"She's taking quite a shine to you," Carol said to Pat. "Her name is Bonya, which means pretty."

"Kind of like the word bonnie which is the Scottish version of pretty," Eric pointed out.

About five minutes later, the storm had let up and the sky started to brighten. The wind's speed had decreased to a moderate breeze. The windows started to fog up a little, suggesting the temperature had dropped a lot because of the hail.

A few minutes later, Steve came back, looking rather down, which led the others to believe Maili had taken a turn for the worse and hadn't make it.

Chapter 7

Maili

"How is Maili doing?" Carol asked Steve.

"She's doing well and should be out sometime tomorrow." They all breathed a sigh of relief. "The bad news is she's going to return to her home. She misses her fiancé."

Pat felt a wave of disappointment flood through him. He looked on the bright side though, and realized that being in Owega was a trip from home. Meeting someone here would be like travelling overseas, and meeting someone there. Inter-dimensional travelling however was even worse. If he met someone on Owega and returned to Earth, he would have no way of communicating with her, unless the Owegan scientists invented inter-dimensional e-mail.

The door opened and Steve and Carol's son, Dave, and his fiancée, Liz, walked in. Steve introduced them to their three guests, and instructed them not to discuss the guests with anybody. The business of travelling between dimensions was supposed to be reserved for royal members, appointed scientists, and government-approved persons.

Dave was tall with short brown hair and thick arms, indicating he worked out in a gym often. His fiancée, Liz, was short with shoulder-length strawberry blonde hair, tied in a high ponytail.

"What's with all the debris out there?" Dave asked.

Carol told them about the severe storm. She also informed them about the lightning hitting the tree and Maili, who had been taking her dog for a walk when the electrical storm came in unexpectedly.

Pat, Eric, and Steve went outside to look at the storm damage. There were hundreds of twigs and branches ranging from finger-sized to a large five-metre branch that had fallen just inches from Steve's car.

Pat remembered the dream about hiding a cache of life-saving supplies and asked Steve if he could go back to Earth to get a few more things for his trip. Steve agreed and Tony went with him because he had forgotten to check his voice mail.

Making sure nobody was around, they returned to their homes on Earth fifteen minutes later. The weather was still chilly in Lavinia, even though the sun was shining.

Pat stopped at the store to buy a dozen condoms, part of the list in his dream. He returned home and gathered his spare laptop computer and first-aid stuff. He took some instant-soup and meal-replacement powder that mixed well with water. In his dream he had also been instructed to put the following two things in: some banana-shaped leaves from the tree struck by lightning, and an atomic clock his grandfather had given him when he was ten. He reset it to the beginning, which displayed: 01-000001. It was designed to keep track of time for a million years and didn't need a battery because it used the Earth's magnetic fields. He mulled this over and the only conclusion he could draw was that there perhaps existed a small chance he could encounter a time warp while going through the gateway, which would leave him on Earth far into the future where humans no longer existed.

The phone rang. Tony had bad news. He couldn't return to Owega with Pat. His father had taken ill and was in hospital. The doctor thought he may have cancer but had to run some tests on him.

"Gee, that's sad. Please tell him I hope the tests prove negative and I pray for a speedy recovery. If you want to come back, leave me a message. I'll check in sometime next week after the trip to Wiktona Beach."

"I will, but it'll probably be a few weeks before I can make a decision about going back to Owega. I want to make sure my dad is okay."

"I thought you had gone on holiday," remarked Pat's neighbour, who happened to be outside when he was on his way out. Pat thought quickly and decided to tell her the flight had been postponed until tomorrow, blushing slightly at telling her a white lie.

"Tony had to stay. His dad is very ill," Pat informed Steve when he got back to Owega.

"We'll stop at the hospital and see how Maili is doing," Steve said as they got into the car.

On the outside, the Serie General Hospital looked like any other. However, the inside looked more like a hotel or resort. The walls were chestnut brown, and the floors yellow, white, and dusty rose mosaic tiles.

Maili's large room was about five doors down from the lobby. She shared the room with three other patients. The room was a light green shade with a large waterfall mural on the wall. It looked as big as Niagara Falls, with palm trees growing nearby. Pat concluded it had to be Rainbow Falls.

Maili spoke to Pat in a language foreign to him. Steve, seeing the look of consternation on Pat's face, explained she was speaking Pihanos and he would translate. She had asked him: "Are you the one who saved me?"

"Yes, I did," Pat replied and Steve translated it back. He told her how he had been walking with his two friends when he saw the lightning bolt hit the tree. His friend had seen her dog acting strangely nearby, which led him to come over and discover her lying there.

"Timko and I will always be in your debt," said Maili. Steve relayed her message to Pat.

"It was nothing – anyone else would have done the same. I wish you two the best   She told Pat she would check with her fiancée to see if it's okay for him and guest to attend their wedding.

"

A nurse with blonde hair, done up in a ponytail, walked in and checked Maili's blood pressure and pulse. While she was busy, she smiled at Pat and Steve saying, "Just doing some routine checking."

"Is it good or bad news?" asked Steve after the nurse marked Maili's chart.

"She's doing well so far, but the doctor wants to keep her overnight just to be sure her condition doesn't worsen. Lightning-strike victims can sometimes be unstable, and experience periods of unconsciousness. The one who saved her sure knew about emergency care."

Maili spoke to the nurse in Pihanos and the nurse responded in the same language. Pat somehow knew she had been explaining to the nurse he had saved her, because she looked at Pat while she spoke.

"Maili says you are the one who saved her," the nurse said to Pat, thereby confirming his earlier deduction. He blushed, embarrassed by all the attention. "Anyway, I have to go and check on the other patients. I'll be back later." She spoke to Maili in Pihanos, then switched back to English and said, "See you later." She winked at Steve and Pat, as she left the room.

"We should be leaving too. We don't want Carol worrying about us."

Maili asked if Pat would be with Steve to pick her up the next day. Steve told her Pat and his friend had plans to go away for a week, to watch the big Bluewood Cup game and would be staying at the Panther Resort. He would give her Pat's e-mail address so she could let him know whether or not he could attend her wedding.

Ten minutes later, Steve dropped Pat off at Carrie and John's place, just as they were having dinner.

Carrie asked how Maili was doing and he replied that she was okay. He told Eric Tony had stayed behind to be there for his father in his time of need.

The dinner was a soup dish called 'mushroom pudding'. It consisted of meat and rice mixed with corn and potatoes. Pat thought the meat was beef, but was informed it was actually deer.

"Back home they would call this venison stew," said Pat, who had never tried it before.

After dinner, Carrie instructed Pat and Eric on operating the computer terminal and the Info-Screen system, which about 90% of the Owegan population had access to. She started on the main menu and spoke these words: "Go to Panther Resort enter."

"This has voice recognition?" Pat queried after seeing the screen change to display the Panther Resort logo and a picture of the resort.

"Most terminals do. It's a lot quicker than typing. The downfall is, the basic phonic sounds have to be dictated for it to learn your speech patterns, and that is time consuming."

They spent some time reading about the resort. They learned it was one of only five six-diamond resorts on the planet. It had all the facilities and activities of any resort on Earth, and more. There were features Pat had never heard of. One of them was a supply of love-tree leaves.

The front page of the site had several options to choose from, such as the rates of rooms and activities. One feature that caught their attention was the ability to view parts of the grounds through on-line cameras. Pat requested Carrie choose the live cameras option.

Carrie selected the camera menu and the main lobby was displayed. It was like watching a silent movie. Carrie chose another icon that showed a still image of the lobby. The time and date were printed on the bottom, in cycles and Owegan months and year. It read 08.59-14/5 13 006.

"Man, those images are crystal clear," said Eric impressed. "We have on-line cameras on Earth, but the images are of poor quality or the cameras are unable to transfer several images at once."

"Our Info-Screen system has various types of these cameras, all over the planet. The computerized cameras can send thousands of sharp images in the time it takes to snap your fingers. The main system, to which the estimated four billion terminals are attached, can send a billion copies of a list of every human on this planet, in one thousandth of a cycle."

"Now, that's fast. If only our Internet backbone lines on Earth were that fast," Eric said wistfully.

"Our network used to be painfully slow in the first ten years of its existence, but that was way before my time."

"How long has the Info-Screen system been around?" asked Pat.

"About a hundred years."

Pat whistled and told her the Internet system has only been around for thirty-odd years. First available only to governments and scientists, then ten years ago to the general public. He asked her what would happen if the system broke down and couldn't be repaired for several cycles or days.

"In the case of a system failure, they would switch to one of the twenty backup systems. They are updated at the same time as the main system. The only difference is the backup systems only run at half the speed of the main one. However, not many would notice much difference in speed."

Carrie let Pat navigate the computer. He switched to a camera in an entertainment lounge. They saw a five-piece band playing and some people dancing near the stage. He zoomed in on an empty table with a menu on it. In the still image, he could clearly see the names and prices of the food items. There's a hotel in Las Vegas that has a camera in their restaurant. When he looked at the images there, they were always snowy because of the dimness of the room.

Since it was too dark to look at the outdoor cameras, Pat went to an information site on the Pihanos language. The site briefly explained the Pihanos language was based on many historical languages invented by different tribes. It was also more common in the northern tropical area and on several of the islands that surround the equator to the west of Corvus, than Corvic or English.

The language was fairly straightforward to learn. The vowels were pronounced in much the same way as they are in Spanish. This meant the last *i* in Maili's name was pronounced like a long *e*. The next screen showed the following table of pronunciations:

	Pronounced
A	m<u>a</u>
E	p<u>ay</u>
I	t<u>ea</u>m
O	b<u>oa</u>t
U	l<u>u</u>te
Ai	t<u>ie</u>
Ia	c<u>a</u>t
C	<u>ch</u>at
Eu	<u>ay-you</u>
Y	t<u>ea</u>

The next screen he looked at had some of the most common words and their Pihanos version.

Corvic	Pihanos	Pronounced
Hello	eylo	ee-lo
Good-bye	adio	au-dee-o
Bathroom	kiamcian	Cam-can
The	za	za
Money	doha	doh-ha

The next subject they looked at was the upcoming Bluewood Cup game. On the sites, they learned the Wiktona Panthers were to host the Clarissa Crows as they had a better head-to-head record with Clarissa.

They studied the background of each team. They discovered that in the last seven years, the Panthers had played in six of the ten Bluewood Cup games and lost every one. Four of them they had lost in the tiebreaker shoot-out contest. The shoot-out occurs when the tie is not broken after a 250 milo-cycle sudden death overtime period. Two 250 milli-cycle periods are then played for the tiebreaker. Two other games were lost by one goal. Only one of those games was played on their home field.

"Well, we shouldn't feel bad for the Buffalo Bills losing in all four their Super Bowl appearances," said Pat, laughing.

The next screen they went to had some information on the Panther Stadium, which was also owned by the family who owned the resort. Pat contemplated that ownership was the explanation for the package deal. The mayor must've received the tickets from the owner himself.

Eric and Pat turned in for the day since it was getting late and they had a big day ahead of them.

That night Pat dreamt he was taking a course on how to get the maximum benefit from the powers, he had received after arriving on Owega for the first time. The instructor was a short elf-like man who reminded him of Yoda in the *Star Wars* movies. He told Pat the most important power he had was called Shape Changer, which was the ability to change objects into different things, whether living or not. He said this could some day be a lifesaver when all the other powers failed to eliminate an attacker. He had Pat test his power by changing a stone into a spider, which Pat had no trouble doing. Then he instructed Pat to change it back, which he achieved by just thinking about it. Pat woke from the dream, making a mental note to try using this power. Before he knew it, he was sound asleep again.

Chapter 8

Wiktona

Pat and Eric awoke, ate breakfast, got ready to go, and said their goodbyes to Carrie and John.

"Remember to have fun and don't do anything I wouldn't. I'll be keeping an eye on you two," Carrie said, laughing.

"What are you going to do, call the desk every day and say you're my mother?" asked Eric, playing along.

"No, I meant I'd be checking the on-line cameras."

"Gee, now I feel like a contestant on one of those reality shows," said Pat, joining the banter.

"Don't worry, guys. I'll make sure she stays away from the computer. I'll make a mess so she'll have to spend more time doing housework," said John in a light, teasing tone.

Carrie gave John a little slap on his right shoulder. "If you do, I'll have to gang up on you like this," she said putting her arms around him and kissing him.

Pat was relieved to find they have similar male-female relationships to Earth. He had been concerned that, if he were to go on a date and give a girl a goodnight hug and kiss, she would be offended. After all, he thought; there are countries where you bow before someone rather than shaking his or her hand.

* * *

It was a good day to get away and travel to a tropical beach. The drizzle had changed to wet snow. The wind was still blowing, adding a bite to the air; a complete turnaround from the warm autumn weather of the day before.

They were at the station parking lot, getting their luggage, when Steve pulled out what looked like a two VCR remotes. "Take these with you in case of an emergency. It's called a QTA or Quantum Transport Activator. One of the things it does is create a portal to teleport to anywhere on Earth, by entering the latitude and longitude coordinates. I have it set up so that you would be transported close to the cave behind Pat's house. The numeric keypad is used for setting the coordinates. The light blue buttons are for storing favourite destinations. The green button activates a portal and shuts it automatically after 90 seconds. The yellow button allows you to shut the portal the instant you step through. This is especially handy when being chased. The orange button is used to create a holographic image of yourself. This is useful when you need to teleport without it being known. In other words, you can still appear to be in one place, while teleporting somewhere else. And lastly, the red button is to cancel."

"So we can slip back and forth to any location on Owega?" Eric asked amazed.

"Yes, but be sure to pick an isolated spot. The QTA's are only in their testing stage and won't be available to people for another eight or ten months. These are two of five prototypes. The last thing we need is curious people on our tails. Once the QTA goes on the market, people would be able to use them to cross to Earth and be overlooked as tourists, thereby diminishing their chances of being discovered or imprisoned."

"Seems like a handy device," remarked Pat.

"Now remember, if anyone asks, you are from Clarissa and live next door to each other."

Pat was about to ask Steve what they would do if asked for i.d., should they decide to go for a drink, when he pulled out a couple of cards stating they had temporary Corvus citizenship.

"If you have any questions or problems you can reach me at this number," said Steve, handing them a business card with his number and what they assumed was his e-mail address (it ended in M*Steve Bloomstein).

Pat guessed the M* was used instead of the @ symbol. Ten minutes later they were on the train. There were no spare seats available when it left the station, leaving them with the impression the tickets had all been sold.

After leaving the station, the monotrain went at a leisurely speed of 60 km/h, which reminded Pat of the monorail trains at Disney World in Florida. Pat computed they could never travel the eighteen-hundred kilometre distance, in time to make it to the game, at their current speed.

Twenty minutes later, they were in the country and the track became elevated. The voice of an attendant came over the intercom system, instructing everyone to be seated and buckled up until the train reached its cruising speed. The announcement was made in both English and Pihanos. Suddenly they felt the train accelerate at the same rate as a jet plane going to mach-speed would.

Five minutes later an announcement was made they had reached their cruising speed of 104 leagues per cycle, which Pat calculated was about 500 km/h. Everything outside passed them by so fast, that objects like trees or weeds near the tracks were completely blurred. The other indication of the high speed was the clouds traveling southwest to northeast now appeared to be going in the opposite direction.

For about the first ninety minutes, they cruised along at this speed. There were no stops as it was a non-stop express train they were on. The weather became a little warmer and the snow had turned to drizzle and fog.

"Ladies and gentlemen, please return to your seats, buckle up, and secure any loose articles. We will be going through a rough area for the next ten centa-cycles," came the announcement.

"Where's the orange lap bars?" joked Pat, because the attendant had made it sound like they were boarding a roller coaster ride.

The pleasant fields and little villages suddenly gave way to a rough rocky and hilly area known as the badlands. The windows to Pat's left had a view of the lake, and judging by the water, the track had to be a good 150 metres above the lake.

Suddenly the train took a dive downward and went through some moderate curves that appeared tight due to the train's speed. The zigzagging curves went on for fifteen minutes, and it was very much like a roller coaster ride. There were even a couple of long tunnels with curves in them. The tracks levelled out and the rough terrain was replaced by pleasant scenery.

One thing Pat was puzzled about was that he didn't see any active farms of any kind. He saw only a couple of run-down barns that looked like they had been abandoned several years ago. Weeds and small trees overran the fields around them. There was no sign of any livestock either. He'd have to remember to check into that, once they arrived at the resort.

Before they knew it, the train slowed to a more leisurely speed and they had arrived at the city of Wiktona. The attendant announced they would be arriving at the station shortly, and the temperature was about 300 degrees, which Pat computed to 30°C or 86°F. He noticed they had arrived to sunny skies.

After getting off the train and boarding the resort shuttle bus, they found the city of Wiktona was as different to Clarissa as night from day. Unlike the modern image Clarissa had, Wiktona looked like an old European city. Most of the buildings looked like they had been built six or seven hundred years ago. It also looked a lot like Venice. There were a lot of waterways with boats of all sizes traveling on them. He also saw a couple of Venetian-style, arched pedestrian bridges.

They passed the stadium, which looked like the ancient coliseum in Rome in its day of glory, about 2000 years ago. It was enormous and seemed to have the capacity to seat just over 100,000 people. The only thing that made it look modern was the large purple neon sign at the main entrance displaying the name: Panther Stadium.

Just past the stadium, they made a left turn and crossed a bridge leading to a narrow, but long island, where the resort city of Wiktona Beach was situated. The Panther Resort was the very first resort, and it seemed to be large and spread out. There was a two-story main building and several small buildings on the grounds. All the buildings were dark-coloured with white roofs. It looked a lot like an African safari resort.

They checked in and were given separate rooms. The two tickets the mayor had given them were actually double-occupancy tickets, since there were no single tickets. Pat favoured this arrangement because they wouldn't have to take turns showering, or lose sleep because of the other person's nightly activities or snoring. The other reason Pat preferred this arrangement was that if either, or both, of them should get lucky and meet a woman, they could take her back to the room and have complete privacy. Moreover, I wouldn't have to worry about sharing the computer, Pat thought to himself.

The computer terminal was the only item in Pat's room that used electricity. Any lighting in the room was provided by candles placed beside the two double beds and a larger candle in a gold coloured glass jar suspended from the ceiling. It reminded him of the big candle that hung above the altar at his Catholic church.

He checked the drawers of the bedside table and found three things. The first item was a brown book that looked like it could be a prayer book or Bible. The second item was a package of condoms, and the last item was a plastic bag full of shredded stuff he figured was incense of some kind. In the bag was a little plastic device.

Pat opened the bag, took the device out, and examined it more closely. It was black with a red button on one end. He pressed the button and nothing happened, or so it seemed. He touched the other end and quickly let it drop — it was red hot. He quickly picked it up at the cool end and checked to see if the other end was still hot. To his surprise it was cool again. He was glad the room had a tiled floor instead of carpet, as dropping the device could have started a fire, or left a nasty burn.

He was a little puzzled about the application of the shredded stuff. He guessed the incense was used for relaxation. He knew it was meant to be burned because it came with the electronic lighter.

Since there were a few hours to kill before boarding the stadium-bound shuttle, Pat met up with Eric and they went to the pool for a swim.

The pool was quite large and built like a small lake with a few small islands, just large enough for one or two palm trees. Some of the trees had dark red palms instead of the standard green. The red was the same shade as the red maples on Earth.

Pat noticed there were a couple of cameras mounted on the roof of the main building. They panned back and forth, which meant that any of the 900 million people who have access to the network could be watching them. Pat made a mental note to have a look through the cameras when he returned to his room.

The water in the pool was pleasantly warm, indicating it had been hot in the Wiktona area for the last few days.

"So what do you think of those lighters in our rooms?" asked Eric.

Pat snorted. "I learned the hard way." He gave a brief account of his experience.

Pat decided to return to his room and do some on-line exploring, since his face was showing signs of sunburn. His skin was used to the cold weather back home, which left it more vulnerable to the sun.

He turned the screen on and the same front page picturing the resort he had seen the previous night at Carrie's, was displayed. The first thing he looked at was the pool cameras. He could see Eric lounging on a chaise chair, smoking a cigarette.

Since the number of people at the pool was decreasing, Pat looked up the site for the stadium. He found it on the Panthers' homepage, along with more camera options. Through one of the cameras, he could see the home team practicing on the field. Their shirts were white, with purple on their sleeves, and the Panthers' logo on the front – a panther with its paws stretched out. It could easily be mistaken for the Florida Panthers' logo, Pat thought.

He checked the seating areas and saw there were already quite a few people there, watching the practice. Pat assumed they had all allowed themselves extra time to get there, considering most of them had probably come by boat of some sort.

The phone rang. Eric said it was time to head down to the lobby to board the shuttle. Just before Pat went down to meet Eric, he quickly checked for e-mail messages using the profile Steve had set up for him. He was surprised to see there was new mail waiting for him. He hoped it was from Maili, about her wedding invitation, but it wasn't. It was just a picture taken under water. The picture appeared to have been taken in the ocean, as the water wasn't as clear as a swimming pool's would be. He could barely make out two little kids in the water. There were no words or explanation. I'll have to have a closer look at it later. Maybe it had been sent to my address by mistake, he concluded.

Chapter 9

Games of Good and Bad

A half-hour later they were at the stadium, entering the gates nearest to their seats. As they went through, a man in his sixties, tore a stub of their tickets, just like they did back home. There was a young girl, probably around ten or twelve, drawing a vertical line on a piece of paper, grouping them by drawing a horizontal line across every four. Pat guessed she was counting the number of people with a ticket. There were probably workers at the other twenty-or-so gates doing the same thing. He assumed they would tally them up and announce the paid attendance to the game during the halftime interval.

Their seats were high up. Pat estimated they were about five or six stories up from the rectangular field. Looking around he could see the place was huge and about two, or even three, times the size of an average NFL stadium. Pat learned the stadium's capacity was larger than he had estimated: it could seat up to 165,000 people. He felt sorry for the people tallying the attendance of the game.

Five minutes before the scheduled start of the game, the announcer asked everyone to stand and join hands for the singing of the national anthem. The anthem was very similar to the old Shakers 'Simple Gifts' hymn, part of Aaron Copland's *Appalachian Suite*. Pat had heard that when the United States had picked 'Star-Spangled Banner' as its anthem, 'Tis the Gift to be Humble' was one of the runners-up. He could understand why. Some of the words described a land of the free or Utopia-like setting. The other words he couldn't make out and assumed they were in Pihanos, just as part of the 'O, Canada' anthem is sung in French at a Toronto Blue Jays game.

Eric struck gold. He had joined hands with a woman. She had long, curly dark hair and hazel eyes and seemed to be in her early 30s. Pat wasn't as lucky. He was seated next to an elderly man with two young boys who appeared to be his grandsons.

"Who do you think is going to win?" Eric asked the woman.

"Oh, Clarissa of course; they're the favourites in this game."

"I'm actually rooting for Wiktona. I always root for the underdogs."

"The what?" she asked, a puzzled look on her face.

"The least favourite team."

"Oh, you mean the sub-cats. Pardon my manners, I'm Joanne." She offered her hand and Eric introduced himself and Pat.

"You're not from this area, are you? You have an accent I don't recognize."

"Pat and I are actually from Canada," said Eric, then realized he had dropped his guard, thereby disregarding their instructions and creating a potentially dangerous situation.

"Where's that country?" she asked, baffled.

Eric thought quickly. "Oh, it's a small island way down south and far west of Corvus," he replied, hoping she wasn't going to catch him in his lie. He hoped her geographical knowledge wasn't extensive and he would get away with it, because apart from the two continents, the planet was made up of millions of islands, ranging from the size of Texas to a couple of city blocks. Some areas on the opposite side of Clarissa had so many irregularly shaped islands, a mariner could get easily lost or shipwrecked during storms.

At this point in the conversation, the Crows scored the first goal of the game, which diverted their attention and diffused the situation. Joanne started cheering and clapping.

"Don't worry, Pat, the Panthers will score the next one," Eric said to tease Joanne.

For the next few minutes, Eric and Joanne chatted up a storm and Pat lost interest in the conversation. He excused himself and went to look for a bathroom.

* * *

The bathroom was unisex and unlike the public ones on Earth. There was a long trough but no toilet that Pat could see. After spending some time, he found the toilet was a bar on which to sit while holding onto a higher bar and placing his feet on a set of pedals. The 'plumbing' was much like an old outhouse. He remembered once going on a blind date with an Italian girl in Toronto. She had told him about going to Sicily the previous summer, where the bathrooms were like this.

Once outside, various mouth-watering aromas assailed Pat's nose. His stomach rumbled. He found a food stand, after walking a hundred feet. While in line he tried to identify something on the menu, but all the names were foreign to him. He decided on Spegilli hoping it would be a Cincinnati-style chilli served on spaghetti. He also ordered a tall draught beer, which was home-brewed at the stadium. The total order amounted to one krayoh.

As he walked over to the condiments area, he heard a woman say, "I'll have the same thing he ordered."

A little thrill ran through him. There was something very familiar about the voice. He glanced towards the food stand to see if she was still there. She must have been served very quickly as she now stood beside him.

"Hi, Pat. Is it really you?"

The woman was Bella. His astounded mind reasoned it had to be an Owegan double of her. He remembered the people on the *Sliders* show had sometimes met their identical doubles on different dimensions. He then considered the possibility she had found a portal and had came over out of curiosity, just as he had.

"How did you come to be here?" Pat asked, while trying to avoid drawing attention to them.

"It was easy. The portal is just down the road from where I live in San Francisco. It brings me, here, to Wiktona."

Pat described coming through a portal behind his house, and how he had only discovered it the other day.

"I've been coming here over the last nine years or so. I actually live in Wiktona. I still go back to Youngstown for family gatherings."

"Do they know you live here?"

"Nope, they think I live in San Francisco, which I did for a while, until I became bored, and discovered this world, which to me is superior to Earth anytime. I still don't speak fluent Pihanos but I'm getting there."

"This must be a bilingual city, unlike Clarissa where English, or as they call it, Corvic, is the dominant language."

"Yep, there's a lot of Pihanos here," she said taking a sip of beer. "There are also a few Kaylahzians who have traveled here to come to the game, because a couple of the Panther players are from Kaylahzee. I would love to chat, but I should get back to Karen before she sends a search party after me." She took out a small business card, "Here's my card with my e-mail and chat-room address. Why don't you page me later this evening, after the game. Maybe we can meet somewhere tomorrow."

"Sounds cool to me. We can catch up."

Pat quickly wrote down the e-mail address Steve had created for him, and handed it to her. He told her he didn't have a chat-room address yet. He also added he planned to use 'Grey Cat' as his handle.

After they hugged, Pat started heading back to his seat. On his way there, he wondered if she had a boyfriend. Over the last ten years he had come to realize she wasn't truly meant for him, and getting back together would mean a chance of getting hurt again. Besides, if he lived here half the time, he could some day find a girl and have a better relationship since it appeared people on this planet were happier. Outside of a few flaws such as Soapy's gang and inclement weather, people seemed to exist in almost perfect harmony, like their ancestors did in Atlantis.

* * *

As Pat walked down the row his seat was in, he checked the scoreboard - the Crows were now leading 2–0, and the quiet audience reflected that fact.

"What happened, did you get lost or something?" asked Eric.

"It took me a few minutes to find some food that looked safe to eat," said Pat as he sat down.

"Don't they have the same food in Clarissa?" Joanne asked, laughing.

"We've only been living in Clarissa for a few months," said Eric. "Anyway, Pat, hold the fort. Joanne and I are going to grab a bite to eat before the halftime rush sets in."

The halftime bell rang as soon as they left. The players exited the field and went to their locker rooms for the, approximately, thirty-minute break. Pat was sure the Panthers' coach was probably giving his team a good pep talk to encourage them to make a contest of the game.

Pat reflected that Eric and Joanne seemed to be hitting it off. Knowing Eric as he did, he wondered if Eric would see her again after the five days at the resort.

His train of thought was interrupted when he saw an airship fly over the stadium. This one was different to the one they had seen two days ago. It had three masts and the boat itself probably had four or five decks. He couldn't determine its true colour as night had fallen in the last hour or so. The only thing he could see was a string of blue light bulbs that gave it a blue tint. The lights weren't enough to illuminate the name on the side.

The halftime show was well performed. The performers were all blonde-haired and pale skinned. They appeared to be in their

95

twenties and were all dressed mostly in shades of blue, but a few wore purple. The stage was blue with blue, purple, and white lights. The song and dance performance reminded Pat of a time, about ten years ago, when he had gone to the annual Friendship Festival in Fort Erie, a town about 60 kilometres from his house. There had been a group of people at the festival ranging in age from early teens to mid-twenties, and they had done a very similar show. He tried to remember what they were called. Then it struck him: 'Up with People'.

In one part, only the women were singing in a foreign language that didn't sound like Pihanos. The tone of their voices was having a hypnotic effect on Pat. Would somebody tie me to my mast, and plug my ears, before these lovely voices lure me to my grave! Pat thought to himself. He could see what the Greek hero, Odysseus had gone through when he sailed by the 'island of the sirens'. He started laughing, which broke the spell.

He took out the binoculars Steve had lent them. They were basically the same as his own, with twenty-power capability. He looked at the stage and could clearly see the women wore light blue outfits.

After taking a look at the stage, he decided to look around at the fans. Sure enough, he spotted Bella and her sister, Karen, sitting ten rows down and ten columns to his left. He started thinking about inviting her to the resort and burning the incense in the drawer beside his bed. He laughed loudly and blamed it on the beer, which he found could be quite potent.

"What the blue hill are you laughing at?" asked Joanne, startling Pat." I think I just got hit by a thunder-" Pat answered, but was unable to finish as he had another laughing fit.

"That's it, Pat, no more beer for you," said Eric.

Pat told him about a scene in a *Godfather* movie, where Michael was in Sicily and had been hiking one day with his cousins, when a beautiful Sicilian girl caught his eye. One of the cousins had laughed and told Michael he had been hit by a thunderbolt.

"Okay, so where's your thunderbolt?" asked Eric.

Pat handed the binoculars to Eric, and told him to look down at where Bella was seated.

A few minutes later, the halftime show was done. The stage was rolled off the field and the second half of the game started.

Pat made a mental note to check the computer for information regarding the halftime performers, hoping he might find out which of the women were single.

The first three quarters of the second half were dull. There was no scoring and very few attempts at a goal. Some of the fans packed up and left.

Pat decided to see if his powers could help the Panthers in anyway. At one point, when a Panther player had a remote shot at scoring a goal, Pat tried to unleash his power. As soon as he did, the player picked the ball up, whipped it towards the goal, and it went flying into the net, past the shocked defender, for a goal. The roar of the crowd was so loud it sounded like a jet plane thrusting down the runway. The fans were now wide-awake with enthusiasm as the Panthers trailed by one goal.

About a minute later the same player was again within shooting distance. Pat tried the same thing again, and sure enough he scored again, bringing the game to a tie, with only 0.001 cycles left in regulation.

The regulation ended and the players went off for another break before starting sudden-death overtime. The fans cheered and anticipated a big come-from-behind win.

Pat looked through the binoculars and saw the player he had helped was light-skinned and blonde, just like the people who had done the halftime show. According to the voice announcing the goal, his name was Zaylis Sozee and his jersey number was 41.

The overtime started and Pat kept a close eye on Sozee to see if he could help him score again. If he does, Pat thought to himself, he would owe me a beer or better yet, an invitation to his place when it was his turn to have the trophy, assuming they did the same thing as the National Hockey League back home.

Sozee had the ball and threw it before Pat could guide the shot into the net. The ball bounced off the goal post. A Crow player retrieved it and kicked it to the other end — to one of his teammates. While running, he threw it in the net for the game-winning goal.

Pat's heart sank, feeling that having used his powers on Sozee had been in vain. The fans became quiet and subdued, knowing the game was a heartbreaker for the Panthers.

Pat looked towards the Panthers' net and could see the defender yelling at one of the officials while pointing at the crease-line. The referee pointed upward and the stadium announcer declared: "The goal is being reviewed."

Everyone cheered. Finally, after three nail-biting minutes, the announcer came back and said with greater enthusiasm, "After further review, the goal has been disallowed!" The crowd stood up and cheered. Pat heaved a big sigh of relief.

After about twenty seconds of play, Sozee had the ball and Pat tried using his powers again. The defender was able to stop it and threw it to one of his teammates. Pat thought perhaps he had tried too hard. The Crow team-mate just missed the ball and it rolled back to Sozee. Okay now Sozee, Pat thought, blow this thing up so we can all go home. Immediately after the thought, Sozee picked the ball up and whipped it with all of his strength. It sailed towards the defender, then hooked hard to the left and went in for the overtime game-wining goal.

"Yes! Yes! Yes!" Pat yelled while throwing his hands up in the air. The crowd was cheering so loudly he didn't even hear himself yelling.

Eric and Pat thrashed their arms in imitation of a panther's tail.

A few large fireworks were set off, but their explosions were muffled by the noise of the celebrating fans. Finally, after fifteen minutes, the cheering settled down and the president of the league walked onto a blue strip of carpet laid out on the field. He took a microphone and announced the award for the most valuable player went to Zaylis Sozee for scoring the only goals for the team. Sozee received his trophy and held it up high to the fans. Pat could tell this wasn't the trophy he had waited, all his life, to hold. The one he wanted to hold was the next trophy to be presented to the team.

"Now, it is my pleasure to present the Bluewood Cup!" said the president.

Sozee took the cup and holding it high, ran around the perimeter of the field, so the fans could get a good look at the Panthers' first-ever Bluewood Cup.

The Bluewood Cup was about the size of the NHL Stanley Cup. There were two different things about this cup though. It was made from a mixture of blue topaz and metal, giving it a blue hue, and the neck of the cup was shaped like the ball used in the league. Under the neck was a trunk section engraved with all the names of the last several championship teams and their players.

After Sozee finished his victory lap, he gave the cup to his teammates to carry around. It was at this point that Pat, Eric, and Joanne left the stadium and took the shuttle back to the resort. There weren't many people returning with them. Most had remained to participate in the celebrations at the stadium and in the streets.

* * *

At the resort, Eric and Joanne retired to his room, while Pat went for a walk on the beach. It was a lovely, warm, sultry evening out. Over the lake, Pat could see lightning in the distance. It didn't surprise him at all. It had been hot and humid all day and a weather front must be drifting towards them.

Twenty minutes later, Pat stopped at the pool bar to have one last drink before turning in for the night. There were mostly older couples sitting around the bar watching the post-game show and highlights of the game on a large Info-Screen.

A couple, around Pat's age, sat down beside him. He turned to them, "A real exciting game tonight."

"Oh yeah, we watched it earlier at my cousin's Bluewood Cup party," the man said.

Pat introduced himself and remembered to say he was from Clarissa.

"I'm Chris Wisestone and this is a good friend of mine, Anne."

Chris and Anne were both skinny. Chris had short, straight brown hair. Anne had short, curly brown hair and wore glasses.

"Did you travel here by yourself?" asked Chris taking a sip of his beer.

"I came with a friend who met someone at the game and is spending time with her now."

"Oh, okay," said Chris, gave Pat a brief wink, and asked if he had met anyone yet.

Pat mentioned running into his former girlfriend, whom he hadn't seen in nine years, at the stadium.

"Mmmm," Anne murmured, taking a puff on her cigarette. "Did you get her number?"

Pat said he had gotten her e-mail address and planned to send her an e-mail the next morning, about meeting for a drink or something. He gave her name, and they both remarked that it was a nice name.

"Maybe tomorrow night it'll be your turn," said Chris. "Just invite her to your room then light up a zizi bomb."

Anne laughed, took a deep drag of her cigarette, and asked, "Are you trying to teach him bad habits?"

"What if she invites her sister along, like she used to when we were dating?" asked Pat.

"Then it'll be a two-for-one special."

Anne gave him a soft slap on the arm. "You're terrible." She turned to Pat, "Don't mind him; he must have had a few too many. He's not — "

A large lightning bolt hit close by, seemingly in the lake, followed instantly by a large crash of thunder, cutting off Anne's sentence. Pat realized the storm was much closer to them than he had thought, and it was intensifying since it was spawning lightning a good 10 kilometres from the main rain source. He remembered reading on-line how thunderstorms could produce lightning as much as 15 kilometres from the main source, and that if outdoors when hearing thunder, one should seek shelter as soon as possible or else stand a good chance of being zapped.

"I think it's time to go to the indoor bar, before we get drenched," suggested Anne

"Or fried," said Chris.

Pat went with them to the indoor bar, even though he was rather tired and wanted to head back to his room. He decided to wait out the storm at the bar, rather than walk the hundred-or-so metres to the building where his room was located.

Shortly after settling in at the bar, the wind and rain became fierce and they could hear rain mixed with hail hitting the windows. The lightning became fierce too, and one bolt knocked the power out for a few seconds. By the thundering noise of the falling rain and hail, it seemed the hailstones were getting larger. Pat was now glad he hadn't gone to his room as not only would he have been drenched but also bombarded by the hail.

"This will put a big damper on the victory party," said Pat.

"The storm will probably be moving over there too," said Chris. "Just after the game they flashed a severe-thunderstorm warning for all of the Wiktona area until zero cycles, or midnight."

The storm let up as fast as it had roared in. Pat was wondering if Eric and Joanne had been riding out the storm by hiding under the covers.

"Well, we should head out now," said Chris. "Anne has to get up early for work in the morning."

Pat asked where she worked and she informed him that she worked as a part-time secretary for a female doctor. After they had wished Pat a good remainder of his vacation, he headed back to his room. The heavy rain and hail had tapered off to a light drizzle, and the thunder was in the distance and heading further away. When he looked at the ground he could see large hail stones, the size of golf-balls. There were also a lot of branches and twigs lying on the ground. Pat had to climb over a large branch to get to his door.

In his room, the large ceiling candle was the only one that had been lit. He decided to light a few more with the electronic lighter. He turned on the Info-Screen and checked to see if Bella had sent him an e-mail, but there were no new messages. He called up her chat-room and sure enough, she was there and had been waiting to chat for the last 0.03 cycles or four minutes. Her handle-name was the one she had given to him earlier: 'Sketch-lady'.

```
Grey_Cat> Hi, Bella.  How's it going?
Sketch-lady> Pretty good, Pat.  Karen and I just
got back from the game.  That was some game, huh?
Grey_Cat> It sure beats that Bills one-point Super
Bowl loss we saw at the bar (LOL).
```

102

For the next fifteen minutes, they chatted about some of the stuff that had gone on in their lives during the nine years they hadn't seen each other. Pat told her about the divorce of his one friend they had often visited. She told him about seeing someone, while she lived for a short time just outside of London, England, five years ago. He was tied to his work as part of the film crew for a BBC drama series.

They made arrangements to meet at the hotel lounge the day after tomorrow. She couldn't make it tomorrow as she had made plans with Karen to go to a nearby art festival.

After signing off, Pat decided to turn in since he was exhausted from the long day, and the next day would probably be long again: he would most likely go over to the mainland and check out the planned victory parade, at the stadium.

Pat decided to burn some of the incense provided by the resort. He put the dried leaves in the container and lit them with the electronic lighter. The smell wasn't as strong as he thought it would be, but it was a familiar scent. It took him a moment to realize it was the same smell that came from burning leaves back home. Ten minutes later, he didn't feel any different, so he put the incense burner out and crawled into bed.

* * *

Carrie and John were finally alone after their guests had decided to return to their respective homes. They had held a Bluewood Cup party and were left with a fair amount of cleaning to do. Fortunately, the majority of their guests were Clarissa

103

Crows fans. Their high spirits had evaporated when the Wiktona Panthers were led to victory, in overtime, by a rookie. Had Clarissa hung on for victory the party would probably still be in full swing. An elderly guest had earlier been temporarily housed in Pat's room for the night, when the party became too much for him.

Carrie started the vacuum and began cleaning the carpet, when the door chimes sounded.

"Honey, do you want to get that?" she called to John, who was putting his coat to go out and cover the plants. The weather bureau had issued a hard-freeze warning for the general area.

John opened the door and was shocked to see two gangsters. They stormed in, first rendered John unconscious with a zapper, and then Carrie, before she could scream for help. The elderly man, came rushing down the stairs as fast as his cane allowed, to see what all the noise was about. The shorter of the two gangsters used his zapper on the old man. He gave the old man a large dosage to ensure he didn't recover until after they were long gone.

The taller gangster waited outside while a large truck reversed into the driveway. He went to the truck and helped carry a large square, transparent, oversized phone booth into the house.

A few minutes later, the booth was set up in the living room. The gangsters dragged the still unconscious John into it. They placed him on the full-length body board, similar to ones found in a gym, and quickly strapped his arms to a horizontal crossbar, making it look like he was being crucified. They tied a wire around his waist and another one around his thighs. Once he was completely strapped in, the tall gangster sat on the nearby sofa with an oversized laptop. He pressed a few keys and a bunch of lights went on in the booth.

"Wait until he wakes up!" the shorter gangster, who appeared to be in charge of their assignment, barked out.

In Clarissa there was a famous game show called *The Tank*, which was broadcast continuously over a dedicated Info-Screen site. Contestants were strapped into the tank and asked a series of questions while they braved the elements of the tank. Some of these elements were: hot or cold air, an agitator simulating an earthquake, foul odours and wires used to make leg and lower-back muscles go into painful spasms. After a segment of time, the players entered the next level. There were eight levels and on each, the elements became more intense. If the contestant answered two consecutive questions incorrectly or their vital statistics reached critical level, they came out of the tank and lost half their cash winnings. If they made it through all eight levels, they would win the grand jackpot starting at 10,000 krayohs and incrementing by a 100 each time a player lost.

The tank the gangsters were about to use on John was a more sinister version to the game-show tank. This tank had more twisted features: temperature controls that could change by as much as 70°C in ten seconds, hoses to spray acid at the victim's face, mechanical arms capable of hitting the victim at deadly speeds. The gangsters' tank was named 'T-tank' or 'Torture Tank'; it was highly portable and lived up to its name.

Fifteen minutes later John was awake and disorientated. He discovered his hands and legs were strapped to a bar behind him. There's something familiar about this, he thought to himself. Then he realized what it was. He watched *The Tank*, from time to time. He now realized the rumours about the gangsters' own tank were true.

"Are we a little nervous, Mr. Orangesand?" the mocking voice of the shorter gangster came from a monitor in front of him. The door to the tank was sealed so he would have no way of getting out, should he be able to release himself.

John had heard the gangsters used the tank to torture victims to within an inch of their lives in an endeavour to procure information. He had never thought the day would come when he was put into the tank.

"Now, Mr. John Orangesand," said the short gangster. "My name is Mark Brownbird and I'm going to be your host on the our version of *The Tank*."

Mark began to hum the theme song from the game show in a sinister tone.

"I'm going to ask you just one question and if you tell me the truth, you'll win the grand prize." Mark paused for a few seconds. "The grand prize isn't money — it's your life!"

"What if I don't?" John challenged. He could feel his heart hammering in his chest and for a brief second wondered if it was loud enough for anybody else to hear.

"Then I'm afraid you'll have to suffer some pain and discomfort, like this for example." Mark pressed a key and John felt a brief surge of electricity flow through his legs. He screamed.

"Oh, I'm afraid there's no stopping this game if your vital statistics reach critical limit. If you die it's Este me vistio, or that's life." Mark gave an evil laugh.

"You can rot in Hades," John hissed.

"Wooo, aren't we a brave one," said Mark, laughing and sending another jolt to John's legs.

John heard Carrie call his name and was relieved that she was still alive. "Stay away from my wife!" he yelled.

"She's okay — for now," said Mark. "After all, you don't think I would let her miss the best show of all time, do you?"

"Whoops, I forgot — you have no heart," John blurted out sarcastically.

"Okay, enough bull. Now for the grand question. It's about a guest that stayed with you and checked out sometime this morning. His name is Patrick Silversol. Where is he now? You have one milli-cycle before I show you some of the real magic this baby can do."

John waited for the eight seconds to expire. Suddenly, the temperature rose to 45°C. Beads of sweat began to pour from his near naked body.

"Somebody, please, help!" Carrie screamed at a concealed camera that was on at all times and hooked into the Info-Screen system. She hoped and prayed her yelling for help wouldn't draw their attention to the undetected camera.

"Shut up, or I'll turn him into toast," Mark shouted.

"Are you a little warm in there, Johnny Boy?" Mark taunted.

"Yeah, just slightly."

"Then how about some AC action."

The temperature suddenly dropped to -25°C and hit John like a bucket of snow in the face. He could feel the sweat freezing on his body. He began shaking violently, causing the chair to rattle in its mountings. A hidden fan blew the air at a speed of roughly 40 km/h, adding to the discomfort.

"Just passing through some rough turbulence; please fasten your seatbelts." Mark laughed evilly.

"John, just tell them what they want to know!" Carrie screamed fearing for his life.

"He went to Emeestatz!" John shouted, giving the first name that popped into his head.

"Now, John. It's not nice to fib."

"Why should I tell you anything after your group killed my parents and four hundred other innocent souls, thirty years ago?" John was battling to speak. His jaws were tightly clenched.

"Yakity-yakity-yak-yak. Here, have a shot of special juice."

A burst of liquid acid hit his face and instantly started to eat into his skin. The acid hit him square in the eyes. He screamed in agony. He thought he heard Carrie screaming but wasn't sure. His mind had started to shut down. The stinging sensation went away. The last thing he heard was: "So long, my friend, now it's your sweetie pie's turn."

"Nooooooo!" Carrie became hysterical at the sudden and violent death of her husband.

"Get that bag of crap out and the bimbo in before I put you in there with her! Make sure you clean up the acid." Mark shouted at Pete Redspoon.

Redspoon had recently joined the organization and was learning the ropes. He felt like throwing up. It took all he had to get John's corpse out of the tank, without looking at what had once been his face. He quickly threw John into a body bag, wiped up the acid spill and rushed for the bathroom where he heaved his dinner all over himself, then fainted.

"Man, the help is never good these days," Mark said as he tied Carrie to the board, which still had some of John's blood on it. Carrie was now silent and in a severe state of shock.

* * *

Ellenor Woodhouse, who lived in a village 200 kilometres west of Clarissa, had been browsing for bed-and-breakfast places in the Serie Beach area. She was scheduled to attend a seminar for her company and had to find a place to stay. The company was footing the bill, so money wasn't a deciding factor.

Of the list, she randomly picked John and Carrie's bed-and-breakfast. She checked the live info-cam page. What she saw made her blood turn to ice. There were two scruffy men in the main living room and a third in a tank, almost like *The Tank* game show. When she saw a woman screaming at the camera, and understood the word *help*, she went to the emergency screen and reported what she had seen.

* * *

108

Pete came to, snuck into John and Carrie's bedroom, and found the address to the Panther Resort. He quickly put two and two together, and reported it to his headquarters. He wished Mark had heeded to his suggestion to conduct a search before torturing them. He had guessed John would lie or die trying to protect his friend. With John's death they would have to lie low for a while and tread carefully so as not to stir up the public enough to neutralize the club.

Carrie was strapped into the tank, unaware of surroundings. She was still deeply in shock.

"I'm going to ask you the same question. I suggest you co-operate with us, unless you want to join your husband. Where's Pat Silversol? You have one milli-cycle."

After the eight seconds had elapsed, the temperature in the tank rose to 50°C. Carrie was unresponsive. She just sat there as if she were a statue.

"Answer the question, honey, or — "

A loud knock interrupted Mark. Followed by a bellowing voice, "This is the police. You have to the count of three to come out, or we're coming in."

Mark ignored the officer's demand. A splintering crash followed. Two officers had knocked the door down with a long wooden pole.

Mark placed his finger over a button. "If you move any closer to me I'll kill her." Moving his hand to indicate his finger poised on the button.

The officers froze, giving Mark the confidence he had proven he was in control of this confrontation. However, he had forgotten all about the old man. The old man had regained consciousness despite the dosage he had been given. He quietly snuck up behind Mark, and hit him over the head with his walking cane. Mark went down like a sack of potatoes.

One officer came into the room, handcuffed both Mark and Pete, who had come out of the bedroom at the wrong time, and led them out to the police van. The other officer radioed for an ambulance and asked the old man to wait for the medics.

Steve came over, attracted by the noise. He asked the old man what had happened. The old man explained he had been unconscious for the most part and didn't have any details.

Steve looked through the tank's glass wall and saw Carrie, strapped in and seemingly in a catatonic state of shock. "We've got to get her out of there." He went over to the sofa but couldn't figure out how to operate the control panel. The keys were coded.

He quickly went to his garage and returned a few seconds later with what looked like a flash light. He pressed a button and a violet-coloured light, in the shape of a skinny triangle, shot from the top of the device. He aimed the light at the tank's wall, so the tip of the triangle touched the glass. He pressed another button, the light turned green and started to rotate like a drill. Once he had made a hole with the laser drill, he cut out a rectangular area large enough for him to walk through. He shut the device off, went inside the hot tank and carried Carrie out just as the ambulance attendants arrived.

"It looks like she's in shock. Let's get her to the hospital," said a tall, husky male attendant.

* * *

For some strange reason, the two dreams Pat remembered having were both erotic in nature. In the first dream he was with Bella and they had made passionate love in his room. Pat thought this dream was possibly the result of having run into her at the game and then chatting on-line before turning in.

His second dream didn't make any sense. In it, he was with a blonde-haired woman he had never met before. They were in a garden where there were a few of the trees with banana-shaped leaves. The leaves on these were dark blue, not pink like those near Carrie's place. There were also some large-leafed plants with orange flowers that seemed to glow, like a dimmer-switch-controlled lamp does when set low. The girl was skinny with light lilac-shaded skin that was smooth to the touch. He didn't know what colour her eyes were because she had worn blue-shaded sunglasses. They smoked a pipe that smelled of autumn leaves and made love on the grass. A knock on the door woke him.

He crawled out of bed and opened the door to see Steve standing there. Pat instantly knew he had bad news. Steve's face looked like one who has just seen the devil.

"I need to talk to you down by the beach where we can't be monitored by the on-line cameras."

Chapter 10

The *Blutanikeh*

Pat took a quick shower, got dressed, and walked down to the gardens, next to the Polando Gardens Resort. Eric and Joanne were already there, sitting at a picnic table under a large red palm tree.

"The two of you can't stay here any longer. Your lives could be in danger," said Steve.

"What happened?" Eric asked, trying to stifle a yawn.

"Late last night, a couple of Soapy's men paid Carrie and John a nasty visit. They wanted to know your whereabouts. After torturing John to death and Carric to a state of catatonic shock, they were arrested, but somehow they found the address to this place."

Pat, only half-awake, didn't fully comprehend what he had just been told and asked, "Are they going to be okay?"

"Carrie's in a severe state of shock. However, John" – he paused, took a deep breath to keep his composure and continued – "was eaten alive by the acid in the torture tank they put him in. I'll explain more later, but now we have to get out of here."

"Geez, that's just awful," said Eric.

"You must all check out and come with me. If anyone asks why you are leaving, tell them you had a change of heart and are going further north to stay on Manada Island. Joanne, you must come too as they may add you to their list. These guys have eyes and ears in every corner around here now."

"But why? What do I have to do with it? I've only just met Eric and hey, don't get me wrong, it was fun, but it's hardly like we have a relationship. And what's more, what about my job?" Joanne ranted.

"You could be in danger by association. You would be safer not staying in Wiktona or returning to Clarissa for the moment. I have already contacted your employer and the matter of your absence has been settled," Steve explained.

"Okay, I could do with a holiday, but I want my own room," Joanne demanded, still a little peeved.

Eric breathed a sigh of relief at hearing Joanne's demand. He wasn't interested in having more than a one-night stand. He didn't want to deal with the possibility of a heartache when he returned to Earth.

"Did they plant bugs in our rooms?" asked Pat.

"Possibly, now they know you are here. They can also spy through all of these friggin' cameras in this place. The three of you must make up code words to use when you're in public, or on-line."

While packing Pat quickly sent Bella a message telling her he had to leave unexpectedly and would not be able to meet her the next day. He added that he would send her another e-mail once he knew his destination. He asked her to delete the message as soon as she had finished reading it. After checking out, they drove around the city for thirty minutes to discourage any pursuers. They also stopped at Joanne's place so she could quickly pack a bag.

Finally, Steve pulled into the parking lot of a pier for the public gondola. There weren't many people around; it was still a little early for the morning rush. Steve explained *The Tank* game show and the gangsters' evil version of it.

"Here are tickets for the next airship departing at 5 cycles or high noon," said Steve, handing them blue tickets for three queen size rooms on the *Blutanikeh* airship. He also gave the guys zappers as Joanne already had one.

* * *

Steve instructed them to take the second-longest boat route to the ship terminal, in an attempt to avoid their pursuers, just in case the thugs were watching the shortest and longest routes. Steve left and the three boarded a gondola that had just arrived.

114

"Can one of you please explain what this all about?" asked Joanne a little angry.

Since there was no one within earshot, Eric explained how they had come from Earth and accidentally collided with one of Soapy's men, which had led to his arrest.

"I suspected you had made up the story about Canada Island. I had never heard of it. This means you're quantimnauts, or people who travel through dimensions."

"Have you ever traveled to another dimension?" Eric asked.

"No, when I was growing up, my parents and teachers told me I would probably never return if I were to use the portals, especially when unauthorised. They also said our world is clean and in good harmony, the last thing we needed were people going to other dimensions and bringing back deadly germs or dirty habits."

"We came over with no problem," said Pat, defensively.

"That's because one of you was pre-authorized to come over. Otherwise, you would have been transported to worlds that may not be comfortable to live in, in any of the other dimensions."

The gondola pulled in at a pier. Some older people boarded and the conversation ceased. Pat took this time to think up code words to use while on the airship. He thought of using hours rather than cycles to indicate the time and to add six hours, whenever stating the time for an appointment. He had once seen this used in the movie *Casino*.

He also looked at his ticket. It stated their destination was a place called Emeestatz, in a country called Kaylahzee. This sounded like a country where the people didn't speak English or Pihanos.

An hour later, they arrived at the terminal for the *Blutanikeh* airship, which was in a large grassy field. The four-story depot building was dwarfed by the size of the *Blutanikeh*, anchored to the ground by several ropes.

They entered the depot, checked in their baggage, filled out forms, and received their boarding passes. Pat thought it was much like checking in to go on a cruise. To board the airship, they went up to the fourth floor and walked through a chute connected to the airship. At the end of the chute, they handed their passes to the purser, and received the keys to their suites, which were one floor down and adjacent to each other, according to the purser.

Pat's suite was a lot larger than he had anticipated, based on the average size of cabins and suites on any Earth cruise ship, which were a lot smaller than those at the Panther Resort. There was a time, Pat had been on a Carnival cruise ship where he had noticed the luxury rooms appeared to be as big as the rooms at the Panther Resort, but two or three times the price.

His suite had three rooms. One with the Info-Screen and some chairs, of which one could fold out into a bed. The other room was the bedroom with a queen-sized bed. Both rooms had an entrance to the four-piece bathroom. Each room had a round airtight window because the airship was built to fly as high as 40,000 feet.

He looked out the window at all the people who were there to see off friends or loved ones and to watch the airship take off. Seeing the people made Pat feel he was on an important cruise. It reminded him of the beginning of the *Titanic* movie; old-fashioned black-and-white footage of people waving and cheering as the ship set sail.

A knock at the door brought him back to the present. He looked through the peephole before opening the door to reveal Eric and Joanne.

"Joanne and I are going up to the observation deck. "Do you want to join us?"

"Sure. Maybe we can get a bite to eat."

* * *

The observation deck was three decks up. Most of the people were hanging out there while it remained open. Once they reached a height of about five thousand feet, the deck would be closed until they descended in preparation for their landing in Emeestatz.

Pat looked down and could see a few shipmates untying the ropes. He could see people below appearing to shrink, which indicated they were airborne. The people cheered as they rose higher and started to move away from the landing area.

"Did you know the masts of this ship are an actual living bacterial culture?" asked Joanne.

"How is that?" Eric asked.

Joanne pointed at the white masts. "See how the masts appear to be chubby, as if they were a balloon of some sort?"

Pat and Eric looked up and found the masts did indeed look like long inflated balloons.

"There are electrical wires that run into the inner section or tank. The captain sends a small current through the wires attached to the bacteria wall of the tank. This causes the bacteria culture to become agitated and emit a super-light gas into the tank. This gas allows the ship to become airborne and gain altitude."

"Oh, so it's like a hot-air balloon or blimp," Pat declared.

"We call them airships, even though it's technically classified as a dirigible, or a zeppelin."

"Or a Led Zeppelin," chuckled Eric. He told Joanne about the band and how they had chosen the name after their friends had told them they had as much chance of becoming a famous rock band as getting a lead balloon airborne.

The captain announced they were at 5,000 feet and slowly climbing. They were going at a speed of 50 leagues per cycle, or about 240 km/h. This was made first in Pihanos and Kaylahzian, and then in English. He also mentioned the reason there was very little wind on the outside deck was because they were cruising along at the same speed as the wind. He concluded his announcement by asking the passengers on the outside deck to go below, to the lower observation deck, as the air was becoming thinner by the second and they needed to seal off the upper observation deck.

The deck below had walkways around the perimeter of the airship. Along the walkway, it was like any ocean liner. There were large airtight windows on the outside wall. The inside wall had entrances to the two venues on that deck. The larger a casino and the other a small pub.

The next deck down had three eateries. The largest was the main dining room where formal attire was required. The other two had no dress code. The first was a buffet-style place. The last one was a place serving Kaylahzian food.

They decided on the buffet. They weren't in the mood for dressing up and didn't know too much about Kaylahzian food. The buffet place was simply called the Simik Chambek Buffitka, which was Kaylahzian for Boiler Room Buffet. The eatery itself looked like the boiler room of an old steam liner. It had concrete floors, and a lot of different sized and coloured pipes running along the ceiling.

While they were in there Pat noticed what made the Kaylahzian people stand out. They all seemed to have whitish or pale blonde hair and bright blue eyes, a much richer shade than his own. The biggest difference was their skin, which was an off-white magenta or lilac shade. Pat thought the shade was a light pink with a hint of purple, unlike the hint of orange his own skin would have when un-tanned.

118

They were slender, and some even skinny, like someone suffering from an eating disorder. Joanne interrupted Pat's train of thought by waving her hand in front of his eyes. She wrote something on a napkin and handed it to him. It read, "Stop staring at the Kaylahzians, I'll tell you about them after we've eaten. Hand this over to Eric."

Pat handed it to Eric. He couldn't help but blush at the fact that he had been looking at them the way a kid would stare at a carnival freak with three hands. It wasn't so much the colour of their skin that caused him to look at them. It was the beauty of the Kaylahzian women. He laughed within himself at the thought of these ladies coming to Earth. They would give the super models some stiff competition. They reminded him of H. G. Wells's *Time Machine* novel where the narrator had travelled 800,000 years into the future and met a group of attractive, blonde-haired people known as the Elois.

The food was once again outstanding in taste and texture. Pat remarked on it and Eric suggested they should get the recipes, take them back to Earth, get them patented, and become millionaires.

"Maybe you can bring some Earth recipes to us and get an Owegan patent on them," Joanne countered, half-jokingly.

"Well, shall we go?" asked Eric, who was craving for a smoke, and felt it would be rude to smoke in front of the others.

"No, wait. We have to get our fortune sticks," said Joanne. "It's a Kaylahzian tradition."

"Kind of like the Chinese fortune cookie popular on Earth," said Pat.

The waiter came over and handed them their fortune sticks, which were very similar in size and taste to the Mexican churro sticks sold by street vendors in southern Californian parks, or gardens, as they are called on Owega.

The fortunes were inside the sticks and were easy to get out once the stick was half-eaten. Eric's said he was a wise person, while Joanne's said she must take a journey, which was already coming true. Pat's said, "Help someone in distress and you'll make a life-long friend."

"That's rather interesting. I hope you realize that these are for entertainment purposes only," Joanne said.

After lunch, they went down one deck to Eric's room where they played around on the Info-Screen. They discovered that even the airship had its own on-line site, which showed some of its history and information on all the venues. Here too the zoom and pan spy-cams, like the ones at the Panther Resort, were available.

"So what's the scoop regarding the Kaylahzians?" asked Pat.

"They're a race of people that used to live on a planet, in a different dimension from Owega or your Earth. About five or ten thousand years ago they were led here by the same supreme beings that had brought our ancestors from, what you on Earth called, Atlantis."

"Is their planet still there?" asked Eric.

"No, it was blown up by a bunch of little quasar stars that spun around and burned the surface of the planet with gamma rays. The rays finally penetrated the planet's inner energy core and caused it to blow up like a huge firecracker. They named their country after their planet: Kaylahzee."

"They seem to enjoy wearing blue or purple outfits," Pat commented.

"Oh, that's because on their planet the colours blue, indigo, and violet were invisible. Their ozone layer was bright orange and blocked out blue to ultraviolet."

"Sort of like blue-blocker sunglasses. So that would mean their sky would appear greyish orange and anything blue or purple was grey," Pat concluded.

"Exactly. They were only able to see blue if they used a white light such as a flashlight or regular light bulb. When they came to our world, they were amazed to see the various shades of blue and purple. They were astonished to see the blue sky and flowers in all their colourful splendour. About a thousand years ago, our ancestors used them as slaves. They classed them as being simple because of their skin colour. Eventually slavery was outlawed but the two nations remained hostile towards each other. It wasn't until after they had had a large and costly war that they declared peace and became allies."

The three continued using the Info-Screen and saw on the airship's info page they were still over Corvus, but the eastern shore wasn't too far off. Pat went over, looked out the window, and saw the land below looked like a dark green carpet with some brown and light green spots here and there, which could have been small villages or flat, treeless areas. He asked Eric how high they were.

"Five thousand cubits and climbing," he answered shortly, after looking at the screen. He also added they were traveling at 51 leagues per hour and increasing. Pat did the math in his mind quickly and figured the altitude and speed to be about 9,167 feet at 245 km/h.

Suddenly, Pat let out a large belch, which startled Eric and Joanne. He quickly excused himself while blushing.

Joanne laughed heartily and said, "That's okay, Pat. You remind me of this guy I work with. He always burps and farts just after we come back from lunch."

Pat excused himself and went to his room to have a short nap. He felt a little tired from being wakened early that morning. After failing to fall asleep half an hour later, he figured he wasn't as tired as he had thought.

He walked over to the window to have a look at the view. He faintly saw the coastline in the near distance. He felt the ship being pushed upwards as it entered different air pockets where the air had been rapidly rising from the day's heat. There were cumulus clouds around. Eventually some of these clouds would stack up enough to develop into thunderstorms.

He went back to the Info-Screen and decided to have a look through the spy-cams. He went to one in the casino and saw it was quite busy. A lot of the people there were Kaylahzians playing the slots. Most of them were women.

Watching this casino is like watching people in the water on a hot day. It makes me want to jump in and join them, Pat thought. He turned off the Info-Screen, found some change in his wallet, and went up to the casino.

The casino was like any other Pat had been to on Earth. There were no windows or clocks. There was the constant ding-ding-ding sound the empty slots bellowed, as if calling some sucker to come and empty his wallet.

Pat walked around the room to determine where the better machines were. They were also like the machines back home, except they all seemed to display multi-coloured spheres instead of the different symbols such as the red number seven or cherries.

He picked a machine and sat down next to a couple of Kaylahzian women who could be in their late twenties or early thirties. The one next to him had straight blonde hair while her friend had curly blonde hair that made her look like a Norwegian or Celtic goddess.

He put a blue Corvic coin into the slot and the machine spat it right out. He tried this a couple of times with the same result.

He felt a tap on the shoulder. He turned and was the girl next to him saying something he couldn't comprehend. He figured it had to be in Kaylahzian.

Pat remembered when he had taken an Italian course, the instructor had said they must think in Italian to speak or write it. He decided to concentrate on what the girl was saying, hoping to be able to decipher her message. He indicated she should to repeat it, by showing, he hadn't heard what she'd said. He was amazed to find he could understand her. She was telling him that he had to buy tokens to play the machines. He thanked her and was astonished to hear himself reply in her native tongue. It was as if the Kaylahzian language was stored somewhere deep in his subconscious. That doesn't make sense, he thought, while waiting in line at the token counter. It's not like I need to know it on Earth where it would be unheard of.

After buying a krayohs worth of tokens he went back to the machine, but some other guy, who looked to be Corvic, was using it. He walked around again and found an open machine two rows over. Unfortunately, there were no women in his age group nearby.

In no time at all, he was down to his last three tokens because he was doing triple spins and had had no paybacks at all. He decided to see if his powers could help him out. He put in the last three tokens, pressed the spin button, and hoped for a good payoff. He didn't want to try for the jackpot as he felt he would be making a spectacle of himself. His spin was two blue circles and one purple which earned him a payback of ten thousand tokens or a hundred krayohs, which he figured to be the equivalent of a thousand US dollars, after taking into account the average cost of goods on Owega. A staff member came along, gave him a row of a hundred one-krayoh tokens, and congratulated him.

He played for a little while at a one-krayoh token machine and won a whole bucket-full of the purple tokens. He decided he had had enough gambling for the day and went to cash in his booty of tokens. The teller took his bucket, dumped the tokens on a scale, came back, and said in Kaylahzian, "That's 653 krayohs, sir. Congratulations!" He then handed him six one-hundred-krayoh bills and smaller notes for the balance.

He was just walking towards the exit, when he spotted Eric and Joanne coming into the casino.

"So this is where you've been hiding out," said Eric. "Did you win anything?"

"Over 600 bucks."

"You mean krayohs?" Joanne stammered. "That's more than I make in a quarter of a year."

"That settles it," said Eric. "You're coming back with us to help us win some dough too."

The three of them found a slot machine and agreed to split any earnings over ten krayohs. Two hours later, they cashed their winnings in at a different teller so they wouldn't look suspicious. The winnings totalled around two thousand krayohs or two grayohs, which was a little less than what Joanne would have made in a year, at the commodity brokerage.

An hour later, they ate dinner in the same place they had had lunch. Pat noticed the two girls who had been in the casino earlier were now seated across the room.

"So are they going to give us another fortune stick?" Eric asked.

"They could but it's bad luck to receive more than one fortune a week," Joanne informed him.

* * *

Pat went to the buffet table and dished up his meal. While he was there, the girl with the curly hair came up and dished up her meal too. Pat was so dazzled by her beauty, all he could manage was a smile. He kicked himself about this but noticed she had given him a half smile in return. He figured she probably thought he was shy around women. Maybe I'll get another chance to talk to her, he thought. He felt he had already broken the ice somewhat by his earlier conversation with her friend.

After dinner, Joanne and Eric decided they had had enough of this event-filled and stressful day, and went to their rooms.

Pat went to the pub on the deck above. In there, the entertainment sounded like a cross between opera and country music. After a drink that tasted like rum and Coke, he left the pub. He was bored with the honky-tonk music, which sounded like a drunken diva trying to sing an opera.

He decided to go to his room and surf the Info-Screen for a while. He supposed he could have gone back to the casino, but he had done his share of throwing tokens in the one-arm bandits for one day. On the other hand, maybe it's the other way around, he thought; the machines had had their fill of losing tokens to a two-arm bandit. This thought and the buzz from his drink made him laugh.

As he walked along the outside corridor he heard what sounded like a couple having an argument. As he got closer, his stomach clenched, leaving him with the feeling that this was more than just an argument. The sounds were coming from a men's washroom. A man, who looked to be one of the ship's crew, was on top of a woman, who looked to be Kaylahzian, and he was trying to open her dress.

It angered Pat that a crewman thought he could get away with raping an innocent girl. I'll see he doesn't get away with it this time, he thought. Even if I have to kill him!

Chapter 11

Eelayka

Pat rushed in and threw a punch at the guy's head. The guy, hearing Pat's footsteps, threw up his left arm to block the punch. He threw a punch with his right and hit Pat on the corner of his left eye, knocking him off his feet.

Pat contemplated his options as he got up. He could hold the guy at gunpoint with the zapper, but the would-be rapist was likely to grab the girl and use her as a shield. Pat opted for his alternative plan.

He quickly aimed his zapper and fired a constant laser beam at the back of guy's head, until he passed out and fell to the ground. When Pat looked at the girl, he saw it was the curly blonde-haired girl that had smiled at him earlier, at the buffet table. Her dress was only partially torn, and Pat was thankful he seemed to have gotten there just in time.

"Are you okay?" he asked her in Kaylahzian, putting his hand on her shoulder.

"I think so," she said in a shaky voice. She sobbed a little, regained her composure, and asked: "What about you? It looks like he hit you quite hard."

"Don't worry about it, it'll heal. The main thing is that I nabbed him just in time."

"Is he dead?"

"No, but he will be out cold for several hours, I gave him a good dosage."

For some reason, Pat's black eye wasn't healing like the cut had the other day. Oh well, he thought, maybe fate is the driving force in deciding when his healing power would be most effective or necessary.

The captain, who happened to be strolling along, having heard the commotion, came into the men's room, and asked what had happened. Pat informed him about seeing the guy trying to rip the girl's dress, and how he had used his zapper in self-defence.

The captain gave the unconscious crewmember a dirty look and said, "This is the third time he has tried this. He'll be dropped off and tarred, once we land. Leave him to us and we'll deal with him." He apologized to the woman about it happening on his airship and went on to continue his nightly stroll.

Pat wondered if the expression *tarred* meant *fired*. He would have done the same thing, only immediately after the first offence.

"Why don't you come to my room? I'll give you something for your eye."

"I wouldn't want to impose on you."

"Oh no, it's no problem. I have just the stuff to heal that eye of yours."

"Didn't you come with a friend or two?"

"The girl you saw me with in the casino, was someone I had gone to school with. She's with her husband now. He's been suffering from air sickness ever since we departed from Wiktona."

She stood up and led the way to her suite, which was one floor below Pat's. Her suite had the same layout as Pat's with a sitting area near the Info-Screen in one room and a bedroom in the other.

"Have a seat and I'll be back in a second with the stuff for your eye."

Pat sat down in the chair used for viewing the Info-Screen. In no time at all, she returned from the bathroom with a small green tube, and sat in a chair next to him. "This is sap from a zizi tree," she said while rubbing the ointment around his bruised eye.

Through his good eye, he got a close-up look at the girl's face and noticed the blue of her eyes was so strong, it seemed to have a slight glow. Her face in general reminded him of one of those angel graphics he had seen on many personal web sites that have downloadable images designed for use with web-creator software programmes.

While she rubbed the ointment on, Pat sensed a warm vibe coming from her. He had never felt this type of vibe from any other woman before.

"You seem to be rather quiet," she commented.

"I'm sorry. I find myself left speechless by the beauty of your eyes." He blushed. "Pardon me for not introducing myself, my name is Pat."

"Mine is Eelayka, which means 'shiny-light'. I'm named after Queen Eelayka, who was head of our country when we made peace with Corvus. You can call me Eelay for short."

"That's too lovely a name to be shortened. Mine is short for Patrick. Some people even call me Patty, which sounds like a girl's name."

"Your name is lovely, too," she said flashing him a nice smile.

"It is an honour to meet you," Pat said reaching for her hand and shaking it. Her hand was long and thin, like a supermodel's. It was soft and warm to the touch, which turned Pat on a little.

"You sound like you've never met a Kaylahzian person before. "You must live far away from here."

"Yes, I have to be honest with you. I'm from another dimension." He told her about Earth, how he had come to Owega by using a portal close to his house, and landed in a garden in the western area of Clarissa. He mentioned accidentally catching a thief, going to the championship game, and being on the *Blutanikeh* due to the danger of being pursued and attacked by Soapy's gang.

No sooner had he finished telling her than he realized what he had done. He had let his guard down and allowed his hormones to control his brain. Regrettably, there was no way to retract this information and he could only hope she could be trusted. He cursed himself for allowing her beauty and personality to get the better of him and his judgement.

"Wow, I've never met anyone from a different dimension. When I was a little girl my papa used to say only someone with royal blood could cross into our dimension, and the rest would cross over to other dimensions."

"Sorry, I'm just a regular Earthling, no royal blood that I know of," Pat said, giggling at the thought.

"There must be a lot to tell about Earth. Why don't we wait until tomorrow and you can tell me more about it, otherwise, we could be up all night. What career do you have for a living?"

"I'm a fulltime science fiction and fantasy writer."

"So you must be famous on Earth?"

"Not really. I still haven't found a big-ticket publisher to buy my stories and make them into novels. Maybe I could bring back my printed manuscript for you, the next time I stop at my house."

"I learned some English at school, but not enough to be able to read your story."

"I could read it to you, or have it translated by the Info-Screen," Pat offered.

"You'll have to be careful when bringing it over. It's illegal to have paper reading material because of the damage to the environment and the fact that it requires the killing of many trees," Eelayka cautioned.

"Sounds like a book I once read called *Fahrenheit 451*, where it was also illegal to have paper books. If you were caught by the police, known as the firemen, they would burn the books and arrest you."

"What does the title mean?"

Pat explained how the title was based on the Fahrenheit temperature at which paper begins to burn. While he told Eelayka about Bradbury's novel, she held his hand and held it.

"You know that was a brave thing you did back there - saving me from being raped and who knows what else." She lifted Pat's hand and kissed it.

"It was no problem. It just burns me up to see somebody trying to take advantage of another like that, especially a crew member, who one would think, wouldn't want to jeopardize his career by preying on passengers."

"I'm going to turn in now," she gave a short yawn. "If you're not ready to sleep yet, feel free to use the Info-Screen."

"I should let my friend know I'm not in my room, else he'll bite my head off."

"Dear me! That would be awful," she said with a concerned look.

"Oh no! I didn't mean he would actually do that," Pat said, laughing. "I just meant he would be upset because we don't want to get separated and not be able to find each other."

Eelayka gave Pat a quick kiss, went into the bedroom, and went to bed.

Pat turned on Eelayka's Info-Screen and signed on to see if he had any e-mail. He had two messages. The first was from Eric and asked him to page or phone when he got the message. The other e-mail was from Bella, informing him she planned to be in the city of Emeestatzlayka next week and wanted to arrange to have tea with him, when it was convenient.

Pat paged Eric because he didn't want to keep Eelayka from falling asleep. They typed away.

```
  Grey_Cat> Blk_Pnthr, are you there?
  Blk_pnthr> Yep, I'm here.  Where are you now?   I
tried to call you earlier.
  Grey_Cat> I'm one deck down at a girl's suite.   I
saved her from being raped earlier, and she wants me
to stay here to keep her company.  She came alone on
the flight.
  Blk_pnthr> Way to go you dirty dog you (LOL)!   I
suppose you'll be having fun with her tonight.
  Grey_Cat> No,  not  tonight.   She's  turned  in
already.   Besides,  she  has  just  been  through  an
```

```
attempted rape - have some sensitivity man.  Anyway,
any news on Carrie?
   Blk_pnthr> Nope.   I'll check with Steve tomorrow.
We  don't  even  know  where  we  are  going  to  stay  in
Kaylahzee.
```

They both signed off and exited the chat-room.

Pat turned in, as he was tired from the long day. While lying down and drifting off to sleep, he realized part of his fortune stick had come true, because he had helped Eelayka who had been in distress earlier. Now, if I play my cards right, the other part will come true as well, Pat thought. He looked forward to starting a good friendship with Eelayka and maybe developing it into something more.

He had the same dream about the blonde girl in the garden. He now realized the girl was Eelayka.

Chapter 12

Kaylahzee

Kaylahzee was made up of 40,000 or so small islands to the east and west of a main island, about the size of Texas. The islands ranged in size from a city block to Lake Erie. Some of these tiny islands were just a sharp pointed piece of rock shaped like an inverted icicle, making them completely uninhabitable. During the early afternoon, the airship passed over the western islands.

Pat spent most of his afternoon watching the islands pass below, and studying the Info-Screen location data. He could feel the ship making a slow descent that would last for several hours. Eelayka was spending time with her friend and would join Pat for dinner with Eric and Joanne, who were very eager to meet her.

Pat went to the gift shop, bought a yellow, daisy-type flower the store clerk had recommended. After walking out of the store, he sniffed it and found it smelt like a tulip.

Holding the flower behind him to surprise her, he rang Eelayka's doorbell. She opened it shortly and, once again, her beauty left Pat dumbstruck. She was dressed in a burgundy-coloured dress, which complimented her complexion.

"A pretty flower for a pretty lady," said Pat, bringing the flower out from behind his back.

"That's sweet of you," she said, giving Pat a quick hug.

Since it would be their last meal on the airship, the four decided to go to the formal dining room. Pat and Eric had stopped at the ships clothing store and bought expensive dinner suits with some of their casino winnings.

* * *

Eric and Joanne were already seated at a table for four, when Pat and Eelayka arrived.

134

Pat acted as translator during dinner since Eric couldn't speak or understand Kaylahzian, and Joanne only knew a little. They learned Eelayka was a computer help-desk operator for a shipping and logistics company with branches all over Kaylahzee, as well as in Corvus.

"Don't they use the Info-Screen for all of their computing work?" asked Eric.

"They use it for sending e-commerce and storing off-site backups of all of their system libraries, which I have to transmit when I work night shift."

"What's the name of the company?" Joanne asked. "One of my cousins works at one of those places in Clarissa."

"It's Harmonkah Izkah Logizkay. It's named after the island the owner and founder of the company was born on."

"Not the same one. He works at a place called Bluewater something."

"That'll be Bluewater and Greengrass," Eelayka said.

The conversation was momentarily interrupted when the ship started bouncing and rolling. The Dinner Master informed everyone that the turbulence was caused by some uplifting air currents while the ship banked from an easterly to a northerly direction.

After dinner, they went to the open observation deck. The ship was at an altitude where the air pressure equalled that of the pressurized ship, allowing the deck to be opened. There were quite a lot of people welcoming the fresh air, after being indoors for the last thirty or so hours.

Pat and Eelayka stood near the front and marvelled at the view below. It was like a postcard scene with the sun to their left, slowly sinking towards the horizon and turning from its daytime white to yellow, amber, and finally red. Directly below was the main island known as Emee Island, which the city of Emeestatz took its name from.

"Hey, there's the island I live on!" Eelayka excitedly pointed to a small island close to the main island. Pat estimated the island to be a few square kilometres in size, going by the size of the houses, which were mostly two-story bungalows.

Pat noticed there wasn't anyone standing at the bow or very front of the airship. He mentioned it to Eelayka and they went to stand at the bow. He saw a platform about 40 cm up from the deck and wide enough to hold a person or two. A bright idea suddenly came to mind. He stepped up onto the platform.

"What are you doing, Pat?" she asked nervously.

"Don't worry, I saw this in a movie back home," he answered releasing the railing and spreading his arms to the side as if they were wings. He could see quite a bit of the island to his left and the aqua-coloured sea to his right. With the view and his arms held out, he felt like an eagle coasting through the fresh, warm, tropical air. He suddenly knew what the Jack Dawson character from the *Titanic* movie had felt like when he had stood just as Pat was standing now. Without giving it a second thought, Pat yelled out in English, "I'm king of the world!"

"Come down there before you get into trouble!" Eelayka demanded.

"I always wanted to do that," said Pat, stepping down. She asked him what he had yelled and he explained the famous line from the *Titanic* movie. "You got to try this, Rose, I mean Eelayka."

"Who's this Rose?"

"She was the girl in the movie who had stood with Jack on the bow. Now it's your turn. I'll hold you so you won't find it scary. It'll be just like the movie."

At first she hesitated, but then figured if Pat were holding her, she wouldn't lose her balance. She stepped up and Pat put his arms around her waist as she spread her arms out like a bird. While doing this, the ship tilted slightly into a left banking turn

136

towards the west. The excitement caused her to yell out, "I'm Queen of Owega!"

"So what do Rose and Jack do at this moment?"

"Well, actually Rose falls over board at this point." Pat started to laugh.

"No, she doesn't. You're just pulling my leg. Tell me what really happens."

"Okay, here's what actually happens." Pat stepped up on the platform, placed his face almost in front of hers, and planted a kiss on her lips. She returned his kiss.

"Hey this isn't the *Titanic*," said Eric, who was holding Joanne's hand.

"You got to try this, guys. It's a real rush," said Pat.

Pat and Eelayka stepped down. Eric and Joanne got up, and she spread her arms out. At this point, the sun had set below the horizon, leaving a bright red and purple sunset in its wake. As Pat stared at it, he thought he saw a brief flash of green. This must be the green flash people can see from the tropics back home, Pat thought to himself.

While Eric and Joanne were up on the platform, a crewmember came along and politely asked them to get down before someone got hurt. They stepped down and apologized to him.

"Look, there's the city of Emeestatz, where I work," Eelayka said to Pat, pointing to the skyline ahead of them.

Pat could clearly see the Emeestatz city skyline and it appeared to be on a separate long and narrow island parallel to the main island.

"Hey, is that a theme park to our left?" asked Pat as he spotted what looked like a few roller coasters of different sizes, and a large Ferris wheel with various coloured lights on it.

"Yes, that's Cryskokah Plykah Gardens or Crystal Beach Gardens. It's supposed to be the biggest park in the world with over fifteen roller coasters and about a hundred or so other rides and attractions. There's the largest roller coaster that's quite high and steep."

Pat took a look at it. The roller coaster looked a lot like the new Millennium Roller coaster advertised on Cedar Point's web site. The first hill looked to be almost as high as the airship's altitude, which he figured to be four or five hundred feet. He saw one of the trains go down the first big drop and imagined he could almost hear the screaming of the passengers on board. From the air, the park looked a lot like the aerial view of the CD game called Roller Coaster. Tycoon.

Pat asked Eric if they had heard anything from Steve about where they would be staying in Kaylahzee. Eric told him they were to meet a shuttle driver from a bed-and-breakfast place they had been booked into, at the terminal. They were to use the phrase 'gravy and doughnuts' as the password to identify themselves to him. He added the driver would be holding a sign that read 'Da zizi Arbik' which meant 'The zizi tree'.

After they passed the theme park, they flew directly over a public garden that had a lot of ponds and trees. There was one large pond with a marina and several docked boats of different sizes and types. They then passed over more trees that seemed to be just below the ship. Pat was worried they would hit one because they were quickly losing altitude and there was no landing area in sight. Then he saw a large open area appear in front of them.

Five minutes later, the airship landed and they watched the workers anchor it with several ropes. There were several people waiting for friends and relatives to step off the airship.

"Are your parents out there?" Pat asked Eelayka.

"No, I came out in my wet boat and anchored it at the main pond at that park we just flew over."

"Do you also have a dry boat, which I assume, is one that flies like the airship?"

138

"Yes, I have one of those, too. I inherited it from my aunt who passed away two years ago. It still runs fine, as long as I don't fly it in stormy weather or try doing fancy manoeuvres."

"Do you have to use your wet boat on those days?"

"Nope, I might capsize, silly one. I drive the dry boat on the stone ways."

Pat explained that on Earth they call their stone ways roads and highways.

"So will I be able to see you again?" Pat asked, after they had disembarked from the airship.

"Here's my e-mail and chat-room address," Eelayka said handing him a small wallet-sized business card that had a slightly different texture than paper. There was a small colour photo of her next to the details.

"Something tells me I'll be looking at this card quite a bit," Pat said and chuckled. "Anyway I have to go with Eric and Joanne to look for our ride. I'll contact you as soon as we get settled into wherever we stay."

"Sure, and I can give you a tour of the local area as well as the countryside." They hugged and kissed. Pat joined Eric and Joanne while Eelayka walked the other way, to the lake where her boat was docked.

They soon spotted their driver, who looked to be in his sixties with a beard and moustache, which made him look like an out-of-season Santa Claus. He was holding a large sign with the name of their bed-and-breakfast on it, in bold, green, neon letters.

He introduced himself as Omtuu Erdvuu and informed them the place, which they had been booked into, was only ten minutes away by dry boat.

"Here we are," Omtuu said in English as they approached a vehicle with a boat-like body, wheels, and a large helicopter-sized propeller on its roof. Eric and Joanne sat in the back while Pat sat up front with Omtuu.

The front windshield was large and concave, which enabled Pat to see out front as well as almost directly below him. On Omtuu's side, above the windshield, was a bunch of gauges that looked much like those of a helicopter.

The aircraft rose from the ground and flew in an easterly direction, through a completely dark sky. They flew directly over the theme park, and below Pat could see all kinds of rides and buildings, decorated with a lot of multi-coloured light bulbs. There were also coloured floodlights shining on the buildings. It reminded him of the Niagara lights festival, which took place during the Christmas and New Year holiday season.

"That park has Owega's tallest, fastest, and longest roller coaster," Omtuu said. They could clearly see a roller coaster's track that had deep blue lights along its side.

"How high and fast does it go?" Eric asked.

"It's about 218 cubits high and can go up to forty seven leagues per ten centi-cycles. Pat calculated that as being close to four hundred feet high and with a speed of 225 km/h.

* * *

Shortly after flying over the park, they were over a small and skinny island. Omtuu started descending and announced the bed-and-breakfast was at the far eastern end of the island known as Slimteeka Island, which had a lot of cottages and some large hilltop mansions in the centre of it.

They landed smoothly in the parking area of the Da zizi Arbik, a large bed-and-breakfast place. It had three stories and the exterior was painted the same shade of blue as the banana-shaped leaves of the tree.

In the lobby, an older Kaylahzian lady greeted them and led them up to their rooms. Pat had a room to himself once again, which he was grateful for. He laughed at this thought because when he had had a cabin to himself on the airship, he hadn't even slept in his bed other than when he had tried to take a nap.

Something tells me I won't be spending many nights in my bed, if it turns out Eelayka lives nearby, he thought to himself. Then he decided he didn't want to rush into sleeping with Eelayka since he had only known her for less than one whole day.

Pat's room was the largest of all the rooms he had stayed in so far on Owega. It was large and spacious with a king-size bed and a purple-coloured bedspread, which was a slightly darker shade than the walls. There was a sliding door, opening out on to a small balcony with an excellent view of Emee Bay, which was just across a bricked road.

Pat went out onto the balcony and decided to see if there were any constellations he could identify. He lay down on a chaise lounge, looked up at the sky, and didn't see any familiar constellations. What he did see though, were a few bright stars that seemed to be even brighter than Venus as seen from Earth. There were several thousand, or million, little stars covering the section of the sky visible to him from the balcony. He estimated there had to be a hundred times as many visible stars here, than there were from Earth. Owega's solar system must be in a denser galaxy than Earth's, he concluded.

There were three other things in the sky that caught his attention. The first was the bright reddish polar lights display on the southern horizon. The second was a full moon that rose, due east and was dark red at the horizon. The final and most interesting feature was a bright white comet with a short yellow tail. He couldn't guess how far away it was, unless he could find out its size. He also figured it was approaching the sun; if it had already circled the sun, it would have had a much longer tail.

Ten minutes later Pat went into his room and logged onto the

Info-Screen so he could e-mail Eelayka and make arrangements to meet with her the next day.

There were two new messages waiting for him. One from Steve, asking if they had checked in. The other from Bella, who wanted to meet with him. She was on her way to Kaylahzee on the *Blutanikeh's* sister airship. After meeting Eelayka, he had no desire to meet with Bella, let alone start a new relationship with her. I'll just have to be frank with her and I'm sure she will understand that I had to get on with my life, he debated with himself. He decided against telling her via e-mail, and thought the matter would best be handled in person.

He took the card from his pocket with Eelayka's chat-room address on it and entered it. Two minutes later, a video window in the chat-room screen popped up and displayed Eelayka as she was saying 'hello'.

"Hi, Eelayka, can you see me on your screen?" he asked after noticing there was a small egg-shaped camera in front of the keyboard, directed at his face.

"Yep, I see you."

"What am I doing?" he asked, fooling around. He lifted his right arm and started patting his armpit with his left hand.

"You are acting really silly," she said, laughing.

"I used to be a member of the Lavinia Jaycees and we would cheer that way at our dinner meetings, instead of clapping our hands."

"What did the group do?" she asked.

"Drink and be merry." He chuckled and continued, "We used to do volunteer work to raise money for community events."

"That's nice. Where are you now?"

"I'm sitting in front of this keyboard and screen, chatting to a beautiful lady."

"You have a way with words. You remind me of a man my grandmamma was always telling me about. He had used words to charm her. He had also played a lot of practical jokes on her."

They made arrangements to meet the next day, at the island's only garden, which was within walking distance of the bed-and-breakfast.

Pat was ready to sign off when an 'incoming call' message popped up on the screen. He checked it and found it was from Bella. Fortunately, her airship's Info-Screen didn't have the camera, otherwise she would have seen him blushing.

"So, what made you suddenly leave for Emeestatz?" Bella asked.

He had to think it over for a few seconds, in case their conversation was being bugged. He finally answered, "It's a rather long story, but don't worry, it has nothing to do with you. I'll tell you more when we're somewhere where there is no risk of eavesdroppers."

"Does it have something to do with that guy you had arrested the other night?"

"Kind of. But there's more stuff that has happened since that arrest."

"Can we meet sometime tomorrow afternoon for tea?" she politely asked.

"We can meet tomorrow but we can't stay out too long. I have made plans for the evening." Pat was glad she couldn't see him, or she might have detected his unease.

They made arrangements to meet at the nearby Slimteeka Garden since she was going to be staying at a place at the other end of the island. Pat felt a little uneasy about this, yet at the same time relieved. He knew he had to settle things; the sooner, the better.

Pat signed off, opened up a can of Kaylahzian beer, and stepped out onto the balcony to look at the night sky once again. The air was still warm and muggy, so he didn't need to wear a jacket. He looked at his watch, which had a built-in thermometer. He pressed the button to display the temperature and it read '21°C,' which was just right, as far as comfort went.

* * *

The moon was higher and yet it was still a sand-coloured shade, a lot like that of the planet Mars, when viewed with the naked eye. The polar lights now ranged in shades of green, cyan, and blue. The blue lights were the highest while the greens extended to the horizon.

Pat was taking a sip of his beer when his next-door neighbour stepped out to take in the fresh air too. It was too dark for Pat to determine if he was Kaylahzian or Corvic. The only thing he could make out was that he was chubby with short, dark hair and glasses.

"Nice night out," he said to Pat in Corvic.

"Real nice out here."

"I'm Kevin Raspberry," he said extending his hand over the wooden rail dividing the two balconies. "So where are you from?" he asked after shaking Pat's hand.

"I'm from Clarissa," Pat said and tried not to make the half-lie noticeable.

"Really? I'm from Doddsville, which is only thirty leagues south of the Clarissa city limits. So are you here by yourself?"

Pat told him he was there with Eric and Joanne, who were in rooms across from him, and how they had met her at the game two days ago. He mentioned that Eric and Joanne seemed to get on very well and were becoming good friends.

Kevin laughed and asked, "Does she have a friend you can pair up with"?

He told Kevin about meeting a special lady on the airship and he planned to see her tomorrow, as well as meeting Bella in the afternoon.

"Wow! You have quite a bit on your plate."

A woman, curious about who Kevin could be talking to, stepped out. She was heavy-set and a foot shorter than Kevin. Kevin introduced her as his wife, Ida.

Pat learned they were on a fifteen-day vacation in Kaylahzee. The zizi Arbik was the fifth bed-and-breakfast they had stayed at. They had rented a wet boat to cruise around the islands.

"You must like to travel a lot, like me," Pat said, considering the trip to Kaylahzee as his trip within a trip, to the planet overall.

"Yeah, we've been to quite of few places during our last five years of marriage. However, this country here is probably the best of them all. I highly recommend you see Spectric Falls. They have tours running there daily. For twenty krayohs they'll strap some wings to your back and you'll be able to fly over and around the falls."

"Did the two of you try it?"

"Just me. She was too chicken to go. Anyway, we're going to turn in soon, so maybe I'll see you again." Kevin and his wife went back inside while Pat stayed out a few minutes longer and watched the dancing polar lights in the southern skies.

* * *

Pat stood on a cliff by the sea, with him was Eelayka. They stood admiring the aqua-coloured sea and the sharp jagged island that seemed to stretch up to the clouds like a large needle. He must have been drinking in the dream, because when he turned to look at her, there were two of her standing beside him. Yet, I

145

see everything else as a single entity; such as the nearby island, he thought.

Suddenly one of the two Eelayka's went to his left and pushed him hard enough to lose his footing and fall over the edge. Pat awoke from his nightmare with his breath rasping in his throat. He replayed the dream in his mind to see if he could spot what it had been trying to tell him. After a few minutes, he drifted off to sleep again.

Chapter 13

Frank Silversol's Computer

Pat joined Eric and Joanne in the dinning room for breakfast. They were eating pancakes with red, sweet-smelling jelly. Pat went over to the food counter, dished up the same, and sneezed a few times. He returned to the table and began eating.

"We could hear you over there, achooing away," said Joanne, laughing.

"It could have been worse. I could have burped or broken a wind."

"What does that mean?" Joanne enquired. "You must mean a dry movie?" she added before Pat could explain.

"A what?" Eric laughed.

"It's the short way of saying someone had a dry bowel movement. If it was wet he would be going back to his room to change his knickers."

Pat silently laughed so hard, tears began to form in the corners of his eyes. Ever since he was a young toddler, he had always found farts and burps amusing.

"Then what do you call a motion film projected onto a big screen?" Eric asked.

"We call them ARV's or Altered Reality Videos."

"I suppose if a movie is a bowel movement, then urinating must be a commercial." Pat said, laughing.

"No, Those are front movies."

* * *

Pat decided to surf the Info-Screen while Eric and Joanne went to the beach to work on their tans. He told them he would join them a little later. Pat was never one to lie in the sun all day, especially after all the hype about getting burned by high UV rays. He wondered if the UV rays were lower on Owega because there wasn't any detectable pollution, unlike Earth,

148

which would mean Owega's ozone layer would be in much better shape than Earth's.

The first topic he wanted to research was the trees with blue banana-shaped leaves. After his search returned a list of trees, it took him a few minutes to find the right one. He had to display the pictures to identify the one he was looking for. He discovered it was a zizi tree; the tree his bed-and-breakfast was named after. These trees grew in both the tropics and temperate zones. In the Clarissa area, which is in the temperate zone, the leaves all turn pink at the same time and start shedding in autumn. In the Wiktona area, which is sub-tropical, the leaves last about 60 days longer before they turn pink and the trees grow new leaves about 60 days earlier than those in Clarissa. In the tropics, the trees keep their leaves all year round, but as each new leaf grows, the older ones turn pink and drop to the ground. The tree was also nicknamed 'the tree of life' as its dried leaves had a substance reported to enhance one's sex drive. Couples would crunch the dried leaves, put them in a container, and burn them. This was more commonly known as a zizi bomb.

Pat laughed when he realized he had burned a zizi bomb in Wiktona. That must be why I had those erotic dreams, he thought. I had been inhaling friggin' Viagra leaves. This made him laugh even more.

He decided to look in the drawers of the desk the keyboard was on, to see if there were any zizi leaves. Sure enough, there was some in a small pink container with red hearts all over it.

The next thing he wanted to look up was what year they were in on Owega. He discovered the year was broken up into two sets of numbers. The first set was the millennium number while the latter set was the year within that millennium. He calculated that if Earth had had the same system it would be the third millennium and year 002, or 3-002. He noticed the screen had the date displayed up top, which read, 14/09, 13-006. This meant they were in the early years of the fourteenth millennium.

149

It also showed a countdown to the New Year, which was 81 days away. He also learned the first day ever in this date system was 01/01, 0-000, unlike Earth's, which started on January 1, AD 1.

Pat went to sit on the balcony for a few minutes and decide what he could do to kill time before meeting Bella for mid-afternoon tea. It occurred to him his poor cat, Pedals, was probably getting lonely without him around. He now had something to do. He would go back home, get Pedals, and see what Tony was up to. However, he had to wait a few more hours as Emeestatz was six hours ahead of Clarissa, which was on the same time zone as his hometown.

Already it was starting to get warm, with a light breeze blowing in from the bay. He checked his watch and it read 25°C. There were some fluffy clouds stacking up, giving a hint of an afternoon thundershower. Pat decided to check the weather for the area and then cross over to his place.

The Info-Screen's forecast called for a slight chance of thundershowers late in the afternoon, with a high near 30°C or 86°F. The next day's forecast predicted a greater chance of showers and thunderstorms as an upper air, low-pressure system would be moving in from the southwest.

* * *

Pat decided not to wear a coat, in case people became suspicious of him wearing a jacket in such warm and humid weather. He quickly put the QTA into his pocket and searched for a secluded spot where he could cross over without being seen. He went into a wooded area behind the bed-and-breakfast and found a spot where the trees were thick enough to block out the view of nearby houses. He pressed the button for the portal

150

near the cave, behind his house.

He thought he would see a spinning vortex like in the *Sliders* show. Instead, he saw a rectangular area about the size of a doorway. In this rectangular spot was an image of the bushes behind his house. It had a bluish tint as if seen through a thick pane of glass. Around the outer edges of the rectangular were seven close lines representing the seven colours of the spectrum, with the inner one being red and the outer being violet. On the outside of these lines were light blue sparks arcing outwards. He could also see it was still twilight on the other side.

Pat stuck his hand through the glass-like texture, as if he were testing water to see how warm it was before getting in. He could see his hand on the other side, and it appeared to be a little lower than his arm, which meant the incoming light was slightly refracted. He pulled his hand back and it looked okay.

He quickly stepped over as if he was walking through an x-ray device at an airport. There were no special effects. It was no different from walking into another room. The temperature was cooler than Slimteeka Island, but not too much cooler, which meant his hometown was having some nice spring weather for a change. Something he noticed was that his ears popped from the difference in barometric pressure. This reminded him of his first airplane flight. His ears had popped when the plane started taxiing to the runway for take-off. He remembered the barometric pressure had been unusually high because of a large dome of arctic high pressure on that early March day.

He went to his house, said hello to his cat, and held her on his lap for a few minutes. While he was holding her, he called his neighbour, told her he was going away again for a much longer period, and had decided to take his cat with him.

He next called Tony, found him home, and filled him in on what they had been up to on Owega.. He told Tony about the girls they had both met, as well as the unfortunate events involving John and Carrie.

"Man, I'm going to have to come over and join you guys pretty soon. My dad's health is improving. He is back home and should be himself in a few days."

"Maybe I'll come back in a couple of days with Eelayka and we can all play Trivial Pursuit or something. If you're lucky she may have a single friend, who speaks English, you could some day meet. I should also mention the Kaylahzian women are so attractive they could give some of our supermodels a run for their money."

"Maybe my dad will be well enough by next week. I'm just dying to see these girls."

"I'll try to stop by in a few days with Eelayka so you can meet her. We'll have to meet in a secluded place. My neighbour might get suspicious." He briefly informed Tony about her lilac-white skin, as well as the story he'd told his neighbour.

After ending his phone call, Pat went into the basement to find the small portable cat cage. He thought he would have difficulty finding it, as he hadn't used it for several months.

He started looking along the wall furthest from the stairs. His grandmother had left stuff there when she moved into the retirement home. Most of it, though, was his grandfather's — anything from tools to old magazines. Some of the magazines were old skin magazines from as far back as fifty years ago. The titles were all old companies that had either gone out of business, or been bought out by Playboy or Penthouse. He had once asked his grandmother about them, but she said she had no idea and avoided them as much as possible. Pat had never gotten around to sorting out the basement because he was always working on a book or going out with his friends.

He found the cage on a shelf just above his head. He got out a small stepladder, stood on the second step, and pulled out the cage. As he did, he brushed against a wooden box the size of a carry-on suitcase, and it fell to the floor with a loud crash.

152

After getting down from the ladder, he saw the impact had popped the box open. He put the cat cage down and took a curious look at the box. A smaller olive-green box had fallen out of it. He picked it up. The texture was like smooth leather and gave off a smell very familiar to him. He thought about it for a second and realized it was the same smell the canvas of the airship he had recently flown on, gave off.

That's strange, he thought, could this be something from Owega? I don't remember bringing it with me on other return trips to the house. He presumed his grandfather had known about the portal and had gone over, keeping it a secret, which he had eventually taken with him to his grave.

He opened the box and found what looked like an antique square-shaped bottle. It was clear white and filled with a dark green liquid. He picked it up and found it too heavy to be a bottle of wine. He shook it, but the dark green liquid didn't budge at all; the substance inside was solidified. He put it back in its box and went upstairs so he could get a better look at it, in the natural light from the window.

In his living room, he took a closer look at it. He turned it around to the other side, and found it had an area where he could see into the centre of the bottle. He peered at it closely and discovered the stuff inside looked like a layer of metal. It lined three of the four inner walls of the bottle. He noticed the wide neck of the bottle had a plastic cork in it, and in the centre of the cork was a hole about 3 cm in diameter. He figured there had to be something that plugged into the hole.

Pat went back downstairs and brought up the wooden box to see if there was anything else in it. He opened it and found another smaller leather box. In it was a small glass sphere-shaped object with a 3 cm neck, the same size as the hole in the cork. He studied it closely and saw it wasn't really a sphere, but instead had several triangular cuts that made it look like a sphere.

It looked a lot like the sphere-shaped building at Disney's Epcot Centre.

He put the sphere to his left eye and looked into it and the bottle. It was like looking through a kaleidoscope because the light rays were duplicated several times by the triangular cuts. Then he looked at it from the bottom. He had to close his eye because the light coming through was magnified several times by the triangles.

Pat put it on the bottle, and it fit perfectly, like an old pair of shoes. He looked in through the open side of the bottle and saw a bunch of little specks, as if he was looking at a miniature universe of stars within the bottle.

"Good day, sir," a female voice said in Kaylahzian behind him - so unexpectedly Pat almost jumped out of his skin. He slowly turned around and saw a tall Kaylahzian woman wearing a skinny, semi see-through bikini. She looked a lot like Eelayka but her voice was a lot deeper and her face had a lot of makeup on it. "How can I help you today," she queried.

"How did you get in here?" he asked her. He thought she might have come into the house while he was downstairs. Then realized it wasn't logical, as she would have had to follow him through the portal when he crossed over. He was sure nobody had been around when he crossed over, or he would have sensed another presence.

"How can I help you?" she asked again. "Say '*help*' and '*enter*' if you're not familiar with operating the KS500 system."

It dawned on him the girl wasn't real at all. She was just a 3D holographic image generated by the bottle, which wasn't a bottle, but a rather complex computer system originally made in Kaylahzee, and imported to his basement when his grandfather had lived in the house.

He took the sphere off the bottle and the image disappeared. This confirmed it was a super computer and was probably so powerful it would make Earth's top-of-the-line computers seem like the old original IBM PC systems of the early '80s.

Pat put the glass sphere back on top of the bottle, and about three seconds later, the image of the woman appeared again and repeated her welcome message.

He said, "Help", and the 'girl' explained the KS500 was a prototype model invented by his grandfather, Frank J. Silversol. Its main purpose was to tap into other computer systems and networks on Owega. It could also be used as a personal computer. It had a superior voice-recognition feature, which meant no worrying about typing skills when using it. She instructed him to log on.

He looked in the wooden box and found a piece of paper with two words on it, which he assumed were the user name and password. The first one word was 'fsilversol' and the second was 'Josephine,' his grandmother's first name. He tried these two words and was logged in.

The image of the woman shrank to about the size of a beer bottle and drifted up into the far right corner of the holographic area, which now had a solid navy-blue background instead of the original transparent background. The holograph was so large Pat could no longer see the wall or sofa behind it.

On the menu there were several options, in yellow text. They ranged from signing into the Info-net to reading e-mail. He picked option "Check E-mail". The holograph turned white with black and blue text.

There was one message: Note for Patty Boy; the name his grandfather had called him. "Read note for Patty Boy" resulted in a smaller window popping up with a digital video of his grandfather sitting on his sofa.

"Hello, Pat. If you are playing this video, then I have passed away into whatever awaits me in the afterlife. If you follow the trail behind our house, you'll find a cave with a portal, which crosses into another dimension, to a planet known as Owega.

It's a lot like Earth, but the oceans and land areas are shaped much different than ours. There are two main countries. The first is Corvus, which has two languages. One is Corvic, which is very much like English. The other is Pihanos, which is like Spanish and Hawaiian combined. The other country is Kaylahzee, where people speak in the Kaylahzian, and Pihanos tongues."

I'm actually one step ahead of you, Grandpa, Pat thought to himself.

"If you have already found the portal and gone over then you already understand the lady in my little computer and why her skin is the colour it is. I will now cut to the chase and tell you that you must be very careful about who you meet. There is a group of bandits whose fathers used to burn villages on some of the small independent islands on Owega. They will be after you because you have the power to control and reshape things to your benefit and to their disadvantage. They'll want to use you to benefit from your powers. You will be better off giving up your life, rather than surrendering to them! They are evil and do not give a hoot how many lives they wipe out in their drive to fulfill their goals."

His grandfather told him to go to Emeestatz. He instructed him to look up a friend, Jonk Villitz, who would be able to explain things much better than he could himself.

"Oh, by the way, you had better watch out for those Kaylahzian lasses. They are quite breathtaking." He winked his right eye, wished him luck, and disappeared from the video window.

Pat closed the window, logged off, put his cat into her box, and took it with him into the woods, where he wouldn't be seen when the time came to activate the portal to Owega.

As he walked into the woods he thought about the bandits. He thought these gangsters were very similar to the terrorists on Earth. He remembered one time back in the early '90s when a bomb had gone off in the basement of New York's World Trade Centre. Later that week authorities had traced the attack to a large terrorist network in the Middle East. Over eight years later the terrorists had come back and finished the job with their 9/11 attacks, which put the whole world in a state of shock and fear.

He quickly activated the rainbow portal and went through to the paradise-like Kaylahzee. He wondered how much longer it would remain peaceful with the gangsters living on some secret island, probably not too far from Kaylahzee or Corvus. The last thing he wanted to see was a repeat of something like the 9/11 attacks, in a world of such beauty.

Chapter 14

The Comet

In the middle of Slimteeka Island, was a well kept garden, rather small when compared to most of the several hundred gardens on the main island. There were still a large variety of flowers, trees, and shrubs to keep anyone with a green thumb occupied for a while.

Pat arrived shortly after returning to Owega, and went to the central pond to meet Bella, who was feeding ducks from a bag filled with birdseed and dried bread pieces.

"These ducks are quite friendly. Just watch." She waved a piece of bread and a couple of white ducks came up to the bench they were sitting on. One of them gently grabbed the bread from her hand. She gave Pat a piece. He held out his hand to the other duck, which also took it gently from him.

"Is this your first time to Kaylahzee?" Pat asked her.

"It's my second. I was here about nine months ago with Karen, and we pretty much saw most of the city, which reminds me of New York because its downtown is on a separate island, shaped somewhat like Manhattan Island."

"Does Karen live here with you?"

"No, she comes over from time to time. She works as a full-time secretary at a veterinary clinic in Niagara Falls, New York."

"Pardon me," said a familiar voice over Pat's left shoulder. Pat turned and saw Omtuu accompanied by a man and woman. He recognized the woman as Maili. The man beside her was tall and muscular. "This couple would like to visit with you," Omtuu announced.

Pat heard Maili say something in Pihanos, which he didn't quite understand. He thought in Pihanos and replied, without thinking, "It's nice to see you again."

"It's nice to see you again, too, Patrick," Maili answered. She pronounced his proper name as 'pah-treek.' "I thought you didn't understand Pihanos."

"Actually, neither did I, until I jogged my memory a bit. This must be your fiancé?" he asked looking at the man.

"Yes, this is Timko," Maili said. They shook hands. Timko thanked Pat for saving Maili. "So who's your friend?" she asked.

Pat introduced Bella.

"We would be honoured to have you both as guests at our wedding."

"Great! You'll have to give me directions," Pat said. He was a little put out that they had assumed Bella would accompany him, as he had intended to ask Eelayka.

"It's on a small island, about a hundred leagues north of here, on Ixlezem, our home island," Maili said

"I hope you didn't make a special trip just to invite me," said Pat.

"When we contacted Steve, he informed us you were here and about the attack on his neighbours. We decided to personally extend the invitation since we were going to be in the area. We came on a pre-honeymoon trip, to see if we would enjoy this area. We really like it, even though we've only been here a day. Steve told us about the attack on his neighbours, and I feel very sad about it. We can't stay long because we have tickets to a show this evening. Let me have your e-mail address so I can send the directions to our island."

Pat wrote down his address on a Kaylahzian gum wrapper and handed it to her.

"Wow, you seem to be quite a hero on this planet," Bella remarked after Maili and Timko had left with Omtuu.

Pat told her how he had saved Maili on the beach behind Carrie and John's place.

"Listen, I have to be honest with you. I didn't come here to see if we could get back together. I came as a concerned friend, to make sure you were okay because these gangsters are bad news. I won't be offended if you had someone else in mind to take to the wedding. After all, I'm seeing someone in California."

160

Pat felt a heavy load had been taken off his shoulders. "Well, actually, in all honesty — there is someone I've met on the way to Kaylahzee, that I wish to ask to the wedding. Her name is Eelayka and she intrigues me as much as her name does. I have to confess, I'm meeting her in a short while."

"That's great. Did she also get hit by lightning?"

"Nope, a drunken airship crewman was attempting to rape her when I came to her rescue."

"Are you, some kind of Batman- or Superman-type figure?" she asked, laughing.

"No, I'm just trying to make my surroundings a better place. I feel this world is so much nicer than ours."

"I wish you luck.".

"Ditto to you. Eelayka, Eelayka I just met a girl called Eelayka," he sang to the tune of a *West Side Story* song called *Maria*.

"Don't push it," said Bella. It was a favourite expression she used when Pat got carried away.

They hugged and Pat went back to his room, feeling much more comfortable knowing she wasn't going to be a factor in his pursuit of a relationship with Eelayka.

* * *

Pat was back in the garden, after having a shower and changing. He had dressed better, and was wearing a light yellow and white striped, fluffed-out shirt and beige pants. He noticed the people in Emeestatz tended to dress up, just as people in Clarissa did.

Five minutes later Eelayka arrived in her light blue flying machine. It had the propeller of a helicopter and a body shaped like a fifteen-foot motorboat. She landed next to the bench Pat was sitting on and alighted with a smile on her face. Pat noticed she was wearing a light blue dress, with darker blue seashell patterns on it, which blended in well with her sky-blue eyes.

"Is that your helicopter, or as you call it, dry boat?" Pat asked.

"Yes, this is the one I inherited from my aunt. She used to fly it all the time, until thirty years ago when she lost an arm in a tragic event. After that, she flew it occasionally but mostly rode the public wet boat to work and back. Hop in and we'll go to dinner at a nice restaurant in the city."

Pat got in as Eelayka started the motor. She pulled on, what looked like a typical steering wheel, and the aircraft ascended to about fifteen feet. She used the wheel to turn the aircraft. When they were pointed westward, she accelerated to around 120 km/h and headed towards downtown Emeestatz.

The short flight was fairly smooth under a calm area of high pressure. When Pat looked towards the northeast, he could see towering thunderheads, which looked like a typical thunderstorm developing.

They flew over the downtown area, which was on a long narrow island shaped like Slimteeka. It reminded Pat of a time when he had gone to New York City and flown directly over Manhattan Island, landing at LaGuardia Airport. The buildings here were all different shades of blue and purple and looked very clean.

"Below us is Centreeka Garden," Eelayka said as they approached an area with numerous green, blue, and red tropical trees. "The place I made dinner reservations at is in the garden."

Eelayka landed the aircraft in a parking lot at the restaurant, which was plainly named Restarkee-vans-Gardeekah, which meant Restaurant-in-the-Garden. "This is one of the city's few five-diamond restaurants." The building itself was circular in shape and had walls of light blue glass, giving patrons an excellent view of the garden while wining and dining.

162

It was hard to tell the difference between the inside and outside. There were many small trees and flowering plants growing in several pots. The air had a nice potpourri smell. An older host led them upstairs to a table for two, against the glass wall.

The table, like all the others, was made of the same light blue glass and had a purple candle on it, adding to the atmosphere. Outside, the sun had just set and it was quickly getting dark.

"There's the green flash," said Eelayka just after the red and purple sky flashed green for a split second. "Make a wish and see if it comes true."

"I wish for our friendship to grow like those trees out there."

"You're not supposed to tell me!" Eelayka chuckled, after playfully slapping him lightly on his right arm.

The food they had ordered was some kind of meat with noodles. Pat found the meal to be excellent, and it would give a five-star eatery back home a run for its money.

After swallowing his food and chasing it down with a sip of wine, Pat asked, "One thing I'm curious about, is where do they get all the food? I have yet to see an operational farm on this planet."

"We get it from our sun, as well as other suns that come out at night."

"Say what?" Pat asked, his face a mixture of consternation and confusion. Eelayka burst out laughing.

"It's all in the light - from the suns, lamps, and anything else that may give off light."

"You mean the light photons?" Pat asked.

"Exactly. Light rays are actually little microscopic photons of energy that travel at super speeds. I don't know how advanced your world's knowledge is of the science of light, energy, and matter, or 'LEM.'"

"We have a limited knowledge of light rays and photons," said Pat, after chewing on another piece of meat. "We use it for

TV's and computer screens. Also, we use it for transmitting computer data at high speeds, to meet the demand for fast data retrieval between different corporations."

"Well, there's a lot more to the nature of light. We have different labs that use large pieces of multi-cut crystal glass to capture the light photons and multiply them as they pass through. They are then directed through a pipe, become compressed into a super beam, which passes through magnetic machinery and is converted into solid matter. The matter is then converted into different types of molecules and can be anything from food to wooden logs."

Pat whistled. "Amazing! If they had this level of technology on Earth, they could wipe out starvation, and any other shortages that come along from time to time. That reminds me. I found a device earlier, in my house." Pat quickly told her about the computer his grandfather had hidden in the basement. "It too must run on light, because it had a crystal top that drew and magnified light to the point that, when I put it to my eye, it was more intense than sunlight."

"He referred me to a man who lives somewhere in this city," Pat said after finishing the last of his meal. "He also told me to watch out for the Kaylahzian lasses. I think I know what he meant."

"And what is that supposed to mean?" she asked, looking directly into his eyes.

"I think he was referring to your beauty. He must have had a romantic fling with a Kaylahzian woman while he was here."

"So maybe that's where you get your blue eyes?" she speculated.

"Does anyone run a farm as a hobby?" Pat changed to the original subject of conversation.

"It's illegal to run a farm for two reasons. The first is that food created from light photons is pure and free of any bacteria usually found in organic food and can be stored at normal room

164

temperature for several days before decaying. I'll explain the other reason when we are done here and in the garden."

After they had finished their meal, the waitress brought them their fortune sticks. Pat opened his and it said "Beware of people with false faces." Eelayka's said "A change is not too far off for you." They quickly exchanged their fortunes and went out into the darkness.

Pat found the early tropical sunsets hard to get used to because in his hometown the sun was normally up until nine o'clock in the months of June and July.

The garden looked a lot like a Christmas wonderland without the snow. Several small and mid-sized trees were draped with strings of small sparkling coloured lights.

They walked hand in hand to a large area where there was a stone wall about 20 metres long and 2 metres high, decorated with a few hundred large light bulbs of different colours and shapes. The most common were shades of blue and purple. There were a few other couples and families strolling along the wall of lights. As they came to the first lights, Pat noticed a person's name and a short inscription. They stopped at a light blue bulb, which said, "Jonk Omee, sadly missed by wife, Jaynah and favourite niece, Eelayka." He now realized this was some kind of memorial wall, for an event, which had resulted in many fatalities.

"This wall was built because of a tragic event that happened in our city about thirty years ago. A cargo airship carrying a bomb had crashed into a monotrain killing about 250 passengers and thirty other people in the vicinity when the track was destroyed with the train. The monotrain had run through this park."

"Holy Toledo! That must have been awful."

"At first they thought it was some kind of engine malfunction. A few weeks later, they found the red box recorder and discovered it was no malfunction. It was a suicide attack instigated by the gangsters. Later that day, they discovered

165

another airship with a bomb aboard, had crashed into a monotrain in Clarissa, with close to the same number of fatalities."

"One thing I can't figure out is: how the train blew up, when the explosives were on an airship?" Pat stated, thinking Eelayka was referring to a type of airship like the *Blutanikeh*.

"The bombs used were made of super-high-explosive material. The actual bomb was estimated to be no bigger than a finger nail."

"That must have been a horrible day!" Pat said, shocked. The incident sounded like a smaller version of New York's 9/11 attacks.

"It was, but, that wasn't all the gangsters did. They also flew around spraying a deadly powder, which killed more people. That's the other reason farming was banned, because some of the farmers had secretly been hired to grow the poisonous plants used to make the deadly powder."

"On Earth, in some countries, in a region known as the Middle East, people have found ways to make a powder form biological weapon called Anthrax. If inhaled, one would die within a few days, unless immediate treatment was received."

"The weapon these basteekahs developed was more potent. One would die from it within a day. They were probably glad to die because the symptoms were very unpleasant such as vomiting, diarrhoea, muscular spasms, and other great pains as the powder destroyed internal organs."

"Did your uncle die that way or from the explosion?" asked Pat.

"My uncle was on the train. He was killed instantly because he had been standing during the rush hour. My aunt who had been waiting at the garden's station for my uncle, was badly injured when the debris buried her. A day later, the rescuers dug her up. She had to have her left arm amputated because it was badly infected from several cuts. Other than that, she had small scars over various parts of her body. She was never the same after that tragic day and her health slowly deteriorated. She managed to pull through the bad times and became the owner of several thriving bed-and-breakfast places over time."

"You must have been close to her," said Pat, who could see her eyes brimming with tears, threatening to spill.

"My uncle's death brought us closer and we spent a lot of time together. When I got my pilot's license we used to love flying to the different gardens and exploring them. Five years ago, she let me have full use of it as she was too frail to fly it alone. When she passed away, I became the proud owner of her dry boat and bed-and-breakfast places."

"What happened after these attacks? Was there a war against the gangsters?"

"Yes, there was a global war against the gangsters who had taken over a few of the small island nations to our north."

"I heard they burnt towns and villages on small independent islands."

Pat remembered Maili had invited him and a guest to her wedding, and decided to ask Eelayka if she would go with him.

"Sure, I'll go with you on condition you come to my girlfriend's wedding, which will be taking place in two days, also in Ixlezem. We could leave late tomorrow afternoon."

"Great. This way, I could get to see what Ixlezem is like. Is it occupied by the gangsters?"

"It used to be until our army, in conjunction with the Corvic army, drove them out. It became free and independent again."

After walking along the wall of lights a little further, they walked over to a large fishpond that had bright floodlights on it, so the fish could be seen at night. They suddenly heard a big splashing which sounded like it had to be from something whale-sized.

"Do they have whales in this pond?" asked Pat, who had gotten splashed in the face.

"No, those are the fish in there, silly. See, there's one near the surface."

Pat looked and saw a goldfish the size of a large dog. If only my neighbours with their little fishpond were here, he thought to himself. His neighbours had fish at least 30 cm long. Most of them were either golden orange or black.

"Fish that size wouldn't have to worry about being attacked by a cat. Unless your cats are bigger here," Pat commented.

Another large, dark red fish jumped up to catch a flying insect near the surface. Once again Pat and Eelayka got splashed.

After viewing the pond, they sat on a bench to enjoy ice-cream. "Tell me, did those people in that *Titanic* movie get married once they got off the ship?" asked Eelayka.

"No, Jack froze to death with fifteen hundred other passengers, while Rose was rescued by the *Carpathian* ship and went to New York, eventually becoming an actress." Pat then explained how the *Titanic* had met its unfortunate end when hitting an iceberg. The iceberg had scraped the hull for 248 feet, leaving a series of small holes and buckled hull plates. Twelve square feet was left open to the sea. Within 40 minutes the ship had taken in 16,000 cubic feet of water. After another 40 minutes, the seaman's quarters, which was forty eight feet above the keel, had taken on water. The ship was doomed and sank two hours later.

"Oh dear, that must have been terrible! Was the news coverage of it on your Info-Screen system?"

"Unfortunately, it happened 90 years ago, around this time of year. We didn't have the technology for video coverage, let alone digital video coverage."

* * *

168

An hour and a half later they were at the beach, where there were no lights to block out the view of the starry night sky. A reddish-coloured moon was close to the southern horizon and the white and yellow comet was once again visible.

"I can't get over how many stars you have in your universe," Pat to said to Eelayka.

"We're in a small galaxy where there are as many stars as in a regular-sized one. It is known as 'the grape' because of its shape. The stars are fairly dense and high in number. There are quite a few within a twenty-light-year radius of our own solar system. The most important is the comet which will pass close to our planet in a few days."

"Has it been around the sun yet?"

"Only after it passes by us. After circling the sun, it'll pass by us again, but not as close as it will on its way out."

"Would you show me the computer you brought back with you?" Eelayka asked.

"Yep, we can go back now," said Pat, who was very curious about the computer himself. They walked, hand-in-hand, back to the check-in lobby area. Pat went up to his room while Eelayka waited in the lobby. Guests weren't allowed to bring anyone up to their rooms.

"We'll need a bright light source to boot it up," said Pat after coming back to the lobby. He led her towards her dry boat on the beach where no one was likely see them.

"I'll turn on my headlamps."

Pat put the bottle computer down in the path of the headlight beam and placed the crystal cork on it. The inside of the bottle started sparkling like a mini universe, and was much brighter now there was no daylight to interfere with the light coming from within the bottle. The hologram lit up and the girl in the computer once again gave her Kaylahzian greeting.

"She almost looks like my grandmother! I have pictures of her at home. I look a lot like her," Eelayka said excitedly

Pat played the message his grandfather had left him. Eelayka was amazed. She told Pat her grandmother had had a short affair with someone from Corvus. To her knowledge, no pregnancy had resulted from the affair.

"I'm pretty tired now." Eelayka yawned. "Jonk is a good family friend. We'll go see him in the morning. I'm sure he would like to know about your grandfather's passing."

Eelayka started up her aircraft and left after they had hugged and kissed for a few minutes. Pat stood watching her fly to the other end of the island, where her apartment was located.

Pat quickly returned the bottle computer and its crystal cork to its wooden case, went back to his room, and decided to turn in. He wanted to be refreshed the next day when they went to see Jonk. To wind down, he sat on the balcony for about twenty minutes, studying the stars and the comet, whose tail was slightly longer than it had been last night.

* * *

It took only five minutes for Pat to get into bed and fall into a dream. In this dream, he was with Eelayka on the beach, watching the comet, which seemed to be several times brighter and bigger than earlier that evening. Its head was white, its tail was orange and yellow and much longer, now that it was closer to the sun.

"That comet is sure getting big. It almost looks as though it's going to hit us." said Eelayka

Suddenly the comet turned towards Owega and appeared to be aiming for Corvus.

"It's going to hit!" Pat yelled, fearful. "I thought it was supposed to miss us."

170

"It will be even more fun if it hits," said Eelayka, who didn't appear to be nervous at all.

The comet dropped to the horizon and they felt like a brief tremor from the impact. They spotted a huge tidal wave, a few hundred metres high, rapidly approaching the island.

The ringing of the phone woke Pat from his nightmare, just as the wave was seconds from hitting him. He picked up the phone. It was Eelayka. She sounded upset.

Chapter 15

Encore Date

"Are you okay? You sound upset."

"No, I'm fine. I just had trouble going to sleep. I thought we could hang out for an hour or so and then maybe I'll be able to sleep."

"Okay, are you at home now?"

"No, I'm standing below your balcony."

Pat stepped out and saw her standing below with a cell phone to her ear. He quickly dressed, grabbed a couple of condoms, just in case, and went quietly down to meet her.

"If it isn't the love birds," said Eric, who happened to show up with Joanne. "Where did you go this evening?"

Pat filled them in on their earlier activities at the restaurant and the memorial wall.

"We were at the amusement park and went on a bunch of rides. We didn't go on the tall roller coaster though, because somebody was too chicken to go on." Eric turned towards Joanne and chuckled.

"Are they still open?" Pat asked.

"They're open until one cycle," said Eelayka. "If you want, we can stop in there and have a few rides. It's only around midnight."

"Why don't we go tomorrow sometime. Maybe Eric and Joanne would like to join us," suggested Pat.

"That sounds like a cool idea," said Eric. "Anyway, we're turning in for the night, so don't you kids do anything we wouldn't do."

"Yeah, and remember to use a parachute if you plan on smoking zizi cigars," added Joanne.

* * *

173

Pat and Eelayka were on their way, in her dry boat, to Grokah National Garden, which was just west of the Emeestatz city limits.

"Here's a map." Eelayka turned on a holographic image that looked a lot like the electronic star point maps different luxury cars and SUV's are fitted with.

"This electronic map is from a satellite and can show our position, at any point, on the globe."

Pat studied the map. When Eelayka zoomed it out, he got a look at the entire island, which was shaped a lot like the Pac Man icon and Emee Bay was its mouth. He was amazed at the size of Grokah Garden, which stretched to the far west coast of the island. He figured it had to be around 800 km long and 200 km at its widest point, from north to south.

"You can now see it up ahead," said Eelayka, pointing out the front window. Pat saw the city lights stretching out beneath them, to where they abruptly ended.

"This garden must be one of the largest in this world," said Pat as they began to fly over it.

"It's the largest in Kaylahzee, but I believe Corvus has one that's two or three times larger."

"They must have quite a staff of groundskeepers for a garden this size."

"About seventy percent of the city is employed in the gardens. The government pays them decent wages."

"Wouldn't it be a far trip for those who work at the west end of the garden?" asked Pat.

"The people on the other side commute on the monotrain from various surrounding villages."

"Here's where I want to land." She started descending to an area with a small village below, which appeared to border a black space. "This is the village of Ahkella and just beyond is Ahkella Lake."

174

They landed in the parking area of a small amusement park, which was towards the lake. Pat looked towards the park and had a sense of déjà vu. He realized he was staring at a park that looked exactly like Crystal Beach Park, a park he had gone to often when he was younger, before it had been closed down ten years ago. At the end of the parking area was a yellow roller coaster similar to the Giant roller coaster in Crystal Beach Park. He looked towards the lake and could see a roller coaster identical to Crystal Beach Park's Comet roller coaster. It's almost as if the founders of my favourite childhood park had come to Owega and built a park just like it, Pat thought to himself.

"This is strange. This place should still be open and look, there's not a friggin' vehicle in sight." She pointed to the empty parking lot.

"Excuse me," said a man dressed in a spacesuit-like uniform with a mask. "You must get back in your craft and leave at once! There's been a chemical leak nearby and we've evacuated the entire park and town."

Pat and Eelayka quickly apologized and ran back, boarded the aircraft and lifted off. They flew back the way they had come, just minutes ago.

"Could it be the deadly biochemical used thirty years ago?" asked Pat.

"Well, if it was we will be dead in a few hours," said Eelayka and burst out laughing at Pat's frightened and worried look.

Eelayka flew the aircraft towards a garden north of Emeestatz and along the shore. She told him the garden was called Eekola, which was named after the glow-in-the-dark flowers.

They approached the garden and landed on the grass. A nice, cool ocean breeze greeted them as they stepped from the aircraft. They were only a hundred metres from the shoreline. It felt much better than the warm, muggy air at Ahkella Lake.

Eelayka led Pat to an area where there were a bunch of large plants with glowing orange flowers. He received a small shock when he realized they were the flowers of his dream in which he had made love to Eelayka.

"Can you tell me about some of the powers you have?" Eelayka asked when they were seated under one of the plants.

"Well, I seem to have the ability to control slot machines in my favour." He mentioned reviving Maili, after she had been hit by lightning.

Eelayka pulled a dark-coloured pen from her purse. "See what your powers can do with this pen."

Pat placed it in front of him and tried moving it with his mind. He pictured it lifting off the ground like a rocket. The pen flew up as if someone had hit it with a baseball bat. It landed in Pat's hand.

"Wow!" Eelayka said in amazement.

Next Pat tried to turn the pen into something else. He pictured it as a ball and, before he knew it, the pen turned into a plastic ball with the ink remaining inside.

Eelayka gave him a kiss on the cheek and said, "You're a regular wizard and magician. Are there any other tricks you can do?"

Pat held the ball in his hand and pictured it turning into light photons. The ball suddenly became hot and he released it as it started glowing bright blue. He moved it up in the air with his mind and it turned into different coloured light photons, which spread outwards like a firecracker.

"I hope you weren't saving that pen," said Pat, who was amazed at this hidden talent within him.

"You should become a magician and do some of these tricks. I imagine you could become famous."

"I don't know about that. I suffer from stage fright."

"And now I'll show you some of my own magic," said Eelayka as she pulled out a bag of dried zizi leaves rolled up like a cigar, and a cube-shaped lighter. She pressed the button on the lighter, lit the zizi bomb, took a large drag from it, and passed it to Pat.

"Wow! You must have read my mind," said Pat, bringing forth a condom.

They began to roll around on the soft grass, kissing. In the soft orange light coming from the flowers Pat noticed for the first time, Eelayka had a small freckle near her mouth.

Ten minutes later, they had made passionate love. A thunderstorm out to sea had developed as if responding to their lovemaking. Pat was a little surprised at the speed of their coupling. He had thought the sex would have been more intense, but put it down to the fact that perhaps Kaylahzian women were not inclined to have leisurely sex.

They quickly boarded Eelayka's aircraft to head back and call it a night. They became airborne and Eelayka flew out to sea, heading straight for the storm.

"Shouldn't we be using the roads in this kind of weather?" asked Pat, who was getting rather worried and a bit nauseated from the turbulence.

"Nah, that would be too boring," she said and started to laugh. "We'll be out of this in a couple of minutes. Besides, if we do go down we could remember we had a chance to make love under the Eekola flowers." She laughed again.

Pat was beginning to think she had smoked too much and was on a high from the zizi leaves.

Suddenly a bolt of lightning hit the aircraft. It sounded like a cannon going off right next to them. Pat's heart started to hammer loudly enough for him to hear it in his ears.

"Don't worry, this thing is lightning proof," said Eelayka. It won't harm us. Besides, we're safer in here than we would be on the ground."

The storm was behind them when they passed over the city and Pat began to feel more at ease now he no longer thought he would be food for sharks or whatever wild sea creatures lurked in the waters below.

* * *

Pat went to his room after Eelayka dropped him off and stepped out onto the dry balcony; an indication the storm had not hit Slimteeka Island at all. He could see some of the stars as well as the comet, which was a little bigger than the previous night. Towards the north, the sky was overcast with sporadic lightning over the horizon.

He checked his Owegan watch Eelayka had picked up for him the other day. The time was 2.2 cycles, which was the equivalent of 5:15 A.M.. This meant the sun would be rising in another hour and a half.

Pat went to bed and it took him a half-hour to fall asleep because his stomach felt a little queasy after the rough flight. He also wondered why Eelayka had been flying so dangerously in the storm when earlier she had flown her aircraft as gentle as a baby. Even when she had flown them out to the Crystal Beach–like park, she had flown the craft as if she was an air ambulance making a fast emergency flight.

The purring of his cat, Pedals, at the foot of his bed, aided him in drifting off into a dreamless sleep.

Chapter 16

The Gangster's Deadly Project

After getting a couple of hours' sleep and having breakfast in the dining room with Eric and Joanne, Pat went outside and waited, in the nice sunny weather, for Eelayka to pick him up. He had heard Emeestatz weather forecast calling for a slight chance of an afternoon thunderstorm. He hoped it would stay dry for their planned outing to the theme park.

Eelayka flew in and Pat stepped aboard. She greeted him with a nice good morning kiss and ascended. Pat noticed she was flying her craft gently, unlike last night when she had flown it recklessly into the storm.

"Have you ever flown an airship before?" asked Eelayka.

"I took flying lessons a year ago while visiting Malaysia. The plane I flew was about the size of your craft but had wings instead of a large propeller."

"How far is Malaysia from your house?"

"It's about seven or eight thousand leagues away. It's so far that when it's morning in my town, it's evening in Malaysia."

"Wow! That must have been quite a trip to get there."

"Yeah, it took a couple of long flights to get there. Then I had to take a few days to adjust to the different time zone."

"What made you want to go so far from home?"

"It's a rather long story," said Pat, feeling a little embarrassed. "I answered a help-wanted ad in my local paper. It was for a person who wanted to travel a lot. It turned out to be a job as a corporate spy for a company called Blue Star Printing and Design. They design the images used on paper currency."

"What does a corporate spy do?"

"They do various things. In my case, I was sent to Malaysia to track down an employee of Blue Star's Malaysian plant in the city of Kuching. The employee was believed to be selling some of the designs to an underground firm, who were making counterfeit money traffic illegal drugs. It wasn't dangerous like the films about spies who risk their lives on a day-to-day basis. All I had to do was act like a tourist reading electronic stories

180

on a Rocket book reader and as a friend to the troubled employee. I had to e-mail any information I acquired from the employee." Pat wasn't uncomfortable describing his job to Eelayka. He felt uncomfortable telling her about Lilly, a local girl who had been vacationing at the resort in Damai Beach.

"Alright, Mr. Spy, why don't you fly my aircraft then? It's really simple. All I do is type in the place I want to go to, and the computer guides the craft there. The auto-pilot system can also adjust rapidly to changing wind currents so there's little chance of crashing while using it."

They quickly changed seats and Pat noticed the dashboard had fewer gauges than the Cessna he had flown in Kuching, Malaysia. Sitting in the cockpit brought back memories of his winter one-month stay in Damai Beach, a resort beach near Kuching, which was on the Borneo Island shared by both Malaysia and Indonesia. The gardens and city below also reminded him of Kuching because of the similar climate. However, Emeestatz reminded him of Kuala Lumpur, which was about the same size. Pat reminisced about the month he had been there and the time he had spent with Lilly, who was petite and had long dark hair and the oriental features most Malaysians have.

"It looks like we're almost there," Eelayka said, about ten minutes later as they started to descend. Below, they could see the Rokojay River, which flows into Emeestatz Bay. "He lives in the west side of the city near the river, in a nice house."

Pat sat and watched the auto pilot land the aircraft safely in the yard of Jonk Villitz's house, which was a light blue bungalow. He had a yard of small blue vines with long skinny leaves, like a blade of grass or corn-plant leaves on a much smaller scale.

They stepped out of the aircraft, walked up to the door, and rang the doorbell, which caused a dog to bark in the house. Pat figured it was a small dog as its barks were high pitched like a

Yorkshire terrier's. The door opened and a man who looked a lot like Leslie Neilson, only thirty pounds lighter, stood before them. At first, he had a puzzled look on his face. After spotting Eelayka, recognition flashed across his face. Eelayka introduced Pat.

"I'm Frank Silversol's grandson," Pat said by way of explanation. "He made me a computer video file and in it he told me to see you for details of his computer." Pat tapped the wooden case that held the bottle-shaped computer.

"Oh yes! Frankie mentioned you when he was here. What is he up to these days?"

Pat informed him that his grandfather had passed away five years ago. He also mentioned his grandmother had passed away only two earth months ago.

"Oh dear, I'm sorry to hear that. He was a funny cat with his practical jokes and smart remarks, only he could get away with. One time my wife and I had gone to the beach and happened to meet him there. My wife, Mareeka, had this new skimpy two-piece swimsuit on and he said to her, "*looks like I'll be seeing more of you*", and we all laughed about it."

Jonk invited them into his living room. It was large and spacious, with a large bay window. The walls were painted light blue with a purple patterned border, halfway between the ceiling and floor. Jonk went into the kitchen and brought out three cups of a sweet tasting, dark blue liquid. It must have had something in it like caffeine because after a few sips, Pat felt energized.

"This is zizi tea. It has a substance in it to give one a jolt of energy. Don't worry – it's from the zizi nut which is a lot different than the leaves, if you know what I mean," Jonk said, winking at them.

Pat took the computer out of its case and booted up. The holographic imagine of the Eelayka-like image appeared.

"Frankie was a genius when it came to making computers. He

made several of them and sold them on the brown market to the gangsters," Jonk explained.

"Did he become a member of them?" asked Pat with dread.

"Oh no, he sold them the computers so he could secretly spy on them. He built micro-cameras and microphones into the crystal glass tops. He would record their activities and forward them to the O.I.A. or Owega Intelligence Agency. He also designed their system so he could sign into it as a 'ghost user'. This meant the gangsters' computer operations wouldn't be able to see him in their system."

"What about the suicide attack on Emeestatz? Shouldn't he have been able to pick up that info and send it to the authorities in time to prevent them?" asked Pat.

"Unfortunately, the gangsters encrypted the info so much, your grandfather couldn't figure it out in time. However, he did help our military track them down. Their hideout caves were bombed so badly, only a few gangsters survived. They were all arrested on the spot and executed."

"Did they get the chair or lethal injection?" Pat asked.

"No, worse. They were taken to Track Zero, which is the spot where the track had stood before it was destroyed. The four prisoners were all given a dosage of the deadly powder they had made for the attacks. Thousands of people attended the execution and millions watched it on the Info-Screen. The crowds cheered as the prisoners got sick. The cheering got louder eight cycles later when they died. If you want, I can show you the video of it."

"Oh, no thanks," Pat and Eelayka said simultaneously. "We get the picture," Pat said. "I don't think you would want us to throw up on your carpet."

"That was a terrible day. It caught everyone off guard. We thought we had a defence system capable of preventing these things. They caught us with our knickers down by hijacking the two airships and crashing them into the monotrains."

Jonk went on to explain that after the air attack there had been a period when most of the people left the city of Emeestatz and hid in caves on the northern side of the island. "Most of them returned but a few stayed in them, such as my wife and I and your grandmother, Eelayka, when she was young and as lovely as you."

"Is that her on the hologram?" Eelayka asked.

"Yes. That's her when she was about your age. Frankie had quite a crush on her at the time. They dated for a while and then he skipped town when the attacks happened. He was worried the gangsters would find out they had been betrayed because of the bugged computers. He came back a few years later but your grandma had met your granddad and was pregnant with her first child - your father."

Pat felt relieved. He had been afraid Jonk was about to say his grandfather had left Eelayka's grandmother pregnant, which would have made Eelayka a half cousin to him.

"Let's see if we can tap into the gangsters' system," Jonk suggested. "Hopefully they haven't found a way to uncover our secret entrance into their computer."

Jonk commanded the computer to locate the system of the Dendoyhee, which was the formal name of the gangsters, even though they were most often referred to as Soapy's Gang.

The image of Eelayka's grandmother said, "Found request. Do you wish to enter at your own risk?"

Jonk quickly said yes, the girl disappeared, and an image with a graphic logo appeared. Pat had seen the same logo on the thief's jacket, in the West Garden of Clarissa. The logo was an image of two falcons picking up a dead possum, as though they planned to carry it to a nest.

Jonk said "Enter", and a menu came up with a few options. He chose "Project Fireball" and a 3D graphic image of Owega from outer space, with the comet to the far left, came up. Jonk said "Play", and the image became animated. It showed the comet's course past the planet. Then a beam shot up from Owega and went straight to the comet. The effect was the comet changed course and headed towards Owega. It showed a view as though a camera was attached to the comet. The comet was heading towards the city of Emeestatz. "Oh dear!" Jonk said in a fit of frenzy. "It looks like they're at it again, except they're trying to end our world for good."

"There must be some way of notifying the authorities," exclaimed Pat.

"That wouldn't do any good," said Jonk, shaking his head. "These people have ways of silencing you before the police can get to you. Let's see if they have any details for this project."

"Maybe we can find where they plan to do it," suggested Eelayka.

Jonk commanded the computer to open a file in the same folder. The file was encrypted, which was no problem because the computer was able to decode it into Kaylahzian. The document described, in detail, how they planned to make the comet crash into Emeestatz. It explained they had a machine that would send a magnetic beam up to the comet, which would cause it to drift towards Owega as if the planet was a large magnet.

The third and last file in the folder was a map showing the location of the machine, which was set up in Ahkella Lake Garden.

"So that chemical leak at the park last night was just a smoke screen!" Pat said in amazement.

"What chemical leak?" asked Eelayka.

"You know, when we went there and got turned away by the security guard."

"I don't understand. I didn't take you there last night," Eelayka said, perplexed.

"Yes, you did. The zizi leaves must have made you forget about it."

Jonk interrupted. "Check this out. It says here a good chunk of their funding is coming from the Harmonkah Izkah Logizkay Corporation."

"Isn't that where you work, Eelayka?" asked Pat, a little disturbed.

"I meant to tell you yesterday that I had quit outright and had walked out."

"What?" Pat asked, shocked.

"Well, I was fed up with the place. They wouldn't let me stay in Wiktona Beach, where I could have watched my brother in the victory parade. After all he was the most valuable player for scoring all three goals which turned the *Panthers* into the championship team."

"This computer was built thirty years ago. They could have found a way to detect 'ghost users.' You might be in danger now, just by being with me and even more so if they find we were snooping around in their files. I strongly suggest you don't go back to your apartment, and we stick together as much as possible. No telling what kind of trap your ex-boss could be setting."

"I'll need to pack for our trip to Soozay and Domko's wedding."

Pat put his arm around her shoulders, "That's no problem. We can pick out an outfit when we get to Ixlezem. I suggest we leave this evening, immediately after we've been to the roller coaster place with Eric and Joanne."

"Those madmen are going to destroy this area in a few days," said Eelayka in a panicky voice. "I must warn my family to evacuate the city and get as far away as possible."

"Leave that to me," Jonk cut in. "I'll tell them myself, but I won't tell them the real reason. There's no need to panic. Maybe there's still a way to stop them. In the mean time, go ride that new roller coaster: it's supposed to be the highest in the world," Ten minutes later, Pat and Eelayka began their trip to

Cryskokah Gardens.   On their way there, they passed a few different aircrafts and didn't even stop to think; one of them could have been a gangster on the lookout for Pat.

Chapter 17

Cryskokah Gardens

"I never knew Zaylis was your brother," Pat said to Eelayka, twenty minutes later.

"Yep, he's my baby brother. I also have an older brother who lives at the other side of the main island. He's a groundskeeper at a garden."

After passing over Slimteeka Island, Eelayka's pre-programmed flight banked her aircraft towards the right. Ahead they could see the theme park. The super high roller coaster stood out.

Cryskokah Gardens had two types of admission; full admission, which included all the rides and a roll of tickets to be used for at least three rides. Eelayka and Pat chose the latter. They could always buy another roll, but had decided to get to Ixlezem in time for a late evening dinner.

"I see you guys decided to show up," said Eric, holding Joanne's hand.

Pat briefly told them about their visit to Jonk's and advised them that they might want to think about coming with them.

"Nah, we should be fine. Besides, Steve would notify us, if we were endangered. So what should we ride on now, the Makeeta? Eric asked.

"Fine by me," said Pat, who didn't know any of the rides by name.

"Gee, I don't know about that one. Why don't we try some of the smaller roller coasters and save the mother of them for last," Joanne suggested.

Eric informed her that Eelayka and Pat had enough coupons for only three rides and they might want to use the other two for the more romantic rides such as the Ferris wheel or a tunnel boat-ride.

After waiting in line for half an hour, it was finally their turn to get on the approximately 122-metre high roller coaster. Surprisingly, the seats had comfortable padding like any plush car seat. An automated voice instructed everyone to ensure their white lap bars were secured and locked in, and to secure any loose items such as glasses and sun hats.

"No kidding," said Eric, laughing. "It's quite obvious they would fly off at the speed we will be going."

The roller coaster left the station and immediately started its long climb up the first hill. The train didn't jerk when it started climbing the first hill. This was because a wide conveyor belt, which started in the station, was pulling the train.

Thirty seconds later, they were at the top of the hill. They could see the entire park and miles on end all around them. Pat thought it was similar to the view he and Eelayka got when they were in her aircraft. He turned to look back at the loading station, with its bright blue and purple colours. The station looked like a miniature toy, from that height.

"Here we go!" yelled Eric as the train crawled over the top, left the lift belt, and started its first drop on the half-metre-wide blue track. The drop seemed to last forever because they were dropping at an 87° angle. What made it even more thrilling was the fact that they were completely weightless in their seats. When it hit the bottom, it went up a sharp curve banked at 130 degrees, which made them semi-inverted.

They finally came back to the loading station, after going over several hills, semi-inverted curves, and over three kilometres of navy blue steel track.

"There's one thing I want to show you guys," said Eelayka, with Pat translating. "It's a walk-in exhibit called the Walkway of Life. They just opened it the other day while I was in Wiktona. It's the only free attraction for people who didn't buy an all-day pass."

As they walked to the attraction, they went past two roller coasters. One had suspended cars that spun around at random so that one could be riding forwards down the first hill and backwards and inverted in a loop up the next. The other one was wilder. The trains were mounted on a platform beside the track. As the platform went around sharp curves, the train would spin around like a giant propeller.

Eelayka pointed to it. "If you guys thought the Makeeta was bad, try riding that while sitting in the far right or left car after having three cocktails."

"Were you able to keep them down?" asked Pat.

"No, I threw up in the ladies room, after getting off. It was on my birthday and I was on a blind date at the time, too. Don't worry dear, I didn't hear from him again after that night," she said, patting Pat on his shoulder.

* * *

Jonk did his daily exercise to stay in shape - a walk around the block. He greeted various neighbours who were out trimming the vines of grass growing over the sidewalks, or watering their lawns. He also wanted to calm his mind since he was desperately thinking of ways to stop the gangsters from steering the comet into Owega.

For the last twenty years, Jonk hadn't bothered to lock his house when he went for his daily walk or when he went to the corner store to pick up his groceries. He used to lock it in the troubled times when the monotrain Eelayka's uncle had been on, was destroyed. After the threat of the gangsters attacking other parts of the city had evaporated, he began to leave his door unlocked. Uneasy, he was now thinking it may have been wise to lock it, since he and Pat hacked into the gangsters' computer system.

He stepped inside his house and was so deep in thought, he didn't see the masked stranger standing next to the door. The masked man put a gloved hand over his Jonk's mouth to prevent him from calling for one of his neighbours to come to his aid. In the other hand, the gangster held a laser gun, which he placed, against Jonk's left temple. Jonk now deeply regretted not locking up before going out.

"Alright, old timer, we are going to do this nice and easy," the masked man said as he led Jonk into his basement. "I'm going to ask you a few simple questions and if you answer them, you won't die slowly and painfully."

He had Jonk sit down on his basement floor and said, "Okay here's the scoop, we caught you stalking around in our computer system, and we want to know how you gained access to it."

Jonk saw the masked man was wearing a jacket with the gangsters' logo. His blood turned to ice in his veins.

"Well, start talking! I don't have all friggin' day you know," the gangster said and gave him a kick in the side.

"I don't know what you're talking about. If it was us, we would've ensured you weren't able to detect us in the first – ". The gangster gave him a hard backhand, making his lip bleed.

"Look, wise cat," the gangster hissed. "That program was written thirty years ago and since then we've found a way of detecting 'ghosts' in our system. The tracer program gave us this address. So I suggest you start talking before I lose my patience."

"It was with that computer there," Jonk lied, pointing to his own bottle computer. The last thing he wanted to do was betray Eelayka and the grandson of his old friend, Frankie.

The gangster powered the computer up and the main menu popped up as a holographic image. Jonk's system was very basic compared to Frank's, which had all the bells and whistles on it. There was no image of a younger version of Eelayka's grandmother.

"This isn't the computer you used!" the gangster said after giving Jonk another swift kick. "This is a KS200 and the one our tracer showed was a KS500, which has the memory and capability to tap into other computers. Now you used the term 'we', so you had accomplices. Who has the KS500? Is it by any chance a blonde Kaylahzian chick with a white male in his thirties who has healing, foresight, the ability to influence shapes of objects, and who knows what other powers?"

"Yes, it is and they went east to Floreedoh Garden," Jonk lied in the hope of buying more time.

"I don't totally believe you. I'm going to take you to see Soapy and he will decide if you are being honest or not. If he catches you lying the ashes of your remains will be shipped in a jar to your home." The gangster's chuckle held such a pure evil tone it almost turned Jonk's bowels to water.

The gangster led Jonk to his parked aircraft. He kept his gun hidden in his pocket so the neighbours wouldn't be alarmed. However, he kept a hand close to it, just in case Jonk tried to make a sudden move.

* * *

"Here it is," Eelayka said as they arrived at the entrance to the Walkway of Life.

"Hey, is this path made of gold?" asked Eric, who was looking down at the bricks, which were a shiny golden colour.

"They probably are. Many of the pathways in most gardens are made of gold and silver, as there's an abundant supply of those minerals," said Joanne.

"How much for a brick?" asked Eric.

"In Clarissa you can buy a load for your driveway at five krayohs."

"You've got to be kidding! In our world gold is the equivalent of three or four krayohs for just enough to put in your eye. Maybe I should take a few bricks back with me and pay

193

off my mortgage and if there's anything left over, I could find something on my world that's rare in Owega," said Pat.

"Shhhhhhhh," hissed Eric. "Keep it down: we don't want everyone to know we're aliens here."

The Walkway of Life consisted of several stops. The first stop was about birth and there were newborn kittens and a Corvic woman holding her newborn baby. A doctor cut the umbilical cord.

"If we were here a bit sooner, we could have watched the baby being delivered," said Eelayka.

The second stop had kittens about a month old. They were orange; like the newborn ones. There were also a few five-year-old kids playing with toys, like in any typical day-care centre.

After a few more stops, they came to one that showed animals coupling. There was an art deco-style sign advertising there would be a couple getting married, under a light blue wooden gazebo with blue-leafed vines growing up its six support poles, in one cycle.

Pat wished they had more time so they could stick around and watch the wedding. That way, he could see how they're performed in Kaylahzee, just in case it turned out Eelayka was the right one. There's still Eelayka's friend's wedding to look forward to, he reminded himself.

When they arrived at the last stop, there was an old orange cat that looked like it was on its last legs of life. There was also an old man who looked to be close to the 100-year mark. He was lying in a bed and his family of loved ones were gathered around. They appeared to be in some sort of deep prayer.

"This is where we can watch a person pass on," Eelayka murmured. "Anyone can volunteer to take part in any of the exhibits along the path."

Pat glanced towards the art deco exit sign when something, from the old man's direction, caught his attention. He looked over and could see a glowing pinkish smoke-like substance lifting from the man's chest. It disappeared shortly. He knew then the man had passed away. A female priestess came over to perform some kind of prayer, which was probably similar to a last rites sacrament.

"Did you see the man's soul depart his body?" asked Pat when they were out of the walkway and sitting on a park bench at a large red palm tree.

The others all gave negative replies.

"You must have the gift to see people's souls depart," said Eelayka, excited.

"Maybe I could get a job recording the official time of death for people," Pat said, half joking.

Pat and Eelayka decided it was time to leave for Ixlezem. They stopped at a washroom next to a haunted-house attraction. The washrooms weren't co-ed like the ones at the *Panthers* game. Pat was done first and patiently waited for Eelayka, who seemed to be spending more time than normal in the ladies room. While he waited, he could hear some of the sound effects from the haunted house, such as howling winds and evil laughs. There were also sounds of the odd woman or two screaming.

"All done, love," said Eelayka when she finally returned.

"Geez, I thought you'd fallen in," teased Pat.

Eelayka cupped Pat's cheeks in her hands and planted a kiss on his lips. While she did, Pat was so caught up in the moment, he didn't see two men in black and grey jackets with the Dendoyhee logo, give a quick wink towards them. Eelayka took Pat's hand and led him away from the thugs and towards the park exit.

They left the park, boarded Eelayka's airboat, and headed out. Eelayka flew out rather fast and gained altitude as if they were being chased.

Chapter 18

Captives

Cumulus clouds towered into thunderheads, threatening heavy rains, frequent lightning, and possibly hail, darkened the skies over Cryskokah Gardens.

Pat and Eelayka were a few kilometres north of the gardens when they saw the first flash of lightning behind them.

"Looks like we got out of there just in time," said Pat, who was a bit leery about flying in rough weather, after their stormy flight a little more than twelve hours ago.

"You mean to say you're afraid of a storm but not the Mateeka?" asked Eelayka, incredulous.

"Well, at least the roller coaster is on a track regulated by a computer system. Whereas these storms are only guided by the hand of God."

"Hey, why don't you show me your world before we head for Ixlezem," Eelayka suggested, changing the subject.

"Yeah, that sounds good. I'll even introduce you to my other friend, Tony. He is quite anxious to meet you."

Ten minutes later, they were on the ground. Pat activated the portal with his QTA. It was the same as before; the size of an average doorway and surrounded by the rainbow design. They could see it was sunny and pleasant on the other side.

"Take my hand. There's nothing to this," Pat encouraged.

She held his hand and they stepped over. Pat hadn't changed the coordinates and they exited at the same spot he had before. The drastic difference in temperature hit them like a bucket of ice-cold water. The temperature on Pat's watch dropped from 28°C to 15°C in only a few seconds. Pat figured it would easily reach 25°C or higher, since it was only mid-morning in Lavinia.

"Is it always this cold here?" Eelayka asked, rubbing her arms to keep warm as she was used to the tropical heat in Emeestatz.

"It's our typical warm, spring weather in Lavinia. Yesterday was fairly warm, too. This weather can easily spoil one, because it doesn't last at this time of year. Sometimes it could be as warm as Emeestatz and the next day turn cold with windy conditions, and snow flakes in the air."

They stopped at Pat's house for a little while so he could show her his PC and the Internet. He displayed his website, which featured a brief description of himself and the three self-published e-books he had written.

"Wow, is it ever slow in bringing up the screens. I don't know how you can stand waiting like that, as well as the small screen," Eelayka declared.

"Believe it or not, this is one of the top-of-the-line home computers. The Internet connection is done through a fibre-optic cable line, which is the fastest connection, a home user can get. The other major connection facility is dial-up, which uses the phone line and takes forever when it comes to downloading a five-minute music file."

"I have an idea," said Eelayka. While standing behind Pat, she put her arms around his shoulders and joined her hands below his chin. She half-whispered, "Why don't we go to your downtown area and browse around the stores."

Pat tried to be diplomatic. "You've got to understand that people in my world have never met someone from Owega. What I'm trying to say is the people in Corvus look a lot like Canadians, Americans, or any English-speaking nation. However, people in Kaylahzee don't look much like any nationality on Earth, except possibly Swedish people who have blonde hair and blue eyes similar to yours, though not as bright."

"Then tell them I'm Swedish and have a rare pigment disorder which has caused my skin to turn purplish."

"Okay, but first I'm going to give you one my spring jackets to wear. It looks good on a man or woman. There's no need to show more skin than you have to. I don't think you would like people staring at you."

Five minutes later, they were briskly walking since downtown was only a few blocks away.

* * *

Eric and Joanne ran towards a Cryskokah Garden gift shop in an attempt to get out of the heavy downpour, which had started in a matter of seconds, as if someone had flipped on a switch. There was some thunder and lightning as well. They stepped into the gift shop just before the rain combined with pea-sized hail started to fall.

"Can I help you two?" asked a polite, rather tall, youngish Kaylahzian saleswoman.

"Oh, we just stopped to look at the shirts and stuff," said Eric, so they wouldn't be asked to go out into the rain.

"We have some special sales in the back. Step this way, please." They followed her to the back room, which had a lot of boxes and looked more like a storage room.

Suddenly the sales lady pulled out a zapper gun and before they could react, stunned them with enough force to render them unconscious for several hours. She quickly removed her fake sales uniform and put on a black leather jacket with the Dandoyhee logo on the back.

She bundled them into a couple of sacks and called for assistance by using a two-way radio. An elevator in the corner of the room opened up. The two gangsters, who had earlier spied on Pat and Eelayka kissing, stepped out and each took an unconscious body. They went back into the elevator, and one of them pressed a button marked 'B2'.

A few seconds later, the elevator opened to reveal a large room, two levels below the main floor. The room encompassed the entire theme garden. This level served as a shipping and receiving area for all the food, souvenirs, and other inventory items. The computers and other electronics, which controlled the rides, were below them, on a third sub-level floor.

Eric and Joanne were placed in a black aircraft that looked a lot like a military jet. They were placed beside two other unconscious people who had also been stuffed into sacks.

The aircraft, which ran partly on electrical power and partly on human waste, lifted off the ground and flew quietly to a large exit in the far back of the park, where only certain employees were allowed.

The craft flew out the exit, climbed quickly to a high altitude, and headed north towards the island the gangsters used as their headquarters.

* * *

The town of Lavinia was an old town, founded in the early 1800s. Victoria Street was where all the gift shops and businesses were located. Most were specialty shops carrying several different gift items. It was the second busiest gift shop street. Niagara-on-the-Lake's Queen Street, which was only a half-hour drive to the east, was the busiest.

The most famous building was the Symphony Hall, the first one to be built outside Toronto, in the southern Ontario area. This hall was the home of the popular one-hundred-piece symphony orchestra known as the 'Lavinia Pops'. They were the only orchestra in a small town anywhere in North America, to produce over a dozen albums and CD's, played on most classical radio stations throughout the world.

The hall also had an outdoor stage used in the summer months. Behind the stage was a broad view of Lake Ontario. At night, one could see the Toronto skyline on the other side of the lake.

Pat and Eelayka went into a gift shop called The North Pole. It was so named, because it specialized in Christmas decorations and small gifts such as Christmas carol CD's and tree decorations suited for that time of year. Hans, and Gretchen Koniginbaum ran the shop. They were Pat's friends since they only lived a few doors from him. He simply referred to them as Mr. and Mrs. K. He had once worked part-time for them when they had run a restaurant called Hans's Family Diner, specializing in German food and home-brewed beer.

"Hey, Patty, how's the writing business treating you?" Hans asked after Pat and Eelayka had walked in. Hans was in his early sixties, but looked more like he was in his late forties. The hair growing on the sides of his balding head was still jet black with only the odd grey hair beginning to show. He also had a moustache and wore black-framed glasses.

Pat introduced Eelayka to him and said she was from Sweden and knew very little English. He told her in Kaylahzian that he had once worked for Hans and had become good friends with him and his wife.

"Why, if it isn't Mr. Pat Silversol," said Gretchen in her thick German accent while walking towards the front area. Gretchen was a short, plump woman with short grey hair and glasses. She was known as the ornament lady because she made most of the custom design tree ornaments by hand.

After Eelayka shook hands with her, she pulled out a small bag and offered Gretchen a small blue and purple scented candle with the unique fragrance from a plant unique to Kaylahzee. She told her the candle was a gift from the two of them. Pat, a little surprised, translated for her.

"Honey, that was sweet of you," Pat said to her.

"It's a custom from my hometown. When we meet someone from a far-away place, we offer gifts to their friends and relatives. However, it's bad luck to light the candles while we're around. So, wait until later to light it and it will bring you a burst of good luck which will last for a whole month."

After chatting for a few minutes, they looked around in the shop and headed out onto the sidewalk, joining a large throng of people who were enjoying the nice warm April weather.

They stopped at the ice-cream shop. Pat asked Eelayka if she wanted to try one, but she declined. Eelayka handed a candle to the young girls working there and told them to wait a few hours before lighting it.

Summer's Delights was a shop specializing in over fifty flavours of ice-cream. It was directly across from The North Pole and was run by Summer and Keith Adams. Neither of them was there because they were attending Summer's brother's wedding in Sault Ste. Marie.

"How are you supposed to eat that?" Eelayka asked when they were seated on a sidewalk park bench.

"You lick it with your tongue. You don't have ice-cream cones in Kaylahzee?"

"There's ice-cream but not on a cone."

"Maybe I should open an ice-cream cone place in Emeestatz," said Pat, thoughtfully. "Maybe I could get a patent there for it and become a tycoon," now joking.

"It's not that easy selling food in our world, silly. The industry is highly controlled by our government."

Their last stop was Tony's apartment, which was only a block from Victoria Street. Tony answered the door and was surprised to see Pat and Eelayka, since it was just yesterday Pat had told him he wouldn't be coming back for a few days.

"It was actually Eelayka's idea," Pat said. "She was over-anxious about travelling into another dimension. How's the job hunting going?"

"Not good. There's just no work in the networking field. The

202

situation is the same as it was a year ago. Are there any jobs in Clarissa or Emeestatz, the place you mentioned yesterday?"

"What I've been thinking of doing is: to import and export goods between Earth and Owega," said Pat. "Maybe we could all form a little business based on Owega and here in my house. I know one could buy a load of pure gold bricks on Owega for the same price as concrete bricks here."

"No shi—, I mean kidding!" Tony said, a little embarrassed about almost swearing in front of Eelayka.

"The big question now is what's here that would be rare and expensive on Owega," said Pat. "We'll have to give that some thought later. There are some problems that need to be resolved first, or else life as we know it on Owega could be destroyed." He briefly described to Tony the gangsters' idea of forcing the comet into a head-on collision with Owega.

"What does Dandoyhee mean?"

"I think it means 'thieves or thugs of a den'."

"Or 'Den of Thieves'," said Tony, chuckling, referring to a cover band they had seen last summer at Lavinia's annual wine festival. The band consisted of four twenty-something guys performing a lot of their own material, which was mainly grunge rock.

For twenty minutes, they sat on Tony's porch drinking tea, which for Eelayka was a little different to the Kaylahzian brand of teas. They mostly chatted about the Kaylahzian area and all its public gardens.

"We have to head back now. We'll be back again sometime." Just before they left, Eelayka gave one of her candles to Tony, telling him to wait until later to light it for good luck.

* * *

As soon as the aircraft landed, Eric, Joanne, and the other two people were carried into a cool and damp underground building. They were all put in separate rooms and the gangsters finally removed the sacks.

Eric looked around in the semi-darkness and could see he was in a small room that looked like an ancient prison cell. The walls and floor were made of rock and the only light came from a narrow barred window close to the ceiling.

Twenty minutes later, the gangsters returned, blindfolded the four captives, and led them down the hall into an even darker and damper room. There were no windows in the room. The only light source was a small light bulb casting an eerie purple light; like the ones in a theme-park fun house.

"The reason you are all here is because you know someone we want, because of his powers and his citizen arrest of one of our members," said a deep voice. "In case you don't know, my name is Drew Soapiosko. I'm more commonly known as Soapy, the name of a legendary bandit who had founded our organization several hundred years ago. We started off just burning villages on small independent islands because they refused to give us 'donations' to keep us away from them."

"Yeah, and now you are also cold-blooded murderers!" yelled one of the other captives. It sounded like an old man.

"Okay, Mr. Villitz, I'll ask you first, since you interrupted me. One thing I despise is being interrupted."

One of the guards grabbed Jonk by the scruff of his neck, brought him to a chair directly across the table from Soapy, and pushed him into it. He removed Jonk's blindfold.

"Jonk, it seems to me you like to play games with us," said Soapy so calmly, it oozed of evil. "I'm going to ask you once, if you don't answer I'll be forced to point this laser gun at your chest and fire at will." He displayed the laser gun while placing his finger near the trigger.

"Go ahead and kill me. Then you'll have another death on your hands, and nothing to show for it - dead bodies won't give you any answers," Jonk said, laughing.

Soapy withdrew the weapon. He realized the threat wasn't going to work. There were other ways of getting the truth out of Jonk. He addressed everyone; "You'll all stay here in captivity until we have Patrick Silversol in our custody. As the days go by, I'll see to it all your food and water rations get cut back. Also, if we don't have Pat in three days, I'll allow one of my men, each cycle, to come in and rough one of you up, on a random basis, until we get Pat. Some of them haven't been with a young lady in a while." Soapy, looking at Joanne, paused for a couple of seconds. "On the other hand, some of them prefer men to women."

At the mention of the possibility the women could be raped, Eric heard sharp intakes of breath and choking sounds from two different angles. He wondered who the other woman could be. It couldn't be Eelayka, he thought to himself. Joanne and I both saw her board her aircraft with Pat. Unless ... His train of thought was interrupted when a guard grabbed him and led them back to their separate cells.

205

Chapter 19

Candle Bombs

Pat activated the portal to Owega. He looked at the QTA and discovered a way of saving the coordinates of the area behind his bed-and-breakfast place. He was curious to see if he would be able to use Lavinia as a midway point between Owega locations. If it could be done, it would take him only seconds to go to Clarissa or Corvus instead of days or hours.

Eelayka nervously grabbed Pat's hand when he finished saving the coordinates; they stepped through and were greeted by the sweet tropical breezes of Slimteeka Island.

While Eelayka waited in her aircraft, Pat went to his room and fed his cat, Pedals. He figured if his idea worked, he could return to Slimteeka by teleporting from Ixlezem to Lavinia and back to Slimteeka. He also took down the address of the resort they had made reservations at.

"And off we go to see the Wizard of Oz," said Pat, joking around shortly after they had lifted off and were flying northward to their destination. He described the classical movie to Eelayka and added that whenever he crossed over to Owega he felt a bit like Dorothy and Toto, when they had crossed over the rainbow to Oz. "You can more or less say some of the people I have met in your world remind me of the characters in the movie. For example, Jonk reminds me of the Tin Man and Soapy is the Wicked Witch of the West."

"And who do I remind you of?"

"Probably the Scarecrow because all he wanted from the wizard was a heart and yours is pretty big."

Eelayka smiled but didn't say anything, as if she wasn't much interested in the conversation.

"Are you okay?" Pat asked, thinking the fear of her planet being doomed in a few days if the gangsters could successfully steer the comet into Emeestatz, and having walked out on her job had left her feeling a little down.

"I just hope everything goes okay. Things are happening a bit fast."

"Hey, not a problem. We can take our time rather than rushing in like fools in love." Pat picked one of the candles from the bag and continued, "I'll light this so we can have a safe flight."

"Oh, no, that's okay," she said quickly. "We'll light one later."

For the rest of the flight they said very little and dozed while the autopilot flew them to Ixlezem.

* * *

Tony finally had a chance to sit down and relax to his pleasant lunch of a grilled cheese sandwich and tomato soup. He had spent most of the morning bringing his father home from the hospital. He had to take it easy for about a week to prevent a relapse.

Tony had just finished lunch when a knock sounded at his door. He opened the door and was surprised to see his next-door neighbour, Jim, who was also his friend.

"Neighbour Tony. I finished up early in the office and thought you might want to join me for a walk to get some ice-cream downtown."

"Sounds good to me."

"Are you off today?"

Tony, who hadn't seen or spoken to Jim in a week, told him he had been laid off and was taking a few days to relax before starting his search for another job.

Jim was weighty and had dark hair with grey streaks in it which showed his age of forty-two. He was a literary agent and Pat had been one of his clients and become a friend. He had put Pat in contact with a POD publisher. He had met Tony three years ago when Pat had thrown a party to celebrate the sale of his 100th book, even though he had made only enough to pay for the POD fee.

As they walked over to Victoria Street, Jim asked about Pat. "I haven't seen or heard from him for a couple of weeks now. He must be shacking up with some new lady friend."

Tony told Jim about Pat and Eelayka's visit, only a few hours ago. Then realized he would have to lie about Eelayka, so he wouldn't divulge the secret of Owega. He said she was from Sweden and Pat had met her while at Damai Beach in Malaysia.

They had just walked onto the Victoria Street sidewalk when a loud bang, like a large cannon being fired, shook the sidewalk so much they almost lost their balance. They paid little attention to the shaking sidewalk because their attention was focused on the Christmas shop that had exploded into bright yellow flames.

"Get low to the ground!" Jim yelled. They quickly hugged the ground. A large piece of glass just missed them by inches.

The people around became excited and they heard a few people call 9-1-1 from their cell phones.

Forty-metre-high flames and black billowing smoke quickly devoured the fifteen-metre-high building; the store and the upstairs living quarters the K's had lived in.

"Well, I guess we'll have to go Niagara-on-the-Lake to buy our Christmas decorations this year," they heard an older man say behind them. His wife scolded him that the matter was nothing to joke about. There was no telling how many people might have perished or been injured in the blast.

"I think we should skip the ice-cream. I don't think I could stomach it while seeing this," said Jim.

Suddenly another explosion, of the same magnitude came from the ice-cream shop and caused everyone to start running out of fear there would be more. Jim and Tony ran with them to avoid being trampled to death, like an unfortunate participant in the running of the bulls. They turned down the side street they had walked from, less than ten minutes ago.

"Let's go back and see if this is on the news. It'll be on the local news for sure. Those explosions were pretty potent and it is my guess they were caused by large bombs. I wouldn't be surprised if it was a terrorist attack," Jim said.

Tony wished Pat had stayed longer to see this. He would have to videotape the news and show it to him when he came back from Owega, if the whole friggin' town didn't blown up.

* * *

For the second time in a ten-minute period, Pat felt a painful spasm in his abdomen, which was starting to make him feel nauseous.

"Are you okay?" Eelayka asked.

"Yeah, I think so. Something I ate earlier doesn't seem to agree with me," he lied. He had a gut feeling that what he was experiencing didn't bode well, but he couldn't figure it out. He decided to look out for Ixlezem, which should be appearing soon. It was dark and ahead of them were some specks of light indicating an island with a fairly large town or city on it. Pat looked at the map on the console and saw it was Ixlezem.

The aircraft circled the island, flew over Ixlezem City, the capital of Ixlezem. At one point, they passed directly over the Ixlezian king's palace.

Shortly after flying low over a dark area, they approached the resort they had made their reservations at. It was called the Xollemar (pronounced zol-lay-mar), which in Pihanos meant 'sun of the sea'. It was also the site of Soozay and Domko's wedding ceremony and reception. The resort consisted of a large white main building with pink and green floodlights shining on it, which was exactly as they had seen it on the Info-Screen site.

Behind the main building were several small cabana-style buildings with a couple of rooms per building.

They walked into the main building, went to the check-in desk, and were given their electronic room key. While they were checking in, Pat glanced at an Info-Screen put there to entertain people while in line. They were showing something about Cryskokah Gardens. Unfortunately, the sound had been muted. He would have to watch it again when they got into the room. He noticed Eelayka wasn't watching the screen at all.

The room they had reserved was the 'king's suite' and was the largest and most expensive room in the resort. The going rate was fifty krayohs a night.

"Are you sure this isn't too much?" Eelayka asked as they walked into the suite, which occupied its own building.

"Heck no, I still have a lot of the money I won on the airship left. Might as well spend it. It's useless to me on Earth."

The suite consisted of two large rooms. The living room itself was larger than Pat's entire house in Lavinia. The other room was the bedroom with a bed that looked big enough to hold ten people.

"I'm going to take a quick shower and then we can go and grab something to eat," said Eelayka.

While Eelayka showered, Pat turned on the Info-Screen and searched for the story on Cryskokah Gardens. He remembered seeing people running towards the exit as if a large T-Rex dinosaur was chasing them, on the lobby Info-Screen.

He found the story, and played it. The news lady reported there had been a big scare in Cryskokah Gardens. A couple of kids had found a candle on the same bench Pat and Eelayka had been sitting on earlier. The reporter was holding the candle in her hand, saying it wasn't any ordinary candle. The gangsters were known to produce this type of candle. It was designed to explode shortly after being lit. Inside the wick was a liquid made from different acids, which exploded when heated. The candle bomb was potent enough to totally destroy an average two-story house, in a matter of minutes.

Suddenly, Pat remembered Eelayka handing out similar candles while she was in Lavinia. He decided he had to go back and ask the people to give the candles back, before it was too late. He had a sickening feeling they were bombs and some of them may already have gone off. He hoped and prayed Tony hadn't lit his yet.

He also realized his relationship with Eelayka would be destroyed if it turned out she was a gangster. If she was, she had probably been hired to turn him in, as well as destroy his hometown.

* * *

All that afternoon and evening, Tony was glued to his TV, watching the news about Lavinia's explosions. The event had already become big enough to be shown on the international news. It even interrupted the regular programming.

The two bombs had burned down six shops altogether, and damaged other shops a few doors down on either side of the Christmas shop and ice-cream parlour. The fire fighters estimated the temperature at the core of the explosions to have been several times hotter than an average house fire. There wasn't a definite victim count, but the estimated number was around twenty-five. So far, they had recovered ten bodies burned beyond recognition.

When evening came, it clouded over and began to rain, which was highly welcomed as it helped put the last of the fires out. Once the fires were out or under control, the fire fighters from Lavinia and several surrounding towns could start searching for survivors, and the recovery of bodies. The fortunate thing was that no other explosions had occurred, but people were on edge and fearful.

Tony would have loved to go down and witness the cleanup in person, but the police had the whole street shut down so fire fighters and rescuers could do their jobs without interference from well-meaning spectators. The most important reason for the shutdown was to minimize casualties if there were other bombs. The police advised people to watch everything from the safety of their homes.

He went to look for a match so he could light his candle. His search was delayed when Lisa, a friend he had met in a chat-room and who lived in England, paged him on his instant messenger service. She wanted to make sure he was okay, after seeing the news about the explosions.

"You must check BBC's site. There's a picture posted that was taken by a tourist with his digital camera, just seconds after the second explosion," she typed to him.

He went to the site and found the picture. In the right side of the image, he saw himself and Jim. He told Lisa where to look so she could see what he looked like.

A half-hour later, they ended their chat session since it was past midnight in England. Tony became tired of looking at the news and decided to watch the Leafs at Ottawa game. There were only a couple of minutes left in the second period and the score was tied at one each.

He remembered he had been about to light his candle to see if it did bring good luck. He knew deep down it was only a superstition, such as horseshoes and four-leaf clovers. He had to drive to the Avondale convenience store to buy matches, as he had run out, or Eric had taken his last box of matches.

When he returned home and checked his answering machine, he found the red light flashing off-and-on, in one beat, indicating a new message. It was Jim inviting him over for a beer.

So much for lighting the candle. It'll have to wait until another time. There's no sense in lighting it when I get back. It'll be time for bed, he thought to himself.

After he was outside and had locked his apartment door, he suddenly thought about getting the candle and taking it with to Jim's.

"Nah! Screw it. I've seen enough fire today. It might be hard getting a fire fighter if the candle should accidentally fall over," he said to himself.

* * *

Pat heard Eelayka shut the shower off, which meant she would be out in a moment or two, when she was dressed. He decided to play it cool and pretend he was clueless about the candle's main purpose. He didn't want to accuse her until he was sure the candles she had been giving out, were indeed disguised bombs.

He pulled one of the candles out and studied it closely, to see if there was anything unusual about it. He couldn't find anything on it that wasn't associated with candles. He looked in a bedside drawer and found an electronic lighter in the plastic bag of dried zizi leaves. He activated the lighter and brought it to the wick.

Suddenly Eelayka, now fully dressed, ran over and knocked the lighter out of his hand.

"What did you do that for?" Pat, startled, barked out.

"I don't care for the smell of them."

"You didn't have to knock the lighter out of my hand. What were you trying to do? Start a fire?"

"I'm sorry," she said sadly. "Let's enjoy our trip rather than fighting." She put her arms around his neck and gave him a kiss on the cheek. She suggested they go out and grab a bite to eat.

214

"I want to go back to my house and grab something I had forgotten to get earlier," said Pat, half lying.

"What do you need there, when you pretty well have enough here to keep you occupied for the rest of the night?" she asked, referring to herself as his entertainment for the night.

"I need to get my nerve medication," he lied. "Else I'll get jumpy and won't be able to sleep or perform very well," he said, pointing to the bed.

"Oh, wait until after dinner. I'm rather hungry."

The resort had two main eateries and a smaller breakfast-and-brunch place, which specialized in homemade corn cakes. The first was a buffet-style place that had a different theme every night. Tonight it was Kaylahzian night. Before they sat down at a table, they went and looked over the selection of food. There were things that made Pat's stomach turn, like: hand-sized dragon flies smothered in some kind of light brown sauce, frog-egg soup, and a few other items he thought were more suited for an iguana or snake.

They ended up going to the main restaurant that specialized in Corvic, Pihanos, and Kaylahzian cuisine. There was no need to be concerned at the cost of the meal as it was part of the resort's all-inclusive package deal. Pat ordered a plate of Spegilli, which he knew was safe, as he had eaten it at the game in Wiktona.

Pat didn't finish his food for two reasons. Watching Eelayka eat dragonflies put an end to his hunger and he was too worried about whether or not those candles were really bombs.

* * *

Four hours later Eelayka finally gave up making love to Pat, and gave into her body's demand for sleep.

215

Pat didn't find much enjoyment in the love making. All he had wanted to do, was cross back to Lavinia, where it was still late evening. He would have gone sooner if it hadn't been for the power of the zizi leaves, and Eelayka's persistence.

He put on the clothes he had been wearing when he first entered Owega. Pat also grabbed his grandfather's bottle-shaped computer, so he could store it at his house. He didn't want to chance coming back and finding both Eelayka and the computer missing.

He stepped outside and activated the portal. He had figured a way to alter the coordinates on the QTA so he could use his living room as his entry point.

The first thing he did was call Tony. After leaving a message on his answering machine to call back, he decided to drive over to Victoria Street. He got into his car, started it up, pulled out of his driveway and onto the road. The car sounded a bit rough because he hadn't driven it for a while. He drove into the country to give the car a good run and turned onto the road that would eventually turn into Victoria Street.

As he approached the downtown section, he knew something bad had happened, when he encountered a roadblock manned by a couple of policemen. He couldn't see the shops as the detour was too far away from them. He decided to drive up to the roadblock and asked the officers what was going on.

"Sir, you must turn," the officer said shining a flashlight into Pat's face. "The downtown area is closed off until further notice."

"I was away all week. What happened?"

"Two bombs destroyed The North Pole and Summer's Delights."

Pat felt like he had just been stabbed in the chest. He had to think of something to say. He asked if the owners were okay.

"Sorry, I'm not allowed to give out any information at this time."

216

Pat went home and saw Tony hadn't returned his call. He put the TV on and found the game was in overtime. Two minutes later, Toronto scored and eliminated Ottawa from the first round of playoffs.

Pat had almost drifted off to sleep when Tony called. Pat asked about Victoria Street and was told what they had seen earlier.

"When I was over earlier, did Eelayka give you a blue and purple good-luck candle?" Pat asked.

"Yeah, she did. I was going to light it earlier but Jim invited me over to watch the game."

"I need to get the candle from you. It's very important we get rid of them."

"Why? What's wrong with them?"

"I'll tell you in a few minutes when I stop in." Pat didn't want to tell him over the phone, because anyone with a radio scanner could listen in on the conversation.

Pat locked his house and walked over to Tony's. First, he had to explain about the candles and then return to the resort to grab a few hours sleep. He brought Tony outside and quietly told him that he believed the candles were actually bombs in disguise.

"What makes you think that?"

"Because the K's had been given one, as well as the young girls filling in for Summer and Keith at the ice-cream place."

"So I guess this means it's over between you and Laya, or whatever her name was."

"As soon as the wedding is done, I'm going to ditch her."

"Won't that be risky? All she would need to do is slip something in your drink while you weren't looking."

"I think she would have done that already if she had been hired to kill me. They want her to eventually turn me in or something."

"Keep an eye on her or she could put some drug in your beer.

You take a sip. Boom! You wake up in the terrorists' headquarters."

"Maybe I should just ditch her. It's not going to be easy, but it's better than being six feet under or in the hands of those murderers," said Pat

Shortly after, Pat left with Tony's candle, returned to his house and discovered she had left a candle there too. He took it with him.

Pat changed the coordinates on the QTA to enter his bed-and-breakfast room on Slimteeka Island so he could check his e-mail without disturbing Eelayka. He also wanted to send an e-mail to Eric and Jonk, telling them about the Victoria Street bombs.

Two minutes after crossing, he was in his room and logged into his e-mail. He quickly e-mailed Eric and Jonk regarding his discovery of Eelayka's betrayal.

He crossed back to his house and then back to the grounds, near their suite at the Xollemar Resort. He didn't know how to teleport between points on Owega. Going from A to C on Owega via point B in his house worked just as well.

He entered their suite and quietly crawled into bed and was fast asleep before he could think of a way to dump Eelayka without causing hard feelings or raising suspicion. Pat figured if there was a bad break-up; it would be exactly what she deserved for betraying him.

Chapter 20

Xollemar Resort

Eric sat in his cell the next morning and realized the guards hadn't bothered searching for weapons when he had been taken captive. He still had the QTA device on him. He could teleport to Earth and return to a different location. Then he could rescue Joanne and the other captives and return to Slimteeka. However, several guards, who could easily turn him into pulp, stood in the way of fulfilling this task.

Then suddenly an idea struck him. He could pop over to Earth, grab Tony, and go to Slimteeka and round up Pat. He would tell them where they were being held captive. Then he could backtrack through the stops and be back in his cell as if he had never left.

His heart suddenly sank as he remembered Pat telling him he was going to some island up north with Eelayka. He had to find them before it was too late. He also had to go and return as quickly as possible, because if the guards found him missing, the other three would be as good as dead.

He had only seen a guard when a dinner consisting of two slices of bread and some sour wine, had been delivered. There's always the chance one of them could come in to rough me up worse, remembering Soapy's parting words.

He looked at all the buttons on the QTA and remembered Steve telling them the orange one could be used to make Owegans think he was still there.

He pressed the green button to activate the portal behind Pat's house. He was amazed to see the image of the woods. He pressed the orange button and nearly jumped out of his skin as another Eric appeared. He went to the image. His hand passed through the other Eric. He realized the orange button simply created a holographic image of himself. The guards could be fooled into thinking it was the real Eric, as long as they didn't enter his cell.

He quickly stepped through the portal, which had a rainbow frame around it. He was surprised at how easy it was to cross over. There was no wind like he had first experienced in the cave.

It was around two in the morning when Eric walked to Tony's house. He was surprised to see Victoria Street blocked off. He asked a policeman why the street was closed and was told about the two explosions the previous day.

He arrived at Tony's, who was quite surprised to see Eric at such a late hour.

"Tony, you need to come over to Owega and help us escape."

"What are you talking about? How can you be there if you are here?"

"The guards will see a holographic image of myself." While Tony quickly fixed them a glass of ice pop, Eric filled him in on their captivity and who their captors were.

Tony told Eric about Pat's discovery that Eelayka was a member of the gangsters, and was the one who had planted the two bombs disguised as candles.

* * *

When they arrived at Eric's bed-and-breakfast place on Slimteeka Island, they went into his room and found the name and number of the place Pat and Eelayka had reservations at. He quickly looked it up on the Info-Screen and got the address. The last screen he looked at was a site that had detailed maps with latitude and longitude coordinates. He called up a map of Ixlezem and zoomed in until he found the resort. When he clicked on the resort, the coordinates were displayed and he wrote them down.

Just before logging off, he quickly checked his e-mail and read the message Pat had sent earlier. He typed a quick reply telling him to stay at the resort and they would shortly be over to meet up with him.

They quickly teleported back to Lavinia where it was now raining. Eric keyed in the coordinates and then activated the portal. They were greeted with a dark scene of the grounds of the Xollemar Resort. They passed through and ended up in a large shrub only 50 metres from Pat's suite.

"Tony, I need to leave you here so I can get back to the cell before they discover my trick. You get Pat and talk him into coming to get us. I know he would want to deal with Eelayka, but this is more important."

* * *

The guard, who had only recently been hired by the gangsters, delivered the bread and water breakfasts to the four captives. He noticed the last one, called Eric, didn't say a word when his food was dropped off. He just sat on his bed with a blank look on his face, as though in a deep trance. The guard thought of punching Eric around but decided not to. He decided instead he would satisfy his needs with the brunette in the adjacent cell. He understood she was Eric's woman. However, he would wait until later when he was really in the mood.

Eric returned to his cell and found nothing looked different. The holographic image was still there with a blank look on its face. He pressed the orange button and the image disappeared. He sat down and ate the breakfast one of the guards must have left for him while he was bouncing back and forth between the two dimensions.

* * *

Pat awoke to the wake-up service phone call, and was surprised to find he felt refreshed, considering he had only slept for an hour after returning from Earth. Eelayka awoke too, gave him a good morning kiss, and went to have a shower.

Pat had just signed on when he heard a knock at the door. He looked through the peephole and was surprised to see Tony standing there with an anxious look on his face. He opened the door and stepped outside to avoid any possibility of Eelayka finding Tony there, or hearing their conversation.

"Pat, we have to help Eric. He, Joanne, and two other people are being held captive by the gangsters."

"You're kidding," said Pat with a shocked look on his face. "How did that happen?"

Tony repeated everything Eric had told him.

"Why don't you go to the breakfast-and-brunch eatery and grab something to eat," suggested Pat. "Here, it's on me." He gave Tony a two-krayoh coin. "That should cover it. Wait there. I don't want her to know you're here, or else she'll know I'm on to her."

He led Tony to the restaurant area, to ensure he didn't get lost on the grounds. For as long as he has known Tony, he has known him to have a poor sense of direction.

Pat went to the beach and took a forty-minute walk. He needed to figure out a way of breaking it off with Eelayka. He hated being the dumper more than she would hate being the one dumped, he reasoned.

Pat returned to their room. He figured it was time to cut to the chase. He felt he had to find the right way to do it, or risk the chance that she could pull out a laser gun and shoot him.

Pat found Eelayka in the midst of a chat session. "Whom are you chatting with?" Pat asked Eelayka, who was in the middle of a chat session in her chat-room on the Info-Screen.

"Oh, nobody," she replied nervously.

"Are you chatting with your buddies about those candle bombs you were given?" asked Pat, his voice spiced with sarcasm.

"I don't know what you're talking about," she said quickly, which led him to believe she had been trained to say that.

"Eelayka, those candles you gave my friends are bombs. I saw on last night's news they had to close the theme park early yesterday, because they found a candle-bomb on one of the benches. It was the same one you and I had sat on just before we left. The bomb looked exactly like your candles," said Pat firmly.

Eelayka remained silent. She had a guilty look on her face.

"You can confess to me. I won't turn you in. However, I'd rather not see you anymore. I don't like or respect anyone who could betray their friends, family and country."

Eelayka walked out and Pat followed her. Tears began to form in her eyes. She blurted out, "I can't take this anymore! I don't know why I took this assignment in the first place. For heaven sakes! I apologize if it has caused you a great deal of trouble."

"You should be saying that to the friends and loved ones of the people you killed yesterday. Frankly, if I was them I would want to see you burned at the stake!"

"I don't blame you," she said between sobs. "I'm not the Eelayka you want to be with."

Pat remembered her telling him when they first met her name meant 'shiny-light'. He figured she was telling him she wasn't his true 'shiny-light'. He would later find out he had misinterpreted her meaning.

She started to run towards the front parking lot, where her aircraft was parked. She didn't notice the man in a dark Dendoyhee jacket until it was too late. Pat saw a bright flash of light hit her, knocking her to the ground as though hit by a cannon ball.

Pat pulled out his zapper gun, intending to knock the sniper out cold for a while, so he could make another citizen's arrest. However, the sniper, from experience, was faster and fired first.

Pat saw a bright flash and felt a sharp pain in his chest. He realized he had been shot in the heart. He felt the pain spread down his left arm, which he associated with a major symptom of cardiac arrest. He tried to shoot the sniper but couldn't get a shot off. Everything around him started to fade out, as if someone was slowly dimming the lights. He vaguely heard another shot but couldn't tell where it came from. He decided it didn't really matter as he was already well on his way to being another victim of the deadly terrorist group. Everything was black now and the last thing he heard was a female voice yelling for someone to call 511. The voice sounded familiar but he couldn't place it before his oxygen-starved brain shut down.

* * *

Maili was surprised when she woke up early that morning. She and Timko had spent the day before flying home to Ixlezem. When they got back to their ocean-view house, they were both exhausted. She figured she would sleep until midday and awake with that run-down feeling one normally experienced after being really busy the previous day. However, she woke up feeling rather energetic. She also had a wild craving for pancakes at the Xollemar Resort, which was only a kilometre or two down the road from their place.

She woke Timko up and forty minutes later, they were at the Cazza Le Maizetort restaurant, which was the small restaurant that specialized in over one hundred kinds of corn cakes.

They waited in line with another gentleman who looked familiar to Maili. Then she realized he looked like one of Pat's friends. She spoke to Tony in broken Corvic and asked if he remembered her.

"Aren't you the one recently hit by lightning?" Tony asked, a little uncertainly and slightly surprised.

"Yes, that's me." She introduced him to Timko. She asked him if he was alone.

Tony explained he was waiting for Pat to join him after breakfast. He didn't want to alarm her by telling her Eric and Joanne had been captured.

Maili invited Tony to share a table with them, so he wouldn't have to eat alone. He accepted the offer. The three of them ordered regular corn cakes with Xule-flavoured (pronounced as zoo-lay) syrup on them. The syrup was pinkish and tasted like passion fruit.

They finished eating and received their bill, at the same time Pat was having it out with Eelayka. After settling their bills, they went out into the warm salty air. They were exchanging e-mail addresses when they heard the first laser shot. A few seconds later they heard the second shot.

Maili whipped out a laser gun she carried with her on a regular basis. She spotted the sniper and shot him before he had time to shoot her. He went down and a puddle of blood formed around his head.

She looked around for the targets he had been shooting at, saw a Kaylahzian woman, and just beyond her, Pat lying on his back with bloodstains on his shirt. She quickly told Timko to call 511, the Owegan emergency number.

She ran over to Pat, felt for a pulse, and found none. She tried to revive Pat, even though she knew he was beyond repair. Through teary eyes, she looked up towards the sky as if searching for a miracle.

226

"They're on their way, honey," Timko said running towards Maili, who had her hands on Pat's heart and appeared to be in some kind of trance.

Maili started to feel a vibrating sensation go through her hands.

* * *

Pat started to feel like he was floating and was amazed when the blackness was replaced by dazzling colours, fluttering around like animated computer-art graphics. He knew he was having an after death experience. His chest pains had vanished.

Suddenly, he saw a large garden with all kinds of people wearing light-coloured clothes. They all had very peaceful expressions. He tried to get closer to them, but bumped into an invisible wall.

A woman with long golden hair stepped from the wall and walked towards Pat. "I don't think it's your time to be here. You must save her before it's too late."

Pat was confused; surely Eelayka couldn't have survived the shot to her head.

"Oh no, she is well and alive and needs you to rescue her from her captors," she said, reading Pat's mind. "Then you must save our world from the comet."

Suddenly Pat knew what she was talking about, and how to save the captives. It was as if the answers were planted into his deep subconscious mind. He turned away from the garden the woman had come from, and started to will himself back to life. The garden scene faded and once again, everything went black.

An image of a woman with long dark hair appeared, which Pat thought was an angel, until he felt the pain in his chest again. He

227

recognized Maili. He realized she was trying to save him and felt a vibrating sensation in his chest.

"Come on, Pat, don't leave us now," Maili said in Pihanos. Pat felt one of Maili's teardrops hit his face. His chest pain began to disappear and he felt his heart beating irregularly for a few seconds. Shortly it regained its natural rhythm.

"I'm alive!" Pat said and he suddenly felt like the guy in *It's a Wonderful Life* when the angel had given him his life back. He heard a roar of cheering come from a group of spectators attracted by the commotion.

"We thought you were a goner," Maili said.

"You have the power to heal, like I do," Pat said excitedly.

"You must have passed it on to me when you saved me."

Pat looked around and saw about fifty or so people, including Timko and Tony, relieved and amazed at Maili's healing power. Then he saw a few medics carrying the bagged body of 'Eelayka' towards the ambulance airboat.

"That's not Eelayka!" he blurted out, without thinking. "She's with Eric, Joanne, and Jonk. We must go and save them before it's too late."

One of the medics, wearing square-shaped dark glasses, came over to Pat and put a device on him that looked like a mouse doctors use for ultrasound readings. The device had a wire running to his glasses. Pat assumed the glasses were a special monitor.

"He's as good as new," the medic announced a few seconds later, and took the device off Pat's chest. "There's not even a scratch to be seen."

Pat stood up and felt like he had never been shot. He gave Maili a hug, thanked her, shook hands with Timko, and told him he had a very special girl.

"I was just returning the kindness you had shown me after the lightning strike," she said. She then knew she had been drawn there to save Pat, rather than to satisfy a craving for corn cakes.

Pat knew now why Eelayka had appeared to have two personalities. The Eelayka that had flown her airboat recklessly through a storm the other night, was the same girl who had just perished. He figured she had been hired to act like the real Eelayka and turn him in. He guessed they had probably intended to shoot, and dispose of her after she'd completed her mission.

Twenty minutes later Pat checked out, went with Tony to say their good-byes to Maili and Timko, and told them about saving the captives at the gangsters' quarters.

"We're going to have to return to Slimteeka and get some weapons and maybe explosives," Pat said to Tony as he activated the portal.

"Wait! I'm coming along too!" they heard Timko shout as he approached. "These thugs killed my brother five years ago. Now it's time we give them some of their own medicine."

"Timko, what we are about to do is very risky and the last thing we need to do is lose you," Pat tried to reason with him.

"No, I need to do this for Roverto."

"Come along then," Pat told him as the rainbow portal appeared. Pat quickly explained how the portals worked. They all stepped through to Slimteeka by stopping over in Pat's house, where he grabbed his grandfather's computer. A few minutes later, they went through a second portal, which returned them to the bed-and-breakfast place.

Chapter 21

Escape

They returned to the Cryskokah Gardens parking lot to check one more thing out. Two minutes later Pat confirmed Eelayka's airboat was still in the parking lot. It occurred to him the gangsters must have kidnapped her when she was in the ladies room. The scream he had heard had been hers, and had not come from the funhouse attraction as he had originally thought.

"Timko, is there a private place on Owega, where we could tap into the Dendoyhee's system and any other central intelligence?" Pat asked.

"We can always go back to my place," suggested Timko.

"It's too risky. The last thing we need to do is put Maili in danger too."

"I know," Timko said, snapping his fingers. "How about Solinga Bay?"

"Where would that be?"

"It's a famous resort town on the northern coast of Corvus. A lot of artists, writers, and poets live there."

"You'll fit right in, Pat," chuckled Tony.

"Yeah, but I usually write science fiction and fantasy, while these other writers probably do historical fiction, romance, and mystery."

"Oh, no. There are writers of all genres there. Just check out their Info-Screen site — it'll blow you away. The place can't be described in words."

"Is it a romantic place?" asked Pat.

"It's the honeymoon capital of the world."

"So it must be like Niagara Falls," said Tony. He told Timko about Niagara Falls and its beauty, which attracts thousands of newlyweds each year. He also added that it was one of Earth's natural wonders.

"Let's go back to my bed-and-breakfast and see if we can get in touch with Steve," said Pat. "He may have some ideas for us."

* * *

Eelayka woke up in her musty and damp cell with a feeling of hope welling up inside her. She had dreamt her late aunt, Jaynah, had appeared before her and told her Pat was okay, and was finding a way to save her and the other captives.

"They may have captured Pat," she heard one of the guards say.

"When will he be here?" she heard a distant voice down the corridor ask.

"It's a bit uncertain. There was a confrontation at the Xollemar Resort. Our hit man managed to take out the phoney Eelayka. However, one of the medics reported there were three dead bodies. The descriptions of the other two bodies sound very much like Pat and our hired man."

"That doesn't make sense. He was told not to bring Pat back or to kill him."

"Maybe he took Pat out in self-defence," said the nearby guard. "Pat must have had tried to shoot him after the slut, he thought was his dream girl, was shot."

"I think the medic is covering for Pat. Remind me to forward this to Soapy. I want to see if we can go and teach that medic not to mess around with us."

Eelayka was shocked at this news. She couldn't see Pat being dead. It wouldn't be fair, she thought to herself. Eelayka had to find a way to escape but had no idea how she would do it. There were probably guards around every corner of the corridors, which were lit by well-spaced, small naked bulbs. She thought of using one of her self-defence moves she had learned in high school. However, it was risky because the guard could dodge her favourite sidekick, and put a move on her. She could only hope Pat would come along soon.

The other thought that ran through her mind was that Pat must have been with someone disguised as her. It was probably a prostitute, whom the gangsters had recruited by offering to pay large sums of money. After she had accepted the offer and failed to bring Pat to the gangsters, she ended up being eliminated. The thought of Pat sleeping with her made Eelayka's stomach turn, but she felt she couldn't blame Pat, as he probably hadn't noticed the difference, especially if they had smoked zizi leaves.

* * *

Eric suddenly had a brain wave. He would use the QTA, teleport to Earth, hunt down anything he could use as a weapon, and return to his cell. Once the guard brought his lunch, he would hit him over the head and flee into the corridor.

He quickly activated his holographic image, jumped through the portal, and was in the woods behind Pat's place. It was only the wee hours of the morning there. He didn't have to worry about adjusting his eyes to the darkness, as his cell was fairly dark.

When he was back in his apartment, he gathered a few things he considered potential weapons if used in the right way, at the right time. Some of the items were a small container of rat poison, a steak knife, and a small but thick frying pan that would be ideal for hitting someone over the head.

Five minutes later, he was back in his cell with his little bag of goodies. He heard the guard serving food to the others and knew he would be next. He got his frying pan ready and held it behind him.

"Your lunch," said the guard while opening the door.

Eric thanked him and tried to distract him by asking for the time. When the guard looked at his watch, Eric took full advantage and swung the frying pan as hard as he could. He knocked the guard out cold. He grabbed the unconscious guard, stripped him of his uniform, donned it himself, and grabbed the guard's gun for extra security.

He stepped into the corridor and went to the nearest cell, where he found Joanne. He signalled for her not to say a word, and brought her out into the corridor.

"What are you doing?" asked a guard.

"Taking her to my quarters."

"Fine, but if she escapes — you will have to answer to the big man. He will probably turn you into shark food. He's getting fed up with your poor work performance."

Eric was relieved to find he had been mistaken him for the unconscious guard. "I'll be sure to bring her back to her cell when I'm done with her." After the guard left, he took Joanne into his cell and whispered for her to tie the unconscious guard's hands behind his back with rope he whipped out of his goodies bag. "Also tie this towel around his mouth."

"No problem," Joanne whispered. "I'm glad I served in the army." She gave Eric a quick kiss and went to tie the guard up while Eric freed the others.

* * *

Eelayka had just finished her lunch when a guard came along and opened her cell door. She thought he must be new because he battled to find the right key. He signalled for her to come with him. She had a bad feeling about this. She sensed something familiar about the guard. Then it struck her it was Pat's friend, Eric, disguised as a guard.

"Weren't you just with the other girl?" she heard a guard in

234

the corridor ask Eric in Corvic (she heard the words but did not understand the language).

"I was undecided on which one to get my pleasure from, so I decided to double my pleasure by borrowing both of them," Eric replied.

"Just don't let them get loose or *else*."

She was led into the cell where Joanne and the tied-up guard were. Joanne explained, in her limited Kaylahzian, Eric's plan to free all of them.

Eelayka was surprised and alarmed when Eric brought in Jonk, who was bruised in the face and had a fat lip. She went over and hugged him.

Eric activated the portal and signalled for the other three to walk through the rainbow frame.

* * *

Pat, Tony and Timko arrived in his living room and keyed in the coordinates for Serie Beach so they could approach Steve for help in rescuing the others from the gangsters.

"Is that your Info-Screen?" Timko asked, pointing at Pat's twenty-five-inch TV set.

"It's basically a receive-only box. My send and receive system, the Internet, is in another room." He led them to his writing room to show Timko his desktop computer.

"We have a network, like your Info-Screen network, but it's not nearly as fast or perfected as yours. In our world, the Internet has only been available to the home user for the last ten years. Before that, we relied on TV, radio and newspapers for the daily news. I would say our world is about ten to twenty years away from having something as powerful as the Info-Screen network."

The doorbell rang and Tony asked, "Who could that be at this hour?"

"Everyone get in the kitchen," said Pat as he went to look through his peephole. A sudden chill ran down his spine as he saw a gangster and three other people he couldn't identify because of the darkness.

"We have company. Four gangsters. Everyone go downstairs while I deal with this." Pat looked through the peephole again and was greatly relieved when he got a closer look at the guard and realized it was Eric. He must have found a way to escape.

"Well, it's about time!" said Eric, when Pat opened the door. "What were you doing, sleeping?"

"I'm not used to having people over at 5:00 A.M.," Pat shot back. Pat let them in and was overcome by joy when he saw one of the three people was Eelayka.

Pat went to Eelayka and hugged her like one would hug a loved one who has just returned from a long overseas war.

"I'm so sorry this happened," Pat said to her through tears of joy. "I thought you had betrayed me and then got yourself killed by the gangsters."

"They must have set you up with someone dressed and disguised like me. I hope you didn't sleep with her, but if you did, I forgive you — you couldn't have known."

"Ugh, Pat and Eelayka, we do have a world to save, you know," said Eric a few minutes later because Pat and Eelayka hadn't stopped hugging and kissing since she'd walked through the door.

"Oh, this is my house. I guess this is your first visit to my world," Pat said to Eelayka.

"Did you bring the phoney one here earlier?"

Pat quickly explained she had caused the deaths of twenty or thirty people when she planted the two bombs.

"I'm so sorry these gangsters brought such tragedy to your town and world."

"I heard on the news the detectives think it had something to do with Osama bin Laden's group. After all, they were the ones who destroyed the World Trade Centre," said Tony.

"Let's go on-line and check it out," suggested Eric.

"Can we make it fast? I'm quite hungry. The food the gangster's served us was rather disgusting." Joanne requested.

"This will only take a few minutes," Pat said as they went into his writing room.

Ten minutes later, they had learned the investigators were still mystified about the type of bomb used. There was some strange chemical detected in the analysis of different debris pieces. They were speculating that the Al-Qa'ida network could have been responsible, because they were known for developing different explosives and biological weapons. The RCMP and forensic personnel also suspected a terrorist group based in Israel might have caused it, because they had discovered the late owner of The North Pole had had a great uncle who had been a member of the Nazi's. The police were leaning towards the Israeli group.

"I guess it's a toss-up now. Maybe we should contact the police and tell them the truth. After all, I hate to see an innocent man go to prison," said Eric.

"Are you crazy?" said Pat. "They would think we're loony and lock us up. Better yet, they'll turn us into some science experiment. Let them arrest the terrorists. Sooner or later they're going to launch another attack on a major city."

"There've been other attacks?" asked Joanne.

Eric filled Joanne in on the attacks that had taken place on September 11, 2001.

"I guess they weren't kidding about your world having such corruption," Joanne answered with a shocked look on her face.

"Let's activate the portal and skedaddle over to Steve's and get him to help us out. He knows all the angles when it comes to spying on the gangsters," suggested Pat.

"Wait," Eelayka cut in. "Pat, you and I need to come up with a phrase we can use to identify ourselves to each other, in case they try to set you up with another phoney me."

"Whenever we've been apart, and get together again, I'll say 'Pedals is her name' and you must reply 'mice is her game.' If not — I'll know I've been set up again. They practiced it a few times, to get it down to pat.

"Pat's a man of many words and ideas," Eric chuckled. "Your typical sci-fi writer."

Pat looked at his QTA and found the coordinates to the beach in front of Steve's place were the last set of numbers on the list of previous coordinates stored into the QTA's memory bank. He entered the coordinates and activated the portal. They could see the other side was dark and rather snowy. "Isn't a bit early for snow in Clarissa?" he asked.

"Not necessarily. We've sometimes had snow even earlier than now. I remember a few years ago we had snow twenty days earlier than today's date," said Joanne.

The seven of them stepped through and the drastic temperature change hit them like a slap in the face. The snow was knee-deep, which seemed even more unusual for the time of year.

"We must be smack in the middle of a band of lake-effect snow," said Pat, who noticed the snow was being driven by a stiff southern wind coming from the direction of Steve's back yard. He was glad it wasn't coming from the north - it would have been more intense since Orthnus Lake was a few degrees warmer than Outhnus Lake.

"This idea had better be good," said Eric. He had to wait few seconds to continue talking because of a sudden flash of lightning followed by a loud crack of thunder. "I'm not freezing my butt off for nothing!"

"Just think of the time we went to Buffalo and got caught in one of their famous lake-effect events on Christmas Eve of

1993, after we went to do some grocery shopping there," suggested Pat.

They walked slowly through the one-metre-deep snow, went up to Steve and Carol's front door, found it locked and rang the bell.

Pat was glad he had taken the time to dig up enough winter coats for everyone. He was cold even in his own parka. Nothing like going from 30°C to below 0°C in less than an hour, he thought to himself. , When he had gathered the coats, he had assumed the temperature would bc around 5 or 6°C rather than below freezing.

Steve opened the door and he had to take a close look at them. He recognized only Pat, Eric, Joanne, and Tony. He hadn't met the other three yet.

"Come on in," Steve said to them. "You must be cold out there. It's quite a bad winter storm out there tonight. Here, this will warm you up." He poured them each a cup of coffee and invited them to sit down in the large kitchen at one of the family-sized tables used by people staying over as bed-and-breakfast guests.

Pat introduced Steve to Jonk, Eelayka, and Timko, who were shivering from the cold. They had lived all their lives in a tropical region.

"Is this the first time you've seen snow?" Steve asked them both in Kaylahzian.

"Jonk saw snow a long time ago when he was here visiting the Clarissa area," said Eelayka. "It's my first time for snow and being in Clarissa. I was in Wiktona Beach a week ago and when it started getting chilly, I left to go back to Emeestatz. That's when I met Pat, who saved me from being raped on the airship."

"This is unusually early for us to get snow like this," said Steve. "Sometimes we get a few flakes, but not a full-blown storm until the final month, or the first month of the new year. The scary thing is the weather people are predicting it will keep coming down heavily for the next three or four days. Sometimes they can be wrong. Let's hope this is one of those times."

"How much accumulation are they predicting?" asked Pat, who has always had an interest in the weather.

"As much as fifteen to twenty cubits or enough to go well over our heads."

"Holy Toledo! Are you serious about that?" Eric exclaimed in disbelief

"I'll show you," he said turning on an Info-Screen in the dining area. He quickly called up an image of a weather map. On the map was an 'L' to the east of Outhnus Lake. Further to the east, was an 'H'. "This 'L' or low pressure system is rather intense and it's drawing cold, frigid air from the extreme south and pushing it over the length of Outhnus Lake. Since the lake is fairly warm for this time of year, it's giving off warmer moist air. When this happens, the warm moist air quickly cools off and the moisture turns to snow and sleet. The winds then force it right towards us. After having a few hundred leagues to pick up even more moisture, it dumps itself all over us. We call it the great white machine."

"We get that back home. The most we get, though, is a few feet or as much as what's out there now," said Eric.

"Well, you see, this low is going to stay put. It is now cut off from the jet-stream currents. This low-pressure system area isn't moving out because the high further east is stacked and blocking the low to the point where it's forced to stay put. The low can't really go around the high, because the high is connected with another high to its south and another to its north. This causes a high-pressure ridge. Think of it as a wall, and the low as a car heading towards the wall. It's forced to stop or crash."

Pat filled Steve in on all the stuff that had happened since they had last seen him when they had left for Emeestatz. He told him about the fake Eelayka — how she had planted candle bombs, her death and his near death experience.

Eric and Joanne also filled him on their capture and easy escape, thanks to the QTA.

"There's more to the story, though," said Pat. "Eelayka, Jonk, and I tapped into the gangsters' computer system and found out about their plans to alter the comet's course so it would crash into Owega. It's like they're turning it into one giant guided missile."

"Our agency has also tapped into their system and found out the same stuff," said Steve. "What I'm confused about is how did you find out, when it's nowhere on the Info-Screen system?"

Pat told him about his grandfather's computer and the e-mail which had sent him to Jonk.

"They caught us in their system," Jonk added. He recounted his capture and the claim that they had found a way to detect ghost or unauthorized users.

"Hey, Pat, can I speak to you in private for a few minutes?" Steve asked.

Pat felt a bit nervous as he followed Steve into a room used as his office. Steve sat at his desk, which didn't have any papers or bills on it. All the bookkeeping was done on the Info-Screen system, for which he rented a storage area in the central mainframe system, in downtown Clarissa, on a monthly basis. Pat sat down in an egg-shaped chair on the other side of Steve's desk. Being called into Steve's office reminded him of being called in to his supervisor's office a few years back, when he had worked at the travel agency. Being called in had meant he was either getting an annual increase or reamed out for something screwing up. Unfortunately, the latter of the two happened more often.

Chapter 22

Solinga Bay

Owega's solar system lay in a cluster of over ten million stars of different sizes. Most of them were about the size of Owega's or Earth's sun. The estimated diameter of 'the grape' was approximately fifty thousand light years. There were about twenty known yellow stars within a light year from Owega. The closest star was about 0.48 light years or five trillion kilometres away and very similar in size and shape to Owega's sun. The closest star to Earth was about four light years away. Within a radius of the same distance from Owega, there were about as many as forty thousand suns. One of them was a green giant fifty times larger than Owega's sun and could be seen in broad daylight, on a clear day.

The advantage of having so many stars close to Owega was that there was an abundant supply of light photons.

The major drawback of being in 'the grape' was the forever-changing fields of gravity between solar systems. Between the systems were large chunks of rock and ice left over from when the star cluster first formed, about six billion years ago, as well as left-over stars that had existed in the area. These chunks would get pulled in by the gravity field of one star, swung around them and shoot out into space with their long tales of fire, only to be pulled in by another star. These chunks were well known as comets and they travelled from one star to another until they either crashed into the star itself or one of the star's planets. Any existing life on that fated planet would perish from the impact.

The particular comet headed towards Owega's sun was about 50 kilometres in diameter.

* * *

"How much do you remember from your childhood?" Steve asked Pat while looking directly into his eyes.

"I can't remember anything before I was eight, because I was in some kind of accident, which left me with amnesia."

"Do you remember anything about your parents?"

"Not a thing."

"You were never born on Earth."

Pat was stunned at this news. "Then, how did I get to be on Earth?"

Steve waited a couple of minutes before replying, as though he was thinking of the best way to break the news. "Your father was the late Prince Alex, who was brother to the present King Alan III."

"I – I don't understand," Pat stammered, shocked.

"Your father used to live a wild life when he was young. He would spend a lot of his allowance on women and travel. His father, King George IV, and mother, Queen Mary V, selected him as heir to the throne. Your dad felt he had to live it up while he was young, rather than live recklessly while he was enthroned.

"His father sent him to a small fishing village on a bay called Northwest Bay. He was there to find a new vacation area since, at the time, Wiktona Beach had several outdated and beyond repair resorts. Once he found the location, he was to e-mail the details to his father, who would have City Planners design an ultimate resort and then commence building.

One day, your father hired a fisherman to take him out on his boat so he could get a view of the shore, which would help him pick the spot for the resort where it could best be seen from sea. Northwest Bay is crescent shaped and about fifty leagues long.

The weather was perfect for sailors that day. However, a remarkable event happened five hundred leagues out to sea. A large subterranean quake took place in a harmless area. A powerful tsunami, or tidal wave, developed and hit the shores of Northwest Bay, about a cycle, or two and half hours later."

"Didn't they see the tidal wave when they were out at sea?"

"No, tsunamis travel under water at speeds of about 166 leagues per hour, or 800 km/h in your metric system. They travel so smoothly, a boat could sail over one without knowing it. Once they hit shallow water, they are forced upward to great heights. When they draw back, they carry anything in their path with them.

Your father and the fisherman were caught in the tsunami's path. The wave pulled them out quite far from the shore. The fisherman drowned shortly after they were both caught in the deadly undertow. Your father would have perished too, but fate was on his side that day.

A mysterious woman, of outstanding beauty, happened to be pulled out with the tsunami too, but somehow managed to stay on top of the wave. She found your dad and carried him back to shore and saved his life."

"Wasn't he already dead like the fisherman?"

"Your mother brought him back to life, the same way you did with Maili."

"You mean to say she had extraordinary powers, like I seem to have acquired since I came to Owega?"

"She had so many powers the surrounding villages felt uneasy about her, some even suspected her of being a witch or demon."

"Was she Corvic?"

"She never truly revealed where she was from. The only thing we know for sure is her name was Solinga. Your dad figured she had to be related to the highly intelligent and powerful race that had brought our ancestors from the lost Atlantis, just before it sank. She once told your father her ancestors had brought ours here."

"They must have brought Eelayka's people here too."

"They were on this planet, just as Maili's ancestors were. What did Eelayka tell you about her ancestors?"

Pat relayed he had been told they had come from a planet called Kaylahzee, and that they had been slaves to the Corvics at one time.

"They were genetically created by our great ancestors as their working- and sex slaves. They were created to live off simple foods such as insects, because then they would then not need any of the light-generated food."

"That explains why they like to eat insects." Pat mentioned the fake Eelayka eating a large dragonfly for her last meal.

"Is that why Kaylahzian women all look like supermodels and the men are built like baseball or football players?" asked Pat, who couldn't believe his ears. "What about the planet they came from?"

"The Kaylahzee planet is an invented story, so the Kaylahzian race would never find out about their true creators. The other two things I should point out are that Kaylahzian mothers-to-be don't bear their babies. They lay eggs, which are then kept in special incubators. This is so the mothers hardly age from bearing their children. The other is a Kaylahzian can mature in ten years, instead of our eighteen to twenty years."

Pat remembered once reading a trilogy series by Anne Rice known as the *Mayfair Witches*. In this series, there was a human race known as the Taltos who had matured from birth in only a couple of days and lived well past a thousand years. He wondered if the Kaylahzians lived for several centuries or only forty years. He asked Steve.

"They have about the same lifespan as we do. They hatch after only three months. Carol sometimes envied them when we had our kids. She thought it would have been nice to have been spared the discomfort of bearing children. Anyway, we're getting sidetracked from the subject of your mom and dad. Your dad gave up his right to the throne and married your mom."

"Do I have any brothers and sisters?" Pat asked, very curious.

"No, your mom died when you were six. Your father was never the same after that. He eventually went insane and disappeared only a couple of days after your swimming incident. That was when your foster grandparents acquired you."

"How did I end up living on Earth?" asked Pat.

"One day, when you were eight, your father took you to one of Solinga Bay's public beaches, for some swimming and sunning. While you were there, a ten-year-old bully tried to drown you. You ended up fighting back with the use of the powers you'd inherited from your mom, and drowned him. It was self-defence and you were never arrested. We learned the bully was Robert Soapiosko. His older brother, Drew, was the lifeguard on duty that day and he had tried to blame you. He thought his brother was only playing around. He vowed he would kill you when you would least expect it. His father was the leader of the gangsters who were, and still are, stationed on a small island due north of Emeestatz. Our agency sent you and your foster grandparents, as well as people to portray the roles of your relatives, to live on Earth. You can say it was our version of the witness protection program. Drew Soapiosko is now the leader of the gangsters. He is better known as Soapy. We knew he would eventually inherit the position, and that's why we sent you to Earth."

"You must have paid them well," Pat speculated.

"We subjected you to a brainwash procedure which wiped out all memories of Owega, and replaced them with false memories of your lives in Lavinia. The gentleman selected to be your grandfather somehow knew where the portal was. He came to Owega and found a way to change the coordinates to Kaylahzee instead of Corvus. He knew he would lose his earnings, if he was caught on Owega. That was where he built his bottle computer.

247

Anyway, now that you are back we have to reverse the procedure. It won't return your memories, but it will unlock the doors and they will return when triggered."

Steve hooked him into a set of headphones connected to a machine the size of a walkman. A few seconds later the process was completed.

"We had better join the rest before they think we have fallen into a deep crack or something," said Steve, joking around to relax Pat.

In the living room, the others were doing research on the gangsters. Eric told them they had found quite a bit of information.

Pat put his arm around Eelayka and she laced her fingers with his free hand. Pat felt the smoothness of her skin and remembered Steve telling him Kaylahzians had been created to be Corvic's ideal sex toys. "Pedals is her name."

She immediately responded, "Mice is her game."

* * *

The Dandoyhee group has been around for over five hundred years. The founder, Jack Soapiosko, a former convict had been released early for good behaviour. He rounded up eleven other ex-cons and formed a small organized crime group on Squid Bladder Island, located about 150 km north of Solinga Bay. Their objective was to have control over the sales of 'pleasure items' such as zizi leaves and alcoholic beverages. They very seldom killed anyone who interfered with their business. Most of the time, an individual would be sent to the Dandoyhees' underground lab and have a finger or toe amputated.

However, at times, a member became dissatisfied with the rules of the gang and broke away. He would round up a few of the other members, and start a more destructive sub-group. Eventually the sub-group was either exterminated by the Dandoyhee or turned over to the authorities.

It was one of these sub-groups that had been responsible for the monotrain disasters. They were also famous for burning the villages of small independent islands and forcing the homeless survivors into slavery.

The latest break-away group of gangsters was the largest number in thirty years, and their leader was Drew Soapiosko, who also happened to be the nephew of John, the president of the Dandoyhee. Their latest project: the steering of the comet towards Owega by using a magnetic device so large and powerful, they had to build and operate it on Red Rock Island where the buildings and homes were all made of stone. A metal adobe would have collapsed from the intense magnetic power. Rob had been sitting at his desk when a guard came in to announce one of the other guards had somehow managed to let their captives escape. Rob demanded the name of the guard responsible for screwing things up.

"I believe it was Pete. He's the one who helped Mark put John and his wife in the tank."

"Bring him in here at once!" Rob barked out. "The fish are going to get another meal this evening."

Pete knew he had screwed up royally, and was well aware of the penalty — dumped into a pool of flesh-eating sharks that spray their prey with acid and then eat the dead victims. I refuse to let them feed me to those vermin. I'd rather end my life right here and now if there is no way for me to escape, he thought to himself. He had the most brilliant idea. He would simply blow the whole fort off the map. He knew where the explosives armoury was stored. If I'm going to die, the rest will die with me. He grinned from ear to ear like the grinch when he had discovered an ideal way to steal Christmas from the Who people.

* * *

Pat, Eelayka, and the rest of his group were at a different bed-and-breakfast at the other end of Slimteeka Island. On the way from Steve's place, they popped over to Ixlezem to get Maili to join them in their quest to stop the gangsters from making the comet hit Owega.

"I'm just glad we're back in the tropics," said Timko, who had never been in a cold and snowy place before.

Pat decided it was a good time to tell his group of friends what Steve had told him earlier, now he had them all together. He gave them the basics and left it at that. They mulled over the information for a while in silence.

Eric decided to change the subject back to the matter at hand and asked, "Have you found a way to reprogram the gangsters' magnetic machine so it veers the comet away from us?"

"What do you mean?" asked Maili, worried.

Pat quickly filled everyone in on the discovery he, Jonk, and Eelayka had made earlier when they tapped into the gangsters' system.

"There has to be a way to stop them. How much time do we have before the comet is destined to reach our world?" asked Eelayka.

"Not very long. The astronomy site said it would be sometime today after dusk, Corvus time. I suggest we all have a nap so we will be refreshed this evening. This jumping back and forth seems to make me feel tired, especially the rapid changes in weather conditions," said Pat.

It was agreed they would nap for one cycle, or 144 minutes, and then meet in the lobby where they would decided on a place for a quick bite to eat.

250

Pat and Eelayka went to their room and as soon as Eelayka got into bed, she pulled out the plastic bag of zizi leaves and waved it at Pat, who was coming from the bathroom.

"That sounds like a good plan," said Pat, smiling. "After all, we never did get the chance to ride the zizi train." Pat said the password and Eelayka answered correctly. "I just wanted to make sure I wasn't going to be sleeping with some fake and not my darling Eelayka." Pat finally had a chance to make love to Eelayka. He found even more intense pleasure in making love to the true Eclayka. In no time at all, they both fell asleep.

In his dream, Pat re-experienced his afterlife experience. The same woman with the long blond hair appeared, and once again said he must save her; which didn't make sense now Eelayka was free.

"No, I am referring to Owega," the woman said reading Pat's mind. "You must save her from a terrible fate."

"What would be the best way to go about it?" asked Pat in the hope she would have a perfect solution.

"You must gather the others you are now with and find Bella. Then go to the pyramid of the city named after me, join hands, and force the comet away with your minds."

"What city is that?" Pat asked, thinking she was talking about Clarissa, which was the only female-named city to come to mind.

"You'll find it, my son," she said and suddenly disappeared.

The alarm they had set earlier, went off and ended Pat's dream before he had a chance to call her back. They now would have to go back to Clarissa and find the pyramid. He had never seen a pyramid in the city.

He quickly went on-line and sent an urgent e-mail to Bella, asking her to meet them as several million lives were depending on them. She happened to be on-line and said she would be there in a few minutes. He was relieved he had been able to get in touch with her, and that she was more than willing to help them out. He realized she would be a loyal friend for life.

Pat suddenly had a wild urge to do some research on his mother. He searched for and found information on the history of Solinga Bay. A picture of his mother appeared on the screen. She looked exactly like the woman in his dream and earlier near-death experience. It suddenly occurred to him the pyramid was not in Clarissa, but in Solinga Bay, where the weather would probably be a lot better than Clarissa. It was now clear they needn't attempt to destroy the gangsters' magnetic machine. He was very anxious — knowing several million lives were at stake if they failed. They had to try anyway. No, he thought. We will not try to destroy it. We *will* destroy it!

Chapter 23

Soapy

None of the Owegan places, which Pat had been to, could have prepared him for the beauty of Solinga Bay. A rapidly growing city with around 800,000 people. The city had three main sections. The smallest section was a high-tech area, featuring homes that could possibly be what houses on Earth would be like in fifty years or so. The middle section was a very popular vacation area with several resorts, bed-and-breakfast places, and villas to choose from. They were all art deco designs in every colour. The last area, to the north of the other two, had the highest percentage of artists, actors, and writers. The locals knew it as Tinselwood.

Pat and the others entered Solinga Bay by programming the QTA to transport them to an area in the hills surrounding most of the city. The area heavily forested and thick enough so no one would see them appear out of the blue. It was about a hundred metres above the city and about a kilometre from the pyramid, which stood above Solinga Bay.

"So, Bella, this being an artists' paradise, you must have been here before," said Pat.

"Why of course, even though I think some of the neighbourhoods are too gaudy looking, and some of the high-tech area is a bit campy."

Pat had to stifle a laugh as he remembered when he used to take Bella out to a movie or museum, she would describe it as being either gaudy or campy at the end of the date when he asked her what she had thought of it.

"Aha, an opening at last!" said Tony, who was a good twenty metres ahead of the rest of the group. The others soon caught up with him and were instantly taken by the view of the well spread out city. They weren't too concerned about the climb down to the city since they were more interested in walking to the pyramid, still not visible because of the trees and thick tropical flowering plants.

254

"Wow, what a view!" said Pat, who now felt like an explorer that had just discovered a new continent. "I'm going to have to get a picture of this some other time when we come back here."

They continued their walk down a path, which appeared to have been there for several years, and reminded Pat of the Bruce Trail, behind his house. So far, they hadn't encountered any wild animals such as cats or wolves, the most common species in the area.

Ten minutes later, the pyramid came into view. Its shape was very similar to the pyramids built in the Mayan area of Mexico, over a thousand years ago. However, this one was made of shiny azure rock, brilliantly reflecting the sun's rays, instead of the white or grey limestone of the Mexican ones. Pat couldn't think of any rocks on Earth that had this particular blue hue.

"I think it's a bit early to destroy the comet," said Pat, glancing at his watch and seeing the time was 10:15 A.M. "We have about nine hours until sundown and less than ten hours before impact. Let's go down into the city and hang out for the day. We should be back here just before the sun goes down." Pat repeated the times in Owegan cycles.

"We had better stay together as much as possible. The last thing we need is someone getting lost and not being able to get back up here in time," said Eric.

"Let's go and check into a large beach-side villa and have an old-fashioned day at the beach."

"Without the alcohol or zizi bombs. We'll need to be clear headed and have all our faculties to divert the comet," said Eelayka.

"We'll celebrate after, then," said Eric.

They walked around the pyramid, got quite a breathtaking view of it, and realized they would have to climb to the top of it later.

The city of Solinga Bay had roads, cars, and a monotrain system too. It didn't have the helicopter-like aircrafts

Emeestatz had. There was a small airport, as the area attracted a large amount of tourists and the quickest transport was airship. Most of the cars had no wheels and were the same style as the cars in Clarissa.

They walked downhill to a parking lot and located a taxi to take them to the resort area. The cab driver took them to a villa rental agency. While they rode to the beach area, they were so intrigued by the city's beauty, they didn't notice the red car following them most of the way.

* * *

Pete had just finished planting the bombs when a couple of the other guards escorted him to the pool of killer fish. They strapped him to a chair suspended over a trap door, operated by the touch of a button.

"Do you have any last words before we let you go for a little swim?" his supervisor asked.

"Yeah, where's Soapy?"

"I'm afraid he had bigger fish to fry in Solinga Bay. That's where we detected the escapees to be."

"Oh yes, there's one other thing. The rest of you here, are going to join me in the afterlife," said Pete.

"And how is that?" the guard asked. The answer became evident when the six powerful bombs, evenly planted by Pete, went off instantly killing and vaporizing everyone. The simultaneous explosion of the bombs created the power of two atomic bombs and could be seen from Emeestatz, which was only 200 kilometres away.

The explosion destroyed most of the island. The island was only inhabited by Soapy's band, which good news to Owegans since most of his gang had been eliminated, as was the console that controlled the comet-veering machine, at Ahkella Lake Garden. The comet, however, hadn't been steered correctly to hit Emeestatz: instead, it would pass over Kaylahzee and hit on the northwest side of Corvus' east continent; the Solinga Bay's area.

* * *

"This is just perfect," said Pat when the agent took them to the second villa. It was painted bright orange and yellow and had seven large bedrooms. A nice large patio gave them an excellent view of the beach and the other villas built along the crescent-shaped bay.

"This is like something from a romantic patio scene painting," Eelayka said to Pat, putting her arms around him.

They had agreed to rent the villa for one week. The agent had Pat sign the rental form, and returned to his office. On his way there, he passed a red car with three of Soapy's gang members, parked along the side of the street.

* * *

Pat momentarily went back to his house in Lavinia and picked up his bottle computer. His plan was to try and sneak into the gangsters' system to see if they had made any changes to their plans after Eric and the others had escaped.

When Pat walked through the portal and into his living room, he noticed the weather outside was overcast with a light drizzle. The forecast had called for it to clear later in the day and remain chilly for the middle of April. He was glad he didn't have to go outside.

Pat heard on the news that Victoria Street was still closed and the investigations into the cause of the explosions were still continuing. The thought of Mr. and Mrs. K brought a wave of sadness to him. It's bad enough we have our own terrorist groups, we don't need any from an alternate universe, he thought.

He returned to the villa and went to the beach after feeding his cat, which seemed to be enjoying the villa because of its large windows with ledges wide enough for her to perch herself on and watch the various coloured birds.

Pat felt sleepy again. He put it down to the inter-dimensional travel. He concluded he would have to cut down on his number of daily trips to and from Earth. He joined Eelayka and the others, and said he needed another nap.

"I'll come with you, my huneekah," Eelayka said and explained 'huneekah' was a fruit eaten fresh off the vine or mixed with rum to form a drink called rumeekah.

"Are you two sly dogs going at it again? Judas priest, you'd think it was mating season or something," Eric commented.

"We're just going to lie down for a while. We could lie out here but the sun is pretty intense in these low latitudes. Besides, Pedals is probably lonely with me being out all the time."

Pat took Eelayka's hand and they walked back to the villa. They went to their room where his cat was curled up, at the foot of the bed.

"Will it attack us while we try to get into bed?" asked Eelayka, pointing at Pedals.

"No, of course not. She's probably more nervous of you. Don't people in this world have cats or dogs for pets?"

"What are dogs?"

"They're a little bigger than a cat and they make a '*wwrraff*' sound."

258

"Oh yes, we do. They are called habruffs," she said.

"What do you call cats?"

"We call them cats, like you do." She reached over to touch Pedals, who, startled, meowed. Eelayka quickly pulled her hand back, thinking she might get bitten or scratched.

Pat picked the cat up and put her on his lap, scratching the back of her ears, which made her purr.

"Have you ever let your spirit fly around?" Eelayka asked, after they crawled into bed.

"I'm not sure what you mean," said Pat, confused. "Do you astral projection?"

"Yes, that's what we call ghost walking. I do it once in a while and it's fun."

"Show me how," said Pat, now curious about it. He once remembered a friend who had done it in college, but he had walked rather than flown.

Eelayka took Pat's right hand. "Just close your eyes and focus your mind on a spot within arm's reach and eventually you'll feel light-headed."

Pat focused his mind on a spot to the right of the bed. He started to feel light-headed. Suddenly he could see himself as though he was standing there. He looked at his body in the bed beside Eelayka and realized he was having his first out-of-body experience.

"You did it!" said Eelayka, whose astral body was on the other side of the bed. She floated towards Pat, took his hand, and the next thing he knew they were drifting upward, through the attic and outside. He saw the others were still on the beach getting sunburned.

"Do you like being out of your body?" she communicated telepathically.

"It's cool. I'm going have to do this more often. That way I can keep an eye on you and make sure you stay out of trouble."

259

Suddenly, they were distracted by a commotion below them. Pat looked down first and saw three gangsters holding the others at gunpoint.

"We must re-enter our bodies and try to save them," said Pat, who was becoming more worried as each second ticked by.

They quickly descended and re-entered their bodies. Pat noticed he felt heavy-headed, after feeling as light as air only minutes ago during his 'aerial' viewing of the beach.

He quickly jumped out of bed and went to the window to see what the gangsters were doing. They were still holding the group at gunpoint, while circling them as if they were playing musical chairs.

"I'm going to try and sneak up on them," said Pat while putting his zapper in his pocket.

"Stay here and hide behind the bed, in case they fire a shot at the window." Pat gave her a quick hug and kiss, went down the stairs and out the front door so the gangsters wouldn't see him.

He quietly walked along the side of the house, peeked around the corner, and got a clear view of them. He pulled out his zapper and aimed it at a spot the walking gangsters kept crossing. He knew one of his friends would probably get shot if he didn't score a direct hit.

A tense minute later, one of the gangsters stopped his pacing, which gave Pat an excellent opportunity to take a shot at him. He aimed and fired, hitting him squarely in the head. The first of the other two reacted by firing off a few shots. One of the shots hit Jonk in his upper chest. The other gangster waited too long to react, giving Joanne the advantage. She got up and using her feet like a karate fighter, hit him a couple of times in the chest. Eric came to her aid by using some of his own karate moves on the gangster responsible for shooting Jonk, who was now laying gasping for air due to a punctured lung.

Pat ran over and zapped the two remaining gangsters now lying on the ground, in pain. He took their laser guns and gave one to Eric, one to Tony and kept one for himself. He instructed Eric to keep an eye on them in case they recovered earlier than expected.

Pat went over to Jonk, whose life was fading fast. Pat placed his hands over Jonk's bloody chest and tried to heal him, assuming a laser beam had a similar effect to a lightning bolt.

"Oh no! Jonk! Don't leave us!" Eelayka cried. "Surely you can save him, Pat?"

"I'm trying — but it doesn't seem to be working." Jonk was unconscious. Attempts to revive him weren't working. Pat saw a violet-coloured cloud rise from Jonk and knew it was too late. He recalled seeing a similar cloud when the old man had died, in the pathway of life. "It's no use. He's gone for good."

"We must get his body shipped home so it can be cremated," Eelayka stammered, breaking into tears and hugging Jonk's body.

"We'll have to notify the police. They'll take him to the airport and ship him out from there," said Pat.

"This place isn't safe anymore. Somehow they knew we were going to be here and were waiting for us," said Eric.

"We'd better get moving before their friends (pointing at the unconscious gangsters) come looking for them," said Pat.

"Let's ride around town and not come back here for a while. We'd be sitting ducks if we didn't stay mobile," Bella suggested."

"That's a wonderful idea. Let's split into two groups, ride the public transit, and meet again in about five hours, at the pyramid," Pat suggested.

"Actually, I just thought of something," said Eelayka. "Jonk's wife died here thirty years ago. He came here twice a year to visit the bay where her ashes were scattered. It would be a great tribute if we scattered his ashes in the same area. I'm sure it's the way he would have wanted it."

"What about your family, weren't they close friends with Jonk?" asked Pat.

"He was the closest to me. I was the child he never had," said Eelayka. She sobbed for a few minutes. Pat comforted her. After she regained her composure, "Why don't we go and get him cremated, rent a boat, and scatter his ashes on the sea?"

"We'd have to wait until tomorrow. We need to focus on destroying the comet before it destroys us," Pat recommended.

"Shouldn't we get a priest for him?" asked Tony.

"You mean a priestess," said Joanne. "Our religious leaders and advisers are all female"

Eric informed them that on Earth, though most religious professionals were mostly male, there were a growing number of female reverends.

They contacted the police, who showed up minutes later, took the three unconscious gangsters into custody, and took Jonk's body to a crematorium.

Pat glanced at the eastern horizon and could clearly see the comet, which appeared white in the cloudless azure sky. He felt as though the whole world was resting on his shoulders. He remembered reading about a comet that had hit Earth around two hundred million years ago, wiping out eighty percent of the planet's life. He didn't want to see it happen to Owega.

* * *

Soapy, in his high-speed aircraft was approaching Solinga Bay's airport. He decided to contact his right hand man on their island. He wanted to let them know he had arrived at 'Da Bay' which was what most Owegans called it. Soapy was angered when nobody answered his call. He had left strict instruction that someone had to be in the communication room at all times.

262

He made a note to have whoever was supposed to have been on duty, fed to the fish.

Soapy was glad Pat and his friends were teleporting back and forth. Whenever they re-entered Owega, the heat sensor device indicated a sudden rise in temperature. Pat's body temperature was usually higher than the air displaced. The heat sensor kept accurate temperature readings of every cubic millimetre of Owega, up to a height of one kilometre.

Whenever the temperature of an area changed, the machine instantly notified Soapy with a beep and a graphic display of the location. The last beep had happened within walking distance of the Zooza temple, one cycle ago.

He hoped his three members had captured Pat and killed his companions. He decided to contact them since the communications operator was sleeping on the job.

He spoke into the built-in mike. "Do you read me, boys?" Static was the only response he received. He had a sudden fearful thought his men has been outwitted and turned them over to the police. Soapy hit the wall of his aircraft and cursed aloud.

He quickly landed and entered the terminal, where he had arranged to meet his men, with Pat in custody. The plan was to return to the island where Pat would suffer a slow and painful death, for drowning his younger brother thirty years ago.

Soapy scoured the terminal but couldn't find his men. He was fretful about the delay in their showing and the lack of radio communication.

"Did you hear about the destruction of the gangsters' fort?" Soapy heard a woman, at a baggage claim area, asking her husband.

"No. When did this happen?" he heard the reply.

"About a cycle or so ago. It's all over the Info-Screen. The place exploded as though a thousand bombs had ignited."

This shocking news became too much for Soapy to bear. He went over and grabbed the women by her left arm, intending to ask her what she knew about it. Before he could say anything, her husband grabbed Soapy's arm . "Let go of my wife! Now! Before I call security!"

"What's this about an explosion at the gangsters' fort?" he demanded.

The husband took a closer look at Soapy and recognized him. His picture was posted all over the Info-Screen: 'Wanted dead or alive — Soapy — 20,000 krayoh reward'. He yelled for security — a bad idea because Soapy shot him and his wife, then fled.

Soapy began to wonder if Pat and his cronies had something to do with the fort explosion. He slowed to a walking pace. He was away from the airport and in a patch of woods with towering zizi trees. He deeply regretted his men's failed attempt, in Clarissa, to shoot Pat and his friend at the inn, their first morning on Owega.

* * *

A few hours later, Pat and his group hailed a couple of cabs and went to the pyramid, locally known as the Zooza Temple. They walked into the woods behind the pyramid where they could get some shelter from the hot sun.

They were about a hundred metres into the woods when Pat smelled the same fragrance that had lured him to Owega. He concluded the smell was a signal. He still hadn't figured out why the fragrance was familiar to him. He was relieved when he heard Tony comment on the scent. It wasn't a figment of his imagination.

"It's coming from over there," said Eelayka, pointing to their right. "Let's follow it and see where it leads us."

"Follow your nose. It always knows," said Eric, giggling over the cereal commercial popular in the early '70s. Eric, Pat and

Tony sang the tune. The fragrance made them feel heady, as if they had smoked a joint. The other's quickly picked up the melody and hummed along.

"Look, there's a house up ahead," said Pat. "The scent is coming from it. Let's go and check it out. Who knows, maybe it'll help us destroy the comet."

"Sounds like the smell is making your brain turn to mush," said Eric.

"I agree. How could a bottle of perfume destroy a comet?" Bella added.

"The odds of killing the comet with perfume are the same as flying a lead balloon," Eric said.

"I sense there's something in there that'll help us," said Pat.

They walked up to the small uninhabited house. It appeared to have been abandoned for a few decades. Most of the window panes were missing, and the roof showed signs of caving in.

Suddenly, Pat remembered why the fragrance was familiar. His mother used to wear it. His mom's spirit must be using it to guide him.

Pat opened the door and saw a large living room with the remains of a sofa and loveseat set, covered in dust and cobwebs. On a wooden floor were several hundred centipede-like insects, crawling around and making a noise similar to chirping crickets. Eelayka, startled by the bugs, quickly gripped Pat's arm. She softened her hold as soon as she realized they were harmless.

"I thought your house was bad when it came to carpenter ants," said Eric, referring to the fact that Pat's house always had a bad case of carpenter ants every year during February and March.

Pat remembered he had lived here before he was sent to live on Earth. He was suddenly overcome by emotions as he began to remember more about his younger life. He sat on the floor. The bugs scattered. Eelayka comforted him until he regained his composure.

The others were speechless. They now knew Pat had been serious when he had said he had a sense about the house.

Pat walked down a dark hallway. The others followed. He came to the room that used to be his and, without thought, he held his hand out, signalling everyone, except Eelayka, to go back to the living room.

The bedroom was that of any eight-year-old boy. It had a single bed and the wallpaper had airships on it, with a bright blue sky in the background, which matched the colour of the bedspread. Time had taken its toll — the paper had faded and peeled in several spots.

On the bed was a tall, skinny, blue-tinted, transparent bottle. Pat wasn't sure if it was a bottle computer or not, as it was a different shape to the one his grandfather had built.

Then he recalled his mom had given it to him just before she died, to use to communicate with her in the after-life. This must be the Owegan version of an Ouija board, Pat thought to himself.

Pat sat on the bed and tentatively touched the bottle. A white cloud began to form within the bottle, rose out of it, and grew into a larger light violet cloud. He was reminded of fairy tales and genies. I wonder what this genie is going to look like, he thought.

The cloud formed a portal similar to the one created with the QTA. This one only had colours ranging from green to violet. Around the perimeter were several white and yellow sparks instead of the familiar light blue ones. Pat peered into the portal and saw a garden with a golden palace in the background.

His mother's image appeared. It suddenly occurred to him she was going to tell him how to destroy the comet drawing closer by the minute.

"Pat, it's up to you and your friends to save Owega," his mom said.

"Is that really you, Mom?" Pat asked, nervously excited.

"Yes son, it's me. You are looking at a window facing into the after-life, or Paradise as the Owegans call it."

"On Earth they call the same place by several names depending on one's religion. I was raised as a Christian. Therefore, I refer to it as Heaven. Other religions call it Nirvana or Utopia."

Pat would have liked to ask her a hundred questions; such as what the after-life was like, and where his dad had disappeared to. However, he had contacted her to find a way to destroy the comet - not to see what Heaven was like.

Solinga gave Pat a list of things to be done. Eelayka took notes so none of the tasks would be overlooked.

"Remember son: this is a one-shot deal. If you fail, millions of lives will be lost. I have absolute faith in you, else I wouldn't have taken measures to get you to return."

Pat didn't need to ask how she had done it. After his mom disappeared, the portal transformed itself back into a cloud. The bottle sucked it back in as though it were a vacuum cleaner. Pat and Eelayka returned to the living room and passed the instructions on to the others. It was only three hours to dusk, which was when the comet would enter Owega's upper atmosphere, turn into a huge fireball, and hit Solinga Bay with the power of a hundred A-bombs.

* * *

For the remainder of the afternoon, the three women went to the closest store and bought sandwiches to be served as a light dinner. They were glad the store was within walking distance since the news of the comet's latest projected path had led the Solinga Police Department to evacuate the city. This would

267

have made it impossible to get a vacant taxi as they were being used to evacuate the city.

When the women returned, they went to pick mooberries behind the pyramid, putting them in containers they had bought at the store as instructed.

The berries were reported to contain a chemical, which had the ability to create a deadly light beam when combined with an electrical charge. The berries also acted as a powerful steroid drug when eaten, which is why they were illegal to have or eat. In the past people were handed the death penalty when caught selling them in the underground market.

The men had the strenuous job of carrying a heavy machine to the top of the pyramid. A two-metre-long glass tube attached to a large coal coloured rock, almost circular in shape. The rock and large tube made it so heavy, it had to be carried by three men. Pat determined that since there were approximately two hundred steps up the pyramid, and four of them, they would stop every fifty steps, take a three-minute break and rotate, so each of them would have a turn at being the guide because the steps had different heights, making it easy to trip and fall. The 'guide' also had to carry a large canteen of a fruit juice around his neck. They managed to get to the top without incident.

"I'm glad that's over," said Tony, as they finally put the device down in its upright position. "There's not a whole lot of room up here," he continued, looking at the size of the platform, which was square and about 4 metres wide and long. It was like the platform on top of the ancient Aztec or Mayan pyramids in Mexico.

Pat's watch indicated the temperature was a hot 34ºC — unpleasant even on the shaded side they had climbed.

"Pat, do we have to carry this back down later?" Timko asked.

"She didn't tell me there were any procedures to follow afterwards."

"Maybe the sucker will be transferred into energy which will eat the comet," suggested Eric. "After all Pat, didn't you tell me you could change objects into different shapes by altering the molecules with your mind?"

"Yeah, I did it the night I was with the fake Eelayka." Pat told them about turning a pen into light photons.

"I think we should head back down," said Pat, after they emptied the canteen Pat had found in the fridge, as his mom had indicated. "The girls should be done picking those berries fairly soon. It's a good thing they didn't try going to the city market - look down there. It looks like they're evacuating the whole area."

They kept hearing air-raid sirens. They had an excellent view from the top of the sixty-metre-high pyramid since the city was another hundred-or-so metres lower in elevation. Pat glanced at the eastern sky. The comet was clearly visible and large. He fancied he could see it with his naked eye, getting larger and closer.

* * *

At the time the men had finished carrying the heavy device to the top of the pyramid, the girls were almost done picking berries.

"So, where did you and Pat meet?" Bella asked Eelayka while they were picking berries from the same side of the tree.

"I met him on an airship." She told Bella about being rescued from a drunken crewman. "Did you take Kaylahzian lessons? Pat told me you were from his world and you entered ours from a place called San Cisco or some name I can't recall."

"I came through a portal in the San Francisco area. I thought I was still on Earth since the part of Owega I had found myself in

269

was very similar to where I had exited Earth. When I exited the park, or garden as Owegans call it, I couldn't see the Pacific Ocean. That's when I knew I had somehow slipped into another dimension. A few hours later, I felt sick and met a man who took me to the nearest hospital. A few days later he explained the situation to me as much as possible."

Bella wasn't able to tell more of her story because a police officer holding a gun appeared out of nowhere.

"What did we do wrong, officer," Joanne asked rather snappily.

"Well, for starters, you're trespassing on private property, and you're also picking mooberries, a capital offence. No telling how many berries you have eaten. All it takes is one berry to make you hyper and destructive. Now, everyone start walking. Anyone disobeying won't live to see the comet pass us by."

The girls walked deeper into the woods, away from Pat and his group.

Pat decided to see if the girls needed help with the picking since the sun was beginning to turn orange, indicating dusk would soon be upon them. He could hear them talking to each other in the thicker part of the woods just behind the house.

He thought about sneaking up on them to scare them as a joke. The thought was short lived when he suddenly heard a male voice telling them they were being arrested for trespassing and illegally picking berries.

He quietly walked over to where they stood. "Officer, is there a problem?"

"There sure is. They were stealing illegal berries."

Pat took a good look at the cop's blue uniform and saw the epaulet: Solinga Bay Airfield Security. "Sir, aren't you a little out of your jurisdiction?"

"What are you talking about?" the officer snapped, aiming the gun at Pat.

270

"Take a good look at your uniform. This doesn't look like the airport does it?" Pat suddenly realized the man was none other than Soapy himself dressed as a security guard.

Soapy suddenly grabbed Eelayka, pointed the gun at the side of her head opposite to where Pat was standing and said, "You say one more word, Silversol, and the Kaylahzian's brains will be all over the ground."

"Let go of her, Soapy. It's me you really want a piece of. She didn't drown your younger brother?" Pat stared at Soapy's gun. With his mind, he tried to make the electrons of the gun's atoms move back and forth. The metal gun suddenly turned as red as an oven element when heated.

Soapy yelled and cursed as he realized he couldn't drop the red-hot gun to the ground, because one of the girls could pick it up when it cooled, so he quickly threw it into the air where it caught on a branch, just out of reach. He let Eelayka go, pushed her aside, and ran towards Pat with every intention of fighting him to the death, ignoring the pain of his burnt hand.

Pat saw him charging at him and was ready with a swift karate kick. It hit him in the chest but not hard enough to have any effect. Soapy hit him just below his left eye. The blow was so powerful Pat lost his footing and fell to the ground.

Pat compared this to a David and Goliath fight and he wasn't playing the role of Goliath since he didn't really have the fighting experience Soapy obviously had. He could reach for his QTA and go back to Earth, but Soapy would have enough time to nail him with more kicks and punches that would certainly do him in.

Pat tried to get up but fell back down after Soapy kicked him, near his kidneys. Pat tried to make the portal appear with his mind, and sure enough, it did. It was a bit shorter and narrower than the one the QTA device would have created.

Pat quickly got up and ran through the portal and into his living room. He hoped to find some kind of destructive weapon such as a steak knife or a can of Lysol. He went into his kitchen and found a can of bug spray, which would do the same trick. He heard Soapy lumber through the portal and into his living room.

"Come out here and fight me like a man, you little fairy!" Soapy yelled just as Pat had the can ready to spray at his eyes as soon as he entered the kitchen. Pat peeped through a rectangular hole in the wall where a furnace had once stood, and saw Soapy drive his foot into the TV screen. He saw him trash his stereo system too. He quickly grabbed a frying pan with his free hand, went into the living room, and shot some of the spray into Soapy's eyes. Pat made use of the golden opportunity to hit him over the head with the frying pan as hard as he could. Soapy, unconscious, fell onto some of the glass from the smashed TV set.

"Well, that's just as effective as using a slingshot," Pat said aloud. "I think it's time I take you back to see the king of Owega. I'm sure he would be glad to see you. He could put on a show for the rest of the world, called "The king of Owega shoots Soapy's ass into space."

Pat activated the portal with his QTA, dragged Soapy over to where the women were starting to panic that Pat wouldn't return alive.

"Did you kill him?" Eelayka asked as soon as they were through.

"No, but I'm sure the king will see to it when we take him there later," Pat said and sat on the ground to catch his breath. He once again felt a wave of drowsiness after going through the portal.

"Pat, look out! He's waking up!" Eelayka cried.

Pat turned around but was a second too late, giving Soapy a chance to get on top of him and push him to the ground.

"Now you're going to pay for what you did to my brother," Soapy said as he put his hands around Pat's neck.

The girls desperately tried to free the gun from the tree. They couldn't reach it by jumping. Bella had an idea. She and Eelayka stood facing each other, their hands linked to form a platform. Maili stepped up while Joanne supported her and was able to reach the gun that had had enough time to cool. Maili could see there was no way she could fire the gun without the risk of hitting Pat, so decided to bide her time.

Pat tried to free himself, but it was next to impossible since Soapy's hands felt like a tight metal vice. He had to think of something before it was too late. He heard Joanne say she was going to round up the guys to rescue Pat.

Then a thought occurred to him. If he was capable of saving Maili by restoring her energy, wouldn't he be able to do the opposite and steal Soapy's energy by putting his hands on his chest? He put his hand on Soapy's chest and imagined his hand pulling energy from the gangster leader's chest. He felt a tingling in his hand, followed by a sudden burst of energy powerful enough to enable him to thrust his knee into Soapy's genitals. Soapy released Pat's neck and howled with pain.

Maili, seeing Pat had a gained a brief respite, quickly yelled at him to catch the gun. Pat spun around to face her and caught the gun neatly. He turned back to face Soapy, holding him at gunpoint. Soapy suddenly growled like a wolf and ran towards Pat aiming to knock him down. As soon as Pat saw Soapy running towards him like a madman, he fired three quick shots, hitting Soapy in the heart. He collapsed just inches from Pat's feet. Pat looked down and could see a large amount of blood oozing out of Soapy's dead body.

"Do you realize what you just did?" Eelayka asked, hysterically excited.

"There was nothing else I could have done," said Pat, feeling guilty. "He would have killed me."

"No, I know it wasn't your fault," said Eelayka. "You have just killed Owega's number one enemy. You're going to be a

273

legend to remember, providing we can save the planet from the comet." She went over and hugged Pat, who felt as if he was on a sugar and caffeine rush.

"Yes, we had better get ourselves up the pyramid and do what we have to do up there. Afterwards we can come down and retrieve Soapy's body, contact the authorities, and all that jazz."

* * *

At the time Pat was fighting Soapy, the majority of Owegans were at their Info-Screens watching the comet, reported under government instruction, to be smaller than it was while the Solinga Bay area was being evacuated.

At the Serie Beach hospital Carrie Orangesand made a sudden recovery from her catatonic state of shock and startled a doctor walking past her room by yelling, "Soapy's gang are all dead!"

Steve chatted with an airship captain who informed him the gangsters' main fortress, a fair 20 kilometres away, had somehow blown its top with such a force it had given the airship a nasty shake.

* * *

Pat and the girls went up the pyramid with their buckets of squashed berries, and dumped them into the tube. He pushed them down to the bottom with a long stick he had found lying in the woods.

"I hope those aren't explosive," Pat joked with Eelayka, who lit a few candles to help keep the bugs away and add some light since the sun had sunk below the horizon.

274

"Don't worry, sweetie, I'm not one of the gangsters' decoys," Eelayka said and put her arms around Pat.

"Okay, I need everyone to grab hold of one of my arms and hang on tight," instructed Pat. "This is the final step."

Eelayka put her arms around Pat's shoulders while Bella, Joanne, and Eric grabbed Pat's right arm. Tony, Timko, and Maili grabbed hold of his left arm. They looked like were executing a bizarre pose.

"Before we start - let's take a moment to pray," said Pat. Pat wasn't familiar with the Owegan religions, but had learned they also worshipped one God. He prayed, "Father in Heaven, we ask that you bless this wonderful world and its peoples and give us the strength to save her from a tragic event brought on by those who had turned against all that is good. We pray to you, Lord. Amen." He repeated the prayer in Pihanos and Kaylahzian.

"That's one of the nicest prayers I've heard in a while. You're going have to teach me some of your religion," said Eelayka.

"Now it's time to rock and roll. Everyone concentrate on me. Picture yourselves as small rivers draining into the sea, which is me. You'll feel a little sleepy afterwards."

Everyone complied with Pat's request and he began to feel a tingling sensation, as though he was touching a low-voltage wire. Pat channelled the incoming energy to the rock the tube was attached to. The juice from the squashed berries started to glow ruby red. Above, the comet was only a minute or so from entering Owega's upper atmosphere.

"Come on, we must concentrate harder," Pat encouraged, when he didn't notice any change in the strength and quality of the glowing red juice. Pat felt the tingling sensation increase and saw the juice glow a brighter pink. Little blue sparks started to arc off the outside of the glass, which startled the others at first because the tube and rock contraption started to resemble a mad scientist's bizarre gadget.

Pat felt his spirit exit his body once again. He looked down and saw everyone huddled around him. He looked for the tube until he realized he was inside it. He knew now he was about to experience something no other person ever would.

The pink light surrounding his spirit in the tube became so bright the grounds below had a pinkish tint. There was a bright blue flash and Pat felt as though he was being pushed towards the comet. He glanced down and noticed the ground was thousands of meters below him. A brief wave of fear passed through him when he looked up and saw he was only miles from the comet and closing.

"Do not fear, Pat," he hear Jonk's voice encourage him.

Pat approached the comet head on and knew he couldn't be harmed because his actual physical body was several miles below his spirit and consciousness. He thought he would coast right through the comet, as though he was a ghost walking through a wall. When he hit the comet, it reacted as though a thousand nuclear bombs had blown it up. He saw sparks and debris of rock and ice all around him.

Pat was once again in his body and awoke to see and feel the coldness of snowflakes falling on him. He thought he was back in Clarissa where it was still snowing, until he looked around, saw the ghostly dark tube apparatus, and realized he was on top of the pyramid.

"Pat, you did it! The comet is no more!" Eelayka cried excitedly.

"What's all this snow? I though we were in the tropics."

"This isn't ordinary snow. It's the comet's ice pack, which must have broken into a zillion snowflakes."

"Where are the others?" Pat asked when he registered they were alone. He felt his heart sink at the dreadful thought that the force had sent the others tumbling down the side of the pyramid. He pictured their mangled bodies scattered to all four sides, along the base.

"They're at the bottom. Are you aware you have been out cold for a good fifth of a cycle, or thirty minutes?"

Pat thought for a few seconds and said, "I had some form of out-of-body experience. I felt as though I went up and hit the comet with my spiritual body. Did you see my spirit rise from the glass tube?"

"What we saw was a huge lightning bolt leave the glass tube and head straight for the comet which blew up like a huge firecracker as soon as contact was made. We thought at first you were dead, until I found a pulse and realized you were only unconscious."

"I've turned my flashlight on and off to signal the others. I sent them down, to hold back the crowd to give you space and time to recover."

Pat stood and saw several people with his friends. He gave a wave and everyone below cheered as though he were a popular rock star.

Eelayka gave him a brief hug. "I once went to a fortune teller known as the Purple Witch. She told me I would meet and fall in love with a hero from a far-away place. Do you think she was right?"

"I guess she was absolutely right," Pat said, planting a kiss on Eelayka's cheek.

"I think we should go down and meet some of your new fans."

"Sounds good to me," said Pat as they started to walk down the steps. "I could go for something to eat."

"We'll go back to the villa and fix something we picked up earlier. We may have people bugging us for autographs on our way back. They may hang out in the front yard with cameras and electronic writers, waiting for you to come out so they could write, what could be the story of the century or millennium for that matter."

"I'll just say 'No Problemo'."

They joined the others and looked for a taxi to take them back to the villa.

* * *

Pat once again had a dream. His mother congratulated him for doing a great job destroying the comet and eliminating Soapy. She also said he would come across other conflicts. Owega wasn't a perfect world, even though it was much nicer and more beautiful than Earth.

"Are you able to see my future and if Eelayka is the one or not?"

"That is for you to decide, my son. I will approve of whoever you someday decide to marry."

Pat's dream ended shortly. He woke and couldn't get back to sleep. He decided to do what he hadn't had a chance to do since he had entered Owega.

He went out onto the back porch, turned on his bottle computer, and started to write a day-by-day journal of his adventures in Owega. Periodically he would pause and look out at the sea and the curving shoreline. He realized if he had never paid attention to the fragrance in the woods behind his house, the northwest coast and Solinga Bay would have been no more. This would certainly make for a good story or movie, he thought to himself.

He looked towards the east, watched the tropical sunrise, and heard the birds singing as though they were giving their creator a prayer of thanks for having a brand new day to live for.

Epilogue

Month 01, Day 05, year 13-007

From the Daily Journal of Pat Silversol

As you can see, I haven't had a chance to make any entries for the last 90 days. It was for a good cause though. I've been constantly busy ever since I was awarded the purple medallion. I now know what it's like to be someone like Paul McCartney or the president of a superpower nation such as America.

To briefly sum up what has been happening, I must go back to the day after I saved Owega, my true native planet.

I was concerned some of Soapy's men would seek revenge. On the Info-Screen, I learned the headquarters had been destroyed. The investigators speculated one of the gangsters was suicidal and had decided to blow himself and the rest of the group up. Whatever way they ended their lives wasn't important. The important thing is the gangsters are now gone and justice has finally been served.

The planet is still not totally free from violence since there are still the Dendoyhees, or Doys, as I like to call them. They're nothing compared to the gangsters. However, they still cause a lot of problems such as some of the rules they enforce upon the small islands that used to be independent before they took them over. One rule is that girls and women can't attend school, or use the Info-Screen for on-line education.

Now I should get back to my friends. Eric and Joanne went their separate ways, partly because they grew tired of each other and partly because Eric got homesick.

Tony, on the other hand, decided to move to Owega on the condition I let him use my QTA since I no longer need it, now that I can open the portal with the power of my mind. He doesn't need to worry about looking for a job because he was hired as an IT researcher at the intelligence agency Steve works for.

Maili and Timko were recently married in their native country. Eelayka and I attended and like most weddings on Owega, it was performed in a public garden. During the ceremonies and reception, Eelayka kept informing me about different traditions and customs of weddings on Owega, which aren't different to some countries on Earth. One example was that instead of throwing her garter to the single men, the bride would be blindfolded and the groom would instruct her to take a different number of footsteps around the line of single men. Finally, she would be told to hand her garter to the closest guy. Then the groom would pick a single lady in the same manner and hand her the bouquet of fresh flowers. She told me at one point she was teaching me all this so I wouldn't have to spend time researching it. However, I think she was dropping me hints because she would say stuff like "I would rather see the bridesmaids and maid of honour wear light purple, instead of light green," or, "I would rather see less guests and a more intimate atmosphere."

I must have given my autograph to everyone there. I was so worried that I was receiving more attention than the bride and groom. When Maili did her thank-you speech, she mentioned that if it weren't for me, at the shores of Serie Beach, she would not have lived to see this day.

Bella and I still keep in touch but only as good friends. She met a guy on Slimteeka Island when she was in the garden doing a painting. I guess she liked meeting men that way. After all, I met her the very same way in a different world (no pun intended).

I was awarded 100,000 krayohs, for the capture of Soapy. The king had increased the reward when he was informed of the plan the gang had had for the comet. This reward amounted to roughly one million American dollars. I purchased a thousand bars of gold, which came to a thousand krayohs. I took them to Earth, sold them to a Toronto bank, and donated the cash to Lavinia for the reconstruction of the devastated downtown area. I read on Earth's premiere news company, CNN, the authorities thought it was done by Bin Laden's network. However, scientists found an intact part of a bomb. They theorised perhaps a couple of meteors had hit the ice-cream place and Christmas shop. The piece was made from a type of metal that matched none of the metals of the atomic charts. The actual piece was sent to the Royal Ontario Museum of Science.

I recently bought a villa for 15,000-krayoh on Slimteeka Island, which is quite spacious. I would have preferred to buy something in Solinga Bay but it would be too far away from Eelayka, who is happy to live on Slimteeka Island, as it is only a few minutes by airboat from her parents and brother. Sure, I could go 10,000 kilometres from Solinga Bay to Slimteeka by using the portals, but it would be tiring. I asked Steve about that and he said the human body was only made to bounce occasionally and not several times in a ten-cycle span, like I had been doing.

The other thing that has been going through my mind was that I actually have royal blood in me since my late father would have been the current king, had he not given up his heir to the throne by marrying my mom. Most likely, I would probably not become the next king since my uncle, King Allan III, has a son and daughter. The only way I could be crowned would be if I were to marry a princess from another nation or if something happened to the royal family such as a terrorist attack. The first option is unlikely since the only other royal family is the one of Kaylahzee and the have two sons. The other one also has a narrow chance of occurring since the gangsters whom were after me are all gone because of gangster Mark's suicide explosion that wipe out every one of them on their little island. I don't mind since I don't know enough about politics and the nature of ruling a nation. Besides, I wouldn't want to have my picture in all those tabloids, like the late Princess Di had.

The only sad thing that happened was my cat, Pedals, died. I guess she didn't adapt to Owega like I did. I currently don't have a cat but when I get another, I think I'll name it either Josi or Pheeny, after my late grandma.

Anyway, Eelayka is once again lying half naked on the bed, calling my name and waving zizi leaves. I must sign off now and ride the train of love. As they say in Kaylahzian, "Kalookah Noctoh," which means good day and good night.